D0014370

THE LIAR'S CHAIR

THE
LIAR'S CHAIR

REBECCA WHITNEY

MANTLE

First published 2015 by Mantle
an imprint of Pan Macmillan, a division of Macmillan Publishers Limited
Pan Macmillan, 20 New Wharf Road, London N1 9RR
Basingstoke and Oxford
Associated companies throughout the world
www.panmacmillan.com

ISBN 978-1-4472-6581-8

1 3 5 7 9 8 6 4 2

A CIP catalogue record for this book is available from the British Library.

Typeset by Ellipsis Digital Limited, Glasgow
Printed and bound by CPI Group (UK) Ltd, Croydon, CRO 4YY

For Rob, Bea and Billy. Always.

And for Terry Whitney, a gentleman and a gentle man.

Alison Marling, we miss you.

PART ONE

1

ECHO CHAMBER

The journey is key, the arrival always a disappointment.

It's half an hour home from my lover Will's place on the coast to the house in the Sussex countryside I share with my husband David. The way back is simple, and I map in my head the journey in front of me: along the clifftops and through endless bland towns until I reach Brighton, with its clutter of cheap hotels on my right, and to my left the sea. At the junction of the pier, I'll funnel through the city then head for the hills. But as I drive down from Will's prefab bungalow, rain thudding the bonnet, instinctively I branch away from the main drag, choosing instead the back route: the near-empty roads that see-saw through the countryside and allow me to drive fast and carefree. After one drink-driving ban I know where to avoid, and the country route means fewer police. Not that it's their habit to stop a woman driver in a top-of-the-range, brand-new Mercedes on a Saturday morning, but the taste of alcohol still furs my mouth and

I want to have some fun. I want to take nine of the ten chances available to me.

The road leads me north, past endless mini-roundabouts and the homogeny of industry that rings every sizeable town. Here the buildings have given up all civic pretence to beauty and efficiency: half-dead shrubs in forecourts fidget in the wind, gates hang heavy with chains, and grey-washed walls wear the tags of bored and artless teenagers. Then, after a final roundabout, the town spits me out into the open relief of green. I head towards the Downs where the route glues to the base of the hills and the land curves up sharp into a heaving sky.

Summer is ending, at last, and all those extended, overheated weeks are finally blowing their top. Windscreen wipers whine at full speed clearing a radar shape on the glass, and outside the morning sun is obscured and the world is compressed to a small frame of black. The wheels of my car hit a puddle and fan a satisfying hiss of water into the air, but the noise is quiet and separate from inside my vehicle; even the motor is soft, its volume cushioned by immaculate engineering. Here in my mechanical kingdom I am insulated, normal life is suspended, and it's only the speed and the distance. Nothing can touch me. Not even David.

I detour down a small wooded lane wide enough for one car, speeding up and slowing down with the smallest amount of leeway, knowing exactly how far to hug the widths and bends familiar to me from years of driving these roads. I swerve past an old horse-box parked up on the verge: blankets at the windows, smoke rising from a tacked-on chimney. Rust-coloured panels patchwork the new-age hippy wagon.

There's no pavement and the tarmac's scraggy edge borders straight on to the soft earth of the woods that lie beyond. If I nudge the steering a fraction too far, the tyres judder on gravel and mud for a few metres until I right them with a playful swerve on to the opposite side. Trees heavy with a late-summer harvest arch over the lane, and their branches entwine overhead to form leafy tunnels. Spatters of roadkill and weeks of fallen fruit mix with rain on the road's surface, so that at times it seems as if the car is skating. I turn the wheel and change gears instinctively, my thoughts of David – and the ten CAPITALIZED text messages he sent this morning – contained and measured by my driving, as if I've capped off my brain and left the worst thoughts behind, to be collected again on arrival. I jumble together an excuse: a surprise call from an old school friend yesterday, too much to drink so a hotel was best – the alibi will have to do, I'm too hung-over to be creative – and I pray my recent good behaviour will be enough to convince David that staying away last night was a one-off, a small error in our otherwise ordered marriage.

My explanation logged, and I'm free to indulge my favourite driving fantasy, which takes me further along the road to a place I've never been – somewhere, any-where – until my car runs out of petrol and fate decides the end point like a pin in a map. The scent of last night is still on my skin and I wonder if, when I've found my new home, I would call Will, or whether it would be best to start afresh. Perhaps today is the day to find out, and I press the accelerator, the country road barely holding the width of my car, and imagine the place where I'll make a new life for myself. Where I'll be effortlessly healed.

Ahead of me is an oak. The enormous trunk would span the girth of two horses, and the branches weave into the sky. A near-perfect U in the road rounds the tree. I change down a gear and steer sharp, wheels gripping the wet road as the engine rises an octave, and each tree and shrub is a streak of green past my window.

Then, a white band of skin. Wide eyes. A crack. The body flips forward – *smash* against the windscreen. Glass shatters. I stamp the brakes, too late, and whatever I've hit flies over the car in a floppy cartwheel, crumpling on the road behind. I skid to a halt, engine still running, my breath panting in and out, sharp and shallow, seconds or minutes. I check my rear-view mirror. On the road behind is a smudge of red from the tail lights; twenty metres from that, a pile. Thick dark liquid spreads on the tarmac. Nothing moves apart from the rain which pounds the ground.

'It's just an animal,' I whisper, then say it loud to make it real. 'It's just an animal.'

Easing the car into gear, I manoeuvre a five-point turn and edge closer until I'm a metre away.

Clothes not fur. Fingers not hooves.

Swaddled in a heavy coat, his face always covered by

a scarf and hat, I recognize him: a local homeless man who trudges the roads near my house.

I teeter from the car, step forward, then crouch a few inches away. Rain soaks me and runs down my face, gathering at my eyebrows and chin. The scarf round the man's face has come loose and it exposes a woolly beard. A long ugly nose.

I shut my eyes for a few seconds.

Who was the last person to be this close to him?

Panic pinballs in my chest. When I open my eyes I tug at the scarf to cover him up and return him to the being he was a few minutes ago, but the fabric is caught under his head. His neck is slack like a broken doll. From my pocket I take out my mobile. It slips like a fish from my shaking hands on to the wet tarmac. I grab it and press random buttons to bring it back to life, then wave it above my head – but there's no signal.

The man's smell is sharp and strong with a feral bite – earth mixed with old piss – and it flips my memory to a time when I saw him at the village shop close to my house, where the same aroma had filled the room. In the shop he had with him his trademark briefcase: his unique and infamous logo of eccentricity. The bag made you look twice when you saw him walking with a gentle limp. It was the kind of case in which a gentleman would take his papers to the office, someone who had important work to do.

Here at the roadside, I check around him. The briefcase is nowhere to be seen.

My legs ache from crouching and I gather my skirt round my thighs, the material wet and clinging. The rain slows but drops have collected in the trees and fall with heavy raps on to the bonnet of my car. I lean closer to the man and lay my palm on his back. No breath. In the distance there's a rumble, a tractor maybe emerging from a barn and on to the road? I sit back on my haunches and my legs wobble, reminding me of the bottle of whisky I shared with Will less than six hours ago.

Breathe. I breathe.

I wait. For what? Nothing changes.

The man is dead.

I have taken something away. I cannot put it back.

'If you can't lie, Rachel,' my mother used to preach, 'then it's best to say nothing at all.'

My pulse slows a fraction and I take a longer breath. A calm of sorts, a lifting away.

I stand and walk round to the man's head. My hands shake as I ease them under his warm armpits; his limbs are loose, and I lever him up to test the weight. His head lolls on to his chest as if he's asleep. He's surprisingly light; malnourished and skinny under the layers of clothing, like a wet dog without the cushion of its fur. I test a drag. It works. I can do it.

Walking backwards, I move him away from the road and into the undergrowth, twisting my head in nervous jerks to see the way. The woods are thick and dark. Trees creak. My shoes sink into the wet earth and brambles scratch my stockings. The further I go, the more difficult it becomes to drag him, and I stumble backwards over a log and sprawl on the ground with my skirt torn. Red liquid streaks down my arm but I don't register pain, so it must be his blood, and I carry on to where, even after the long summer, the ground is boggy and the road disappears from view. Here there is no one, only the daily wars of ants and spiders. I spread him out on the earth and wrap his face with the scarf, as he would have been before the accident, then cover his body with fallen branches and lumps of damp leaves, careful that nothing pokes into his skin. His large blue overcoat is soaked with rain and the laces of his trainers are undone.

The air is still and dense. Watching. I stand for a moment trying to remember something from the Bible, perhaps the Lord's Prayer which we droned through daily in the icy school chapel, 'Our Father, forgive us our daily bread.' It's been a long time. Again a distant rumble, thunder or perhaps a car. I turn and retrace my way along the groove of undergrowth splayed by the body, and a heel breaks off my shoe. As I pluck the inches of plastic from the wet earth, I can't imagine how anything so thin can support me.

Back at the road, the rain has washed most of the blood from the tarmac; only a tiny river of pink has pooled at the edge before dropping off into the earth. In the direction I was headed before the crash, the funnel of trees opens into a circle of light. Back the other way it's silent and dark. The only vehicle I passed earlier was the horse-box, but that was about a mile back, and the smoking chimney meant it was probably moored in for the day. No one else has come. No one has seen. Further up the road though there's something on the ground I hadn't noticed before and I run to it, my actions jumpy and fractured, like a reel of film that's been spliced and sped up. I'm more desperate than before; I thought I was done, I thought I'd made it and the risk was over. As I come close to the object I see it's the man's briefcase, open but empty. I grab the case without a moment's thought and heave it up with arms stretched long, flinging it away from my body into the woods. The case spins like an injured bird, and falls deep in the undergrowth with a leafy crash. Back towards the car now, and as I run my feet kick at something which skitters and sparkles: it's a watch on a broken leather strap, the glass face shattered. He must have kept it in the briefcase instead of on his wrist as the tear on the strap is old and frayed. I hold the watch to my ear. There's no tick. The time reads 10.52 – the time of impact? – but with a couple of winds and a gentle bang against my palm, the second hand starts moving again. I break into a run now, gripping the watch inside my pocket as the second hand pulses against my palm, and only when I'm back inside the safety of my car can I settle enough to try and work out what to do next.

I sit on the front seat for as long as I dare – probably only seconds, but it feels like hours – before shutting the door and starting the engine. All around me, the branches of the trees tumble in the echo chamber left behind by the storm.

2

TINY BOMB OF DISORDER

It's a fifteen-minute journey home from the accident site, but I'm certain it takes longer, though I don't check the time. A few cars pass but the roads remain quiet after the storm. Finally I drive through metal gates and on to our driveway, the rough wet tongue of gravel rolling towards an enormous white cube. The house has never felt less like home.

My car scoops round the semicircle of our driveway, and I park with the boot pointing towards the house, the damage on the bonnet hidden. The rain has stopped but dark clouds still cover the sun. On all three floors of the house, the lights are on. Bright rectangular windows study my approach. I imagine David inside, inspecting the rooms for my presence or absence – though I'm not sure which he prefers – his polished shoes pressing into the thick bedroom carpet, and the wool leaning back up as he passes, his imprint vanishing.

With shaking hands I pull on the hand brake, smoothe

my hair, then step out into the sour smell of wet grit, praying David won't see me before I've cleaned myself up. My breath is short and sharp as I make my way to the house. I open the front door, and our two huskies – David's noisy, needy shitting-machines who've been poised and barking on the other side – pour through the gap, growling. They circle me and sniff the unfamiliar earth which covers my clothes. I shush and stroke them to let them get my smell, then shoo them back to David where they bound happily as soon as they know I'm not an intruder. I hear David on the phone in the sitting room. 'No, no,' he says – his voice pitched soft for such a stocky man, the tone more in line with his height than his weight – 'you can call me any time.' His words carry effortlessly through the polished rooms of the ground floor. 'It's always good to hear from you.' A client, I think, or maybe someone from the club, someone who requires the treacle of his charm. David won't leave a business call halfway through, even to confront his absconding wife. Our dogs yap in the other room, and I suspect they're bouncing up at him to get his attention, probably licking his fingers as he strokes them with his free hand.

The hallway smells of mint, David's signature tea, so he must have a cup on the go. The aroma turns my stomach. An old cardboard box is torn and scattered on the floor – something for the dogs to chew so they don't damage our nice things. David must have been caught off guard by the phone call to have left them in the house without supervision.

Behind me the front door closes with a soft clunk and my uneven shoes alternate a tap and a slide. I slip them off and carry them as I make my way towards the downstairs bathroom. Once inside, I lock the door, and it's only then I take a proper look at myself: the torn skirt, scratches on my legs and blood up my arms. Fingernails full of mud. I hang my jacket on the back of the door then turn on the tall sink tap. Water comes out fast, but the temperature won't adjust quickly enough, and I wash my hands in the scalding liquid. Steam rises in my face as I bend my arm into the stream and scrub the cuts with soap until they sting. A rose whirlpool is swallowed down the plug. The noise of the gushing water bounces from marbled floor to marbled wall and back again; there's room in here for more furniture – towels, rugs or any addition of comfort to help absorb the echo – but we never got round to filling the space.

I slide open the shower cubicle, reach inside and turn on the water. Steam clouds mist the room. Against the wall is a rubbish bin, and I strip off my shirt, skirt and tights, putting everything inside, including my underwear and shoes, then take the liner from the bin and tie it at the top. My hands are still wet as I try to secure a double knot, and I struggle to keep hold of the slippery edges. 'Damn it.' I leave it to one side for later. The knot gracefully unspools as I step under the hot pins of the shower.

With my hands on the glass wall, I bend my head to let the water stream down my face and into my eyes. 'Dear God,' I whisper.

The accident replays in my mind in stop-motion: the man's face as I rounded the corner, his skull denting the windscreen, the dull thud of his bones against the car. Or was the sound a snap? I squeeze my eyes tight but the moment keeps coming at me, more gruesome each time, and I watch him flip and split, blood spraying from his open mouth, until I'm not sure what really happened and what I'm imagining.

I hold my head in my hands.

Tears come, silently at first, then sobs which grow louder above the slash of water until my weeping sounds like it's coming from somewhere else. I retch a couple of times and, on the third attempt, vomit a whisky bile into the shower tray. Yellow strings of phlegm swirl down the plug. I hold my mouth into the jet of water, rinse and spit, rinse and spit.

There's knocking on the bathroom door. I jump. The handle rattles.

'Rachel?' David's voice is muted behind the wood, but I sense his urgency. 'Rachel, what's going on in there? Are you OK?'

Shit. I grab the soap and scrub my body, rubbing the tablet over my head and hair, repeating the action at speed several times, forgetting where I've washed already, until the muddy water turns pale. 'Just coming,' I call. The bottles of luxury hair products that David buys for me skitter under my feet.

'Rachel? Open the door.' The handle shakes. 'Come on, let me in.' I freeze in the jet of water, then the clatter outside the door stops. Silence, so I finish washing and am about to turn off the shower when there's a scraping of metal. David is opening the lock from the other side. He must have got a screwdriver to turn the latch. I press back against the cold tiles.

'Hang on, I'm coming,' I say, reaching to find the dial to turn off the shower, but the bathroom door is open before I've had the chance and David is in the room.

'You don't need to lock the door, baby,' he says, and comes close to the steamed-up screen. 'Where have you been? I was so worried.'

I turn my back and stand in the jet of water, glancing over my shoulder for a second to see his features take on focus in the fog.

'Are you OK?' he says.

'I'm fine. Just finishing up.'

He moves backwards in the room, his body a hazy shape, then returns to me with the glowing expanse of a towel, open and ready in a silent command. I turn off the water and step into the fabric with my head down. Wet hair slicks my face. David wraps me in the cotton and pushes his fingers through my hair to take it back off my face, forcing my head up in jolts as he does so, and trying to catch my eyes with his. I keep my gaze downwards.

'You have no idea how worried I was.' He holds me tight in his arms and kisses my wet head. 'I was about to call the police. Why the hell didn't you return my calls?'

The bassline of my hangover throbs behind my eyes. I nuzzle into his shirt, hiding my face as my nostrils fill with the odour of dry-cleaning chemicals. Upstairs, David has another five identical shirts, plus duplicates of the tailored jeans and brogues that make up his casual weekend uniform. He places his hands on my cheeks and turns my head up to him. I keep my eyes shut.

'Why won't you look at me?' he says.

I open my stinging eyes.

'Have you been crying?'

'No, I've got soap in my eyes.'

He leans forward and kisses both my eyelids then folds his arms round me again. It's good to be held and I want to give in, release everything and hand over to David as I've always done, but this time there's too much to tell and I force the sob back down.

A pause.

'Rachel,' he says, 'I need some answers.'

I take a deep breath and speak into the towel. 'I'm sorry. I met an old school friend, it was last minute, I got carried away. Sometimes, I don't know, I just get sad about Mum, and last night I felt I needed some space. I checked into a hotel to sleep off the alcohol.'

'A school friend? You should have told me, baby, I was really worried, I missed you.' He slips his hand inside the towel and rubs the curve at the small of my back. My skin fizzles. 'It's not how we do things here. Is it? We have an order to things, a duty to each other.'

I look up, though he's not much taller than me. His thick blond hair melts in the steam.

'Well?' he says, holding my chin with his other hand

and looking directly into my eyes. 'You know that, don't you?' This close, the detail in his eyes is magnified, and dark spots pepper the green irises. The whites are bold and bright. 'We spoke about your episodes, and it's not how it's meant to be. It's not our path. I won't put up with any of that rubbish again.' His hand rubs my back with more pressure. 'No more locked doors, no more lies. We were doing so well, weren't we, baby? You need to toe the line. I can't keep bailing you out.'

I look down and move away from him, freeing my arms to grab the towel that's falling from my shoulders. The cuticles of my toenails are darkened by mud, and I remember the man's dirty hands and what looked like blue ink stains on his fingers. I take a breath to stop the urge to vomit.

David paces the floor. His shoes make a rhythmic tap and squeak on the tiles. One of the dogs, the older bitch and David's current favourite, has come in too. She paces with him. He stops. She sits at his side. He holds one of her ears between his forefinger and thumb and rubs the fur gently as if it were a child's soft blanket. The dog cocks its head sideways towards him and sits motionless. David looks down and smiles at the animal. Then he lifts his eyes and scans the ceiling and walls, bringing his gaze to rest on the sink. His fingers stop moving. The dog whines for him to continue but David lets go and turns to me.

'What's this?' he asks, one hand pointing at the thick scum around the edge of the sink. His gesture is poised in mid-air for dramatic effect, and he holds it there a beat

17

too long. 'Why is the sink so dirty?' He moves towards me, and as he gets close I go limp. I stand in front of him as I've learnt to do, not blinking or moving. His breath is hot on my face and he talks softly, in monotone. 'Tell me, Rachel. What's going on? What happened? The truth. Now.'

I take a deep breath. 'I hit a deer.'

'A deer? Where?'

'On Blackthorn Lane. It came out of nowhere. It was injured and frightened and I tried to help but it ran into the woods. I chased it but it got away.'

'Why would you do that? What would be the point of catching an injured deer? Did you think you could wrestle it into the car and take it to the vet's?'

'I'm sorry, I wasn't thinking. It was stupid of me.'

David inhales and exhales loudly through his nostrils, and his eyes skitter around the room, this time coming to rest on the bin liner with the remaining heel of a shoe stabbing through the plastic. 'So why are you throwing away your clothes?'

'Because they're dirty.'

'So wash them.'

'They're beyond cleaning.'

David comes up close again and opens the towel. He holds my arm as he scans the scratches on my forearm, raising the limb higher than is comfortable. Old acne scars pock his cheeks, the silent reminder of the imperfections of his youth. His grip is firm on my upper arm and his pupils jog between each of my eyes. 'Rachel, what's going on? You're a mess. Why didn't you tell me about the deer in the first place?' He leans forward, I lean back, and he sniffs the whisky-filled air in front of my mouth. I turn but it's too late. His jaw drops open. 'Good God, Rachel, you must have drunk the whole bar! Did you have doubles for breakfast?'

'I'm sorry, I didn't realize how late it was when I finished drinking, and then I knew I had to get back to you, I knew you'd be worried, and I thought I'd be OK to drive.'

'You're not making any sense, Rachel. Where were you drinking until the early hours and who is this mystery school friend of yours?'

His face is composed, though my arm stings as David intensifies the pressure and squeezes my skin into white lumps between his fingers.

'Tell me her name. Give me your phone, I want to call her.'

My brain tries to focus on another excuse, but the juggernaut of the accident sidewipes every thought. All I know for certain is that David's reaction to discovering my affair with Will would be more extreme than his response to finding out I've killed a man.

'He was on the road,' I say, my tears spilling out again. 'It was an accident. I didn't mean to. It was raining hard and the car, it . . .'

David moves away to get a tissue. 'Stop crying,' he says, handing me the paper. 'I can't understand a word you're saying.'

I wipe my face. 'I'm sorry . . . there was a man. Oh God, there was a man on the road.' I sob into the tissue then look up to see David's face turn red. I pull my words together. 'The car, I was going too fast. I couldn't stop in time.'

'My God!' He clasps his hair, then seizes me by my shoulders and shakes me. 'What have you done?'

'I didn't mean to. I knew I was over the limit and I panicked.'

He stops still and stares with round, unwavering eyes. 'Rachel, you need to tell me everything.'

'He shouldn't have been there. I mean, not in this weather, not on that road.' I put my arm up to David's shoulder, but he pulls away. 'Hardly anyone walks there, even in good weather.'

'I can't believe this.' He paces up and down, then smashes the flat of his hand against the tiled wall. 'Where is he now?'

'He's gone,' I whisper.

'What did you say?'

I shout, 'He's dead!' The noise makes me wince.

'Jesus!' Again he paces. 'Who was he?'

'I don't know.' I'm gabbling now. 'But I've seen him before. He's a homeless man, the one who walks every-where. No one will miss him.'

'How do you know?' With the heel of his hand, David rubs the frown at the bridge of his nose. 'Did you call an ambulance?'

'No.'

'Where is he now? Is he still on the road?'

'No.' I laugh weakly but David flicks his eyes at me and I stop. 'Why do you think I'm in this state?'

'What have you done with him?'

'I dragged him into the woods, far in, away from the road. You can't even see the cars from where I left him.'

'Good girl. Did anyone see you?'

'No.'

'What about on the way home?'

'A couple of cars. Only a few. No one I recognized.'

'And did you drop anything? Did you have all your things with you when you got back in the car?'

'Yes, I did. I do.'

'And the car itself?'

'It's a mess. The windscreen, the front bonnet's crushed, one of the lights—'

'Enough.' David holds up his hand. 'I need to think.'

The room's growing cold and my skin is speckled with goosebumps, like a plucked chicken. I hold the towel tight round me. David walks up and down, running his hands through his hair, his fingers leaving tramlines.

He stops and stands with his back to me. His shoulders heave up and down with his breath. He's mumbling but I can just make out his words: 'This is not how it's supposed to be.' Then he spins round to face me, his eyes alight. 'I will deal with the essentials, the car, these clothes,' he points at me, 'but you need to keep quiet.' He ties a tight double knot in the bin liner. 'We will carry on as if nothing has happened. This,' he waves his hand around the room like a conductor, lending me a granule of eye contact in the process, 'all that we've built – our marriage, this house, our business – it all stays the same. We cannot let this spoil how far we've come.'

I stand with my head bowed, looking at the muddy toeprints smudged on the tiles.

'Rachel,' he comes close and whispers in my ear. 'If I find out you were with someone else last night, I won't stand for it.' His lips touch my skin, so gently it's a tickle.

He leaves the room and the dog trots after him with her collar tinkling, already having chosen whose side she's on. As David passes the door, he pulls it gently and it winds shut in slow inches, closing finally when his footsteps have passed out of earshot. Facing me on the back of the door is my filthy coat; a tiny bomb of disorder against the smooth white wood. I fish inside the pocket for the watch from the roadside, and find it warm and damp. I hold it to my ear. It's still ticking. On the metal back is a smudge of blood which must have come from my hands after touching the man. The liquid has settled and dried into the letters of an inscription, 'TO MY PA'. I hear David's footsteps coming back and I scan the room for a hiding place, levering up the top of the false shelf which hides the toilet cistern. There is a gap down the side of the tank, and I tuck the watch in there before quietly lowering the shelf and standing back in the middle of the room. I shiver under the towel as a draught of outside air curls up my legs.

3

SMOKE IN THE BEDROOM

In the bedroom I dress into nightclothes and take a sleeping pill. It's afternoon when I lie down, the autumn dusk coming in, and my thoughts scatter and jerk through different scenarios: what if I'd been driving more slowly, what if I hadn't been drunk, what if I'd come home last night instead of staying at Will's? My mind won't settle, continually taking me back over the same questions, as if by repetition the impossible will resolve. All I can do is wait to be pulled into the familiar world of medication, and as the effects of the tablet trickle into my system I have half-waking dreams of a road rolling in front of me and a man leaping at the car. I swerve to miss him but no matter how hard I turn the wheel he keeps being sucked towards the bonnet. Cold panic bolts through me as I watch his body contort into a scrum of bones, and his hands leave inky streaks on the metalwork. The car absorbs him. Over and again these images circle my brain before finally the dream falls away and is replaced by a welcome void.

Six hours later I wake, and the walls of my bedroom have dulled in the evening dark. My back aches as I sit up in the bed, and my scratched arms scuff on the sheets. I take a few seconds to adjust before the vision of the man's face hits me afresh. With a punch of dread I realize that nothing has changed and a man is still dead.

A distant smell of smoke hangs in the room, and with it comes a flash of memory from when I was a little girl at home in my bedroom. Cigarette smoke crept up the stairs from the lounge. Mum and Dad had guests and for some reason I was scared to leave my room and use the toilet. Tonight, though, the smoke is from a bonfire. I put on my dressing gown and, using a chair as support, haul myself out of bed. On woozy legs I cross the room to the unshuttered window. The floor beneath my feet feels fluid as I'm caught in a sticky netherworld between sleep and reality – a third dimension where the edges of my consciousness glow and bob. It's dark but I keep the light off. The stark glare would be too much reality to bear.

On the driveway the roller door of our garage is halfway up and inside the light is on. My car has been driven in, and the bottom edge of the bonnet is visible, dented into a steel drum of fractured colour. A man walks round the car and crouches to examine the damage. My stomach lurches at the sight of him – a stranger already involved in my secret. Then I see David walking across the driveway. His face is lit a soft amber by the light from the garage, and he calls something to the other man I can't hear. The man stands and ducks under the metal door, bumping his head in the process before crossing the driveway towards David. He rubs his crown with a chuckle. David laughs back and looks relaxed, bordering on joyful, in a way I'm not used to seeing, and my legs start to shake. I run for the toilet, banging into the door frame in the process. As I pee I wrap myself tight in my dressing gown to stop the shiver.

When I come out of the en suite I look again from the window and see the two men closer together, still talking, their stance casual, as if they are friends or brothers tinkering with a car on a Saturday afternoon. David doesn't have a brother any more. The one time I insisted on meeting his parents, we went to their house for lunch. The walls and mantelpiece were covered in photos of David's older brother, who died when David was a toddler. Any remaining surface was taken up by china cats, dusted to a shine. His mum spent most of that lunchtime crying in the kitchen, and his dad glowered at the table as he alternated into his mouth forkfuls of roast dinner, sips of tea and drags on cigarettes that were chain-lit from an overflowing ashtray. Halfway through the meal David stood up and left, his chair falling flat on the floor behind him. I waited for him to come back but he didn't. Watching David tonight, he has more ease with this stranger

– brokered through their task of covering up a murder – than he ever gained from a childhood of being the wrong boy.

I turn from the window to light a cigarette and realize that my face is wet with tears. My fingers shake so much it's difficult to line up the match with the end of the cigarette. I haven't smoked in the house before, but now is not the time for domestic niceties. I take a drag and imagine I hear the crackle of the burning tobacco as if I were in a film. I take another drag and the noise gets louder. Ash drops on to the thick-pile carpet and I stare at the mess, willing myself to do something about it, but the message won't send to my muscles. Instead my hand moves towards my mouth, feeding in more nicotine. This same hand lifted glass after glass of whisky to my mouth last night, touched Will's face and pulled him to me. Only hours ago it steered a car round a sharp bend in the road and dragged a dead man into the woods. Deep in the undergrowth where he now lies, his body will be stiff, his skin and muscles breaking down. I wonder how long it will take until all that's left is bones.

Looking outside again, David has disappeared. I scramble through the upstairs rooms checking from each of the windows until I catch sight of him walking from the pool of the security light near our back door towards a small metal incinerator which sits on paving stones near the trees. He pokes a stick through the grille. Sparks whirl up and around him as his face glows from the flames. There's a pile at his side, and from it he picks up a piece of fabric, possibly a towel, and lumps it on to the flames. The material extinguishes the fire for a few seconds, but soon the embers sparkle through until again the flames take hold and tower above his head. He bends down and picks up another item, probably the bathrobe I wore earlier. Next, my shoes and my cashmere sweater. Then small containers, possibly shampoo bottles. I think of the plastic oozing through the gaps of the incinerator and spotting the charred ground underneath. Tomorrow the birds will peck at the hardened globs and take the poison to feed their chicks.

Barking carries from the distant undergrowth that rings our garden. It's too dark to see the dogs but they'll be excited by this unusual nocturnal activity, bounding in and out of the acres of shrubs and trees that camouflage our six-foot fence and buffer this sizeable estate from the outside world.

An image of the dead man's face crashing against the windscreen springs up at me again. From the epicentre of his skull, the glass fractures into a cobweb. I hold my hand over my mouth. My skin still smells of damp earth even though my hands have been scrubbed clean. I squeeze my eyes shut and see the briefcase fluttering into the undergrowth, then with a start I remember the watch hidden in the bathroom.

I tiptoe downstairs, back into the fallout of my earlier entrance: across the hallway my muddy footprints lead the way to the bathroom where inside they turn into a scuffle. The sink is still rimmed with scum, and the shower and bin are dotted with muddy handprints. Tears burst through and I bite my lip to hold in the sobs. From behind the toilet cistern I retrieve the watch. Above the hammer of my heartbeat I listen out for footsteps.

Back in bed, I check the watch is still ticking. The time reads 9.20: only half an hour slow. Twelve hours ago I was at Will's house. I wish I'd been brave enough to do as I so desperately wanted and stayed with him for the day, then none of this would have happened. My head buzzes with exhaustion and I'm terrified I may fall asleep with the watch still in my hand, so I stash it in the divan drawer under my mattress, then take another sleeping pill just to be sure. The remaining foil-wrapped capsules are on my bedside table. If I took them all at once there would be enough for me to sleep for good.

I don't know when David comes to bed but I have a vague recollection we have sex, though it could have been a dream. The rest of the night is swallowed by an oblivion of medication, and when I wake the next day, it seems like only minutes have passed.

Rain falls steadily outside, and even though it's a new day, the stale fumes of yesterday's events hang inside me. I put on my gown and slippers and go downstairs, still groggy and partly sedated, to find that David is out. There are no barks so he's probably taken the dogs for a walk. The hallway has been cleaned and the downstairs bathroom is pristine. A new bar of soap is in the shower along with fresh shampoo bottles, and the hand towel and bin liner have been replaced. There's not a fingerprint of mud on any surface. My errors have been erased.

David must have been in here last night scrubbing the corners with a toothbrush, his OCD cleanliness kicking in as I've seen happen before at times of stress, though haven't witnessed for years. When we were first starting up in business, before the success of Teller Productions, this micro-sorting and deep cleaning was his route towards control and order, and was undertaken in private, like binge eating.

He was more prone to failure at the beginning, his businesses experimental, but he was smart enough to use his mistakes as lessons to springboard the next enterprise. Even though money was intermittent, sometimes only topping up our student grants, when the cash did flow it was a warm blanket for us both. He itemized in a notebook all of our income and expenditure down to the penny, as if by printing the numbers on the page he had more control over their flow. To him the profits were a barometer of success and the more he made the less his need for clinical order. These flushes were used to pamper me through my final years of study. I was dressed and groomed in ways I'd never known before, and from then on there was no reason to go back to the person I had been, scratching around in my bedsit with the thermostat on low, and a trail of one-night stands who substituted for real affection. Instead I shone at David's side; he was my guardian angel and I was his creation. He revelled in my achievements, encouraging me to work harder, to get the best degree of my year group. It was only with me that he wasn't competitive, as if by choosing me he had melded our intellects together, and could claim my better grades as his own. Looking back, I realize that David spotted things in me that I knew nothing of at the time: that I was separate, and malleable, and desperate for anything better.

I check outside the front door. The roller shutter on the garage is now fully open and my car is gone. Next to the front door is my briefcase with laptop inside. I take the bag through to the kitchen and make some coffee in an attempt to clear the fog from my head. The warm liquid does little to take the chill from the house. I stand and sit, then move across the room, but nowhere feels right or safe in the silence, and I'm terrified to go back upstairs. Each time I blink, the dead man's face jolts behind my eyelids.

The back door scratches open and the dogs burst through into the boot room with David behind them. In the dividing door between the kitchen and this other room is a glass panel, and I watch as David takes off his coat and boots. His hair is wet. I'm not sure where to look, but before I decide he catches my eye and smiles. He comes through, puts his arms round me and presses me against the kitchen worktop with his whole body, kissing me in a way he's not kissed me in years.

'It's just you and me, baby,' he whispers in my ear, his

cheek damp against my face. 'I'm going to make everything right.'

A small tear of relief trickles down my cheek. I lift up
my arms and return David's hug. His body is warm, and
I think of the limp limbs I dragged into the woods yesterday. My hands jump away.

He kisses me again. 'You're all mine,' he says.

I haven't heard these words for years, this mantra
from when we were first together, and a spark of pleasure
surprises me as it twists in my gut. For a brief moment
I miss how we used to be, back when David's passion
was needy and he wanted only me for company, ignoring
phone calls and ordering takeaways so that we never had
to leave the bedroom. I wonder if I can fast-track back to
the person I was then and become the chosen one again,
relinquishing control and letting David's rules set order
to the days. When we met, no one else could even look
at me without chancing the wrath of his glare. He gave
me boundaries and curfews, rules for my friendships even
though most friends were long ago dismissed, and the
feminist in me bowed to the little girl who wanted to be
loved. Over time, after the newness between us waned,
instead of resisting I translated the rigidity into love; I
had been smothered but at least someone cared enough to
keep me in line. It was the same up until two years ago
when I met Will and we began our affair. From that point
on, the meticulously crafted machine of my life began to
disassemble.

'Nothing can touch us, baby,' David says.

'I—' I try to say, but David's mouth is on mine again, his hot tongue reaching inside, and there is no room for my words. His eyes are shut but I keep mine open. Just outside my vision stands the man from the road. With icy fingers, he reaches through my skin, holds tight and rocks my bones from the inside.

4

1976

Daddy's left a copy of *Twinkle* magazine on my bed. I run down and hug him but he's cross and sends me back upstairs, saying I should be asleep by now. In my bedroom, I flick through the cartoons of animals and fairies. I'm nearly ten, and this magazine is for babies, but I read it through twice anyway. Mum and Dad's friends arrive while I'm in my room so I don't see them, but I hear their voices in the lounge when I sneak on to the landing. The lady's perfume floats up the stairs and I imagine her long earrings tickling her bare shoulders, like Mummy's earrings do. Mum's dress tonight is pink. It's my favourite one. The man who's here has a deep voice. It's deeper than Daddy's.

Leaning over the banister, I stretch to see how far I can go without falling and I wonder if it would hurt if I fell, or whether I would bounce. My Barbie didn't break when I tried it with her. The floor down there used to be wood, like a puzzle, but Mum and Dad covered it with a fluffy-sheep carpet. 'You're old enough now not to spoil our nice things,' Mum said, 'so maybe we can get back to living like normal people.' Next to the front door is a desk which used to belong to my nanna. Daddy says it's worth lots of money but Mummy wants to get rid of that next. It's old and dark and she says it makes her depressed. On top of the desk is a knobbly orange vase. It's full of flowers from the garden, and some of their stems have bent and snapped. Mum tried to put too many in – she always does because she likes lots of flowers. 'They give the house good vibes,' she says. Under the vase are lots of circles on the wood where the varnish has come off. It's not fair as I always have to be careful putting my cups on furniture, but Mum can do what she wants with Nanna's desk.

Supper was quick tonight – cheese on toast with a tomato on the side. The knife wasn't very sharp so I bit straight into the tomato even though I hate the way the skin pops and the squishy seeds shoot into your mouth. Afterwards I was still hungry but there was no time for more. 'You've had enough, greedy guts,' Mum said. I tidied the kitchen and she hoovered the lounge. 'Don't just leave your plate to drain, Rachel. I want it dried up and put away. The cutlery as well.'

I wiped over the surfaces but my hands weren't strong enough to wring out the cloth and it left big watery streaks on the table. Mum came in from the sitting room and tutted. 'Oh, I'll do it, Cinders.' She grabbed the cloth from me and squeezed it over the sink. Lots of grey water came out. 'If you want something done properly, you might as well do it yourself.' She held her tummy away from the edge of the counter to keep her evening dress dry. Her body curved and her bottom stuck out, so that in her high heels she looked like a beautiful flamingo. She had a bun on her head which puffed the rest of her hair out in a cottage-loaf circle. Ringlets came down at the sides, and round her neck she wore a black choker.

'Where are you going?' I asked.

'Nowhere, we're staying in. And you're not to come down and bother us tonight. Take some water up with you. Daddy has lots of important paperwork to go over with Brian. He'll be very, very cross if we're disturbed. I mean it, young lady.'

On the counter was a bottle of medicine and a spoon. Mum gave me some.

'I'm not ill,' I said.

'Well you might be if you don't take this.'

It was disgusting, and when she went into the other room, I put a chair up to the cupboard to get a glass. I don't need the chair for the sink any more. As I reached for the tap, my school tights slid down my hips and the pant bit hung low between my legs.

'I need new tights,' I shouted through to Mum.

'I'll have to stop feeding you,' she replied.

I hear the adults laughing so I leave the banister and go back to my bedroom, put on my nightie then brush my teeth at the sink in the corner of the room. I can still taste the medicine under the toothpaste. Daddy made me take

35

an extra spoonful. It's eight o'clock now and even though I don't normally go to sleep this early, I'm really, really tired. Lying on my bed, the sounds from downstairs come through the floor. A moment ago there was talking. Now it's quiet. The key to the lounge door clunks as it's turned.

I wake up later when everything is dark, and I'm dying for the loo. There's the sound of furniture being moved downstairs. I slip out of my room and creep along the edges of the carpet to avoid the creaky floorboards, and use the bathroom without turning on the light or flushing. On the way back I peep through the banisters. The door to the lounge is slightly open. Inside a light is on, but it's dim, like the lamp has been knocked over. The hallway is dark apart from a wavy pattern on the front-door glass where the trees outside blow in front of a street light.

A man walks from the kitchen towards the lounge door. He has his back to me and he's holding the ice bucket. Apart from that, he's got nothing on. The glow from the lounge ahead of him lights up fuzzy hair on his shoulders and down his arms, like his body is a dark cloud in front of the sun, and I can see more curls of fur down his back. He reminds me of a bear standing on two legs. I step back quickly and a board squeaks. The man turns his head with a flick and he stares at me. Even though it's very dark, I can tell he's smiling. I stand completely still, holding my breath.

Mum's voice comes from the lounge.

'Brian, darling, what's taking you so long? Come here, you gorgeous creature.'

The man turns his head back to the room and walks in, slowly. There are huge dimples on his bottom as he swaggers through the door. His bum looks as if someone's dug their hands into lumps of wet clay and I think of God making the first man out of the dust of the soil and breathing into his nostrils to make him alive.

From inside the room a woman giggles. It's not Mummy. The door closes and is locked again. I don't know where Daddy is but his shoes are still by the front door.

I go back to bed and pull the covers over my face.

The next day at breakfast, Mummy's already up and dressed with all her make-up on.

'Are you going out?' I ask.

'No, I just woke early and it was such a beautiful day that I couldn't help myself.'

'Help yourself to what?'

She hums and doesn't answer.

Daddy's plate is to one side with only half his food eaten. Mum says he'd had enough and has gone to work early.

I have bacon and eggs with fried bread and freshly squeezed orange juice, but I'm not used to this much. Like Daddy. Mum is smoking, and as she hums she blows smoke from her nose. She stares out the kitchen window.

I recognize the song, it's called 'Killing Me Softly' and it's her favourite. She has the record and she plays it all the time.

'Mummy,' I say, 'there was a man in the house last night who didn't have any clothes on.'

She spins round and looks at me. 'Don't be silly. You must have been dreaming.'

'He looked like a bear.'

'Now I know you were dreaming.'

'But I wasn't. I saw him. I heard you talking to him.'

Her mouth goes all tight and wrinkly. 'Oh, Rachel, you're such a little fibber. If you can't lie properly, then don't say anything at all.'

I stare at my food and go to eat some more, but before I can Mum lifts up the plate and starts scraping the bits into the bin. 'Don't want you getting fat now, do we?' she says. She picks up my bag and coat and hands them to me. The bag is full, so she must have made my packed lunch already, and it's exciting to imagine what she's put in as I normally do it myself. 'Probably time for school now anyway.' She opens the back door.

'But it's only eight o'clock.'

'Oh well.'

I smile. 'Can't I stay with you a bit longer?'

'Sorry, Cinders, but I'm busy busy busy today. You can wait with your friends at the gates.'

I stand on the doorstep until Mum shuts the door and I have to jump off the edge. Her singing gets louder, and I can still hear her through the open windows as I walk round to the front. I tiptoe inside the squares, not on the lines of the garden path, all the way to the gate, which is good, as it means a meteor won't crash into our house while I'm at school.

5

GRAVY

In the week since the accident, the season turns abruptly to autumn, and now it's hard to imagine the late heavy summer existed at all. Days of rain ended the heat, turning the hard ground to mulch. The mid-October leaves are disappearing fast from the trees, and the few that hang on do so in bewildered stoicism. Even though the scratches on my arms have faded, the weather gives me an excuse to cover myself up, the habit of layers a comfort, as if beneath them I will disappear. Tonight I wear a cardigan over my dress and use a shawl when I'm at the table. I leave my hair down how David likes it – it's my best feature and lets me get away with making little effort elsewhere.

We entertain at our house about twice a month; potential clients mostly, but also more random business associates, people with whom it's good to keep up for no other reason than they are rich and powerful and may at some point assist our expanding empire. David had planned to cancel this evening's dinner as he thought I wasn't ready for company, but the lure of schmoozing was too much for him in the end, plus the packet of diazepam he presented me with a few days ago has kept me nicely sedated. 'Where did you get these?' I asked. 'From the doctor, of course,' he replied. But David never gets ill and as far as I know doesn't even have a GP.

I've not been back to work, but if I had the energy to get into the office to deal with the pile of budgets that are waiting to be signed off, the familiar busy routine would be a salve over my darker thoughts. At work it often seems as if I'm acting the part of being in charge but I've been doing it for so long I can't tell any more, and I sense that David has got used to and prefers the pretend me to the real version. In place of being at the office in person, I've been getting as much paperwork as possible emailed over to me, even petty things an assistant could deal with, and for once I've been using my laptop more than pen and paper. At night when the sleeping tablets aren't strong enough to stop the dream of the crash waking me, my planner is on the bedside table where my reading book used to be, and I can switch heads by logging into work zone. David tuts at the bedroom light turning on and off, and he sweeps my paperwork from the kitchen table when he sits down to his morning coffee and broadsheet, but as he's watched his efficient business partner return he's eased off on his monitoring of me. Hence tonight he's allowed what he believes is the only work that should infiltrate our home life: a social event that promises to bring financial rewards at a later date.

This evening we are hosts to Alex and his wife Jane. Alex is a partner in the law firm Hand, Fletcher & Richard. The company has its HQ in London and a satellite office in Brighton. Alex is telling his favourite story, the one about his father being the second of the Richards to go into the family business, after which Mr Richard Senior passed the baton to his son. Hence, with a big laugh that shakes his elongated frame, Alex plays his trump card and calls himself Richard the Third. David laughs too, even though he's heard the story before. Alex's constant gabble meanders into his firm's recent rebranding, their name now abbreviated to HFR. 'More sparky and immediate,' he says. But months ago before the change there was a high-profile court case involving a female employee who'd been passed over for promotion, plus other allegations of sexual misconduct between a secretary and a senior partner. So with HFR the company has swept away the cobwebs of old-school handshakes and inbred misogyny, and updated themselves. 'It cost a fortune. Thieves, the lot of them,' Alex says of the agency who came up with the new branding. 'I'd like to set fire to their Shoreditch offices, preferably with the little art-school cretins inside.'

I take this cue to leave our guests and David in the dining room, and walk to the adjacent kitchen, one of the only rooms downstairs with walls. Much of the internal space in the building is open-plan and divided into zones by shelves and display cases, some of which house pieces from David's toy collection, the valuable ones that aren't in storage: vintage *Star Wars* figures, pristine and still in the box, a Matchbox car collection in height order and rows. David, the little boy who had so few toys, now has everything he wants, but he no longer wants to play.

Walls of windows face a manicured garden of topiary shrubs in zinc planters, where an unused swimming pool simmers blue in the night-time air. The separate kitchen not only relieves me of the pressure of performing to guests while I'm cooking, but it's also one of the only spaces apart from the bathrooms where I'm private and no one can peer in from outside, especially at night when the house is illuminated like a neon box.

I light a cigarette and stand at the worktop for a moment trying to remember what I've come in for. Scratching comes from the boot room where the dogs are kept when we have guests. The animals are muzzled to stop them barking. On the worktop is the notebook we use for our household expenses along with a couple of the pens which live in the kitchen drawer with the book. In the study there's a stack of identical ledgers: new ones to fill in when this one is full, plus a shelf of already-finished books lined up in chronological order. David and I have been keeping a record of our personal expenditure since we were at uni; it helped us streamline as much money as possible into the business while allowing ourselves the indulgences we thought we deserved. Even though we don't have to scrimp any more, we continue the practice out of routine. It's a reassuring nod towards order. The book is open and only the first couple of pages have been filled out in this relatively new book. I flick through the recent entries, the outgoings a diary of the past few days. The wine for this evening came from our cellar and was delivered two weeks ago: £600. That same day I remember I'd been trying to contact Will but his phone was switched off. Another entry from later that week is the dog groomer who came a day before the accident: £80. If only it were possible to rewind time and tamper with these seemingly innocuous events – arrive home late for the wine delivery, forget to walk the dogs so they were too jumpy for the groomer, change the meeting with Will to a different night – then the man on the road could still be alive. His dead face slides across my vision. I shake my head and focus on the book to try and rid myself of the image.

Next on the page there's a break, and the date jumps forward to the food delivery for this evening's meal which cost £189. My new dresses ordered by David: £800. He bought two sizes. We'll send back the one that doesn't fit. I'm wearing the smaller one and I've used some pins round the waist. David's usually pretty accurate but I've lost some weight.

Smash against my windscreen.

There's burning and I turn to see smoke seeping from the edges of the oven door. The pork belly should be crisp on top but it's gone too far. Clearly I've miscalculated. As I open the oven, a food smog stings my eyes and I fumble in blindness, taking out the meat and turning on the extractor fan, hoping to remove this clue to my ineptitude. The meat rests on the worktop as I wipe away the tears. Smoke gulps through the open window into the cold dark of our garden. With a knife I cut the burnt fat from the meat, removing as much black as possible.

Thick dark liquid spreads on the tarmac.

A sauce from the butcher's was going to be a side, but I slosh the liquid over the surface of the meat to disguise the fatty mess, and arrange new potatoes round the edge of the serving dish. The potatoes have split and their powdery innards puff through cracks in their skins – they don't look like the picture in the recipe book. From another pan I drain dark-green broccoli water, and a vegetable sludge clings to the sides. One of David's expectations is that I cook for these occasions, exhibiting prowess and flair so he can bask in the glory of having chosen such a skilled and multi-faceted wife. In the past I've played the part willingly, researching meal plans and making a timetable for the various recipes, but this particular culinary disaster may finally close the door on that duty.

Jane's voice comes through from the other room. Her clipped nasal pitch cuts across the whirr of the extractor fan. 'Not much of an earner, the stables. More pocket money really. Alex likes me to keep busy.'

'I haven't been riding for years,' David says – I don't recall him ever riding. 'I'd love to come and take advantage of your stables sometime. Do you have a horse big enough for a man of my build?' His voice is more of a drone, his words less perceptible above the kitchen noise, but I can tell he's upped his accent to public school, falling in line as he does with whomever he's talking to, mirroring them with subconscious messages of approval and reassurance. Jane titters. I imagine David's winked at her.

My cigarette, balanced on the edge of the hob, burns a streak of brown on the shiny metal. I lift it and notice dirt under my nails.

Fingers not hooves.

My thoughts flip. To the time I saw the homeless man in the village shop, some months before the accident. The shopkeeper kept her eyes on him as she beeped my items past the scanner with blind precision. 'No, put that one back, love,' she shouted across to him, stern but wary as if talking to a teenager with a knife in their pocket. I turned to watch as the man pulled down a pile of cut-price DVDs and I wondered if he even owned a machine to play them. Perhaps a palatial mansion hidden in the countryside with his body fluids collected in jars. The shopkeeper and I exchanged a private smile. She tutted, leant across the counter to me and whispered, 'Came out of a children's home and went straight into prison.' Her husband was refilling the cigarette shelves behind her. He twisted round and joined in the gossip. 'No he didn't, he was a concert pianist back in the day. Got his hands broken over a gambling debt. Probably deserved it.' I paid and stood to one side to sort my bags. The man came up to the counter with a tin of dog food and a sliced white loaf held in a hand so filthy that the mechanism of his fingers had cut white creases around his knuckles and palm. Mixed in with the dirt were blue and red stains, like ink.

I drag what's left of the cigarette dry, blowing the smoke cloud in the direction of the kitchen window.

'You died in here or something?' David's head pokes round the kitchen door. I flick the cigarette into the inch of green water covering the bottom of the sink. The butt hisses and floats above the black hole of the waste disposal. 'You've got panda eyes, Rachel. Better check the mirror before you come back in.'

He returns to the table and I hear the glasses chink, followed by the brittle shot of Jane's laugh. The glass of white wine I brought in from the table has several half-moons of red lipstick round the edge, and the liquid's warmed, but I swig it down anyway with two painkillers. I'm on the highest over-the-counter dose for the pain that crawls up and down my spine but has no single source or intensity. I must have pulled something when I dragged the man through the woods, and the damage persists even though I'd have thought it would have eased by now. I've made and cancelled two doctor's appointments, worried I might cry if she gives me that look and asks me if everything's OK at home. For now the sensation is a reminder, and it takes me back to the woods, safe in the hollow quiet of the trees. I wish I could return and keep watch over the man, be in his company. I wonder if anyone would care if they knew he was dead.

I repair my make-up and take the food through to the table, sitting down next to Alex. Opposite me is Jane. David is at a diagonal. The food smells better than it looks and their disappointed faces glow in the candle-light.

'Isn't this lovely,' Jane says. She wears a peach-coloured dress the near exact match of her skin tone. Aside from the little flush which runs up her neck and into her cheeks, the junction between skin and fabric is confused. Where the material stops above her bust, a nude chiffon continues across her chest and down her arms so that her Dalmatian pattern of moles appear to be woven into the fabric. The dress is the kind a mother would buy a teenage daughter who's going to her first party or a prom – a daughter who's not too racy but is testing her toe in the waters of femininity. And failing.

'You have worked hard, Rachel,' Jane says. 'Tell me, which butcher do you use? I've been buying my meat directly from the farm shop outside the village, but quite honestly, I'm not sure it's all that good. The last time we entertained, the beef was almost green. I mean, I like my meat hung a good long time, but it was just over the edge, don't you think, darling?' She looks at her husband, who opens his mouth to reply. 'Anyway,' she continues, 'I won't bother you for the telephone number now. Our next dinner party is for ten and I always get the caterers in if it's over six.'

David carves the meat and puts it on the plates. *Earth mixed with old piss.* I pass round the vegetables and take a big drink from the fresh glass of wine I've poured myself. The near-frozen liquid chills my throat and the sensation is the only real thing in the room. David looks down at me from his standing position as I top up my glass. I hold his gaze and lift the wine to my lips. He's sober, he's chosen to stay that way, as I used to do on these occasions before the accident; this is a business meeting, not a casual dinner with friends.

While they've been waiting, David has kept the guests' glasses well filled. They attack the food. Jane pushes the meat and vegetables around her plate with small excited prods of her cutlery, making little piles and collecting each of them on the back of her fork then posting the nugget into her neat mouth. Alex eats his vegetables first, saving the meat till last, which he hurls in big slabs into his mouth, talking all the while to David about cases lost and cases won. I'm curious as to how this act of eating together has become such a cultural highlight; all I can think of is the food mixing in their mouths and being squeezed towards their stomachs. Eating is function not fun, it's always been that way, and I prefer to eat in private, only taking the edge off my hunger, if I can be bothered to eat at all. David, as usual, clears his meal with invisible ease. He stares over at my plate, still loaded with food, and my knife and fork stacked to one side. When he was dishing up, he put more on to my plate than anyone else's.

'Come on, Rachel, eat up,' he says in a loud voice, 'the food is delicious.' Then he looks to Alex with another wink. 'Who'll look after me if you waste away?'

Jane and Alex watch as I pick up my cutlery and saw through the large slice of burnt pork fat that David chose specially for me. I put the piece in my mouth, chew, then add a small branch of broccoli.

'I know exactly what it's like when you've cooked,' Jane says. 'By the time it comes to eating, you've completely lost your appetite.'

David smiles at me and refills our guests' wine glasses. Jane puts her hand over hers to signal she's had enough, but too late and the wine splashes her fingers. She giggles, looking up at David with big-girl eyes. She's not his type but I admire his ability to make her feel vital while at the same time keeping Alex firmly in his court. There's no competition between the men – if anything, David's flirtation with Jane is a compliment to Alex on his choice of wife – and the men exchange smiles and winks. Or perhaps there's some kind of readying of Jane, a nod from David to Alex, a telepathic collaboration between two men who understand how to get their needs met, that she'll be easy later. With the food on my plate reorganized and my napkin flung over one half, it looks like I've eaten more than I have, and I hold an unlit cigarette between my fingers and wait for the others to finish. No one smokes any more, but it's my house and I won't stand outside in the cold. And anyway, I'll pay for my bad behaviour later.

Jane wipes the corners of her mouth on her napkin and I spark up. Alex rhythmically chews his last piece of meat with a shut mouth. He puts his cutlery to one side of the plate, then turns his whole body to me, head tilted back as if he's looking through bifocals. One arm is slung over the back of the chair. He swallows the last of his food.

'I used to smoke, you know, before I met Jane,' he says, adjusting his position in the chair to sit taller. Areas of pink scalp show underneath his dark hair, spattered with grey, as if someone has run a paintbrush across his thinning pate. 'I was on twenty a day. Jane has asthma, so I gave up. It can upset her for days afterwards.' He looks at Jane, who's examining the light fitting, then back at me. 'They're bringing in a ban in all public spaces. Good thing too.'

I take another drag and blow the smoke in the opposite direction, away from the table.

'Yes, well, Rachel's only recently started this up,' David says, looking at me with a hard glare. 'Seems approaching forty is a licence to all sorts of bad habits.' The reference to my age is a bold snub in such high company – gentlemen don't openly dismiss their wives – but the slight works as David follows through with a smile to Alex and the men share a chuckle, although I'm not sure either of them know exactly what it is they're laughing at.

'Oh, what will you get Rachel for her birthday?' Jane asks David, popping sparrow coughs into the petite hollow of her fist. 'I suppose it'll be a big surprise.'

'I let Rachel choose her own gifts these days,' he says. He used to buy me fussy jewellery – pieces that would suit his mother – then sulk in silence when they were never worn. 'Open chequebook, you know,' he continues. 'I mean, what do you get the woman who has it all?' David looks back at me. 'Why don't you open a window or something?'

David pronounces the 'th' in 'something' as an 'f'; a tiny lapse in his disguise. Alex winces visibly at the 'somefing' and Jane's back straightens, her breasts push out, and for a flicker of a second she becomes assured, caustic, her social armour falling away. The guests hold a look between themselves but give nothing away. In this parade of class and etiquette around the dinner table, I could fall over drunk, smash glasses, serve up terrible food, and Alex and Jane would forgive all that over David's vocal faux pas.

'That's a beautiful new Aston Martin you have,' David says to Alex, racing into his repertoire of flattery to cover the mistake. 'I've had the Jag for a couple of years but I'm thinking of an upgrade. Would you recommend it?'

Alex coughs into his napkin before answering. 'Yes, it's splendid. Runs very smoothly. Even Jane can handle it on the corners.'

Jane tries to laugh, but the noise comes out like a chicken's cluck. David follows on quickly in his best posh accent: 'Can I get you anything else before we clear the plates?'

I swagger to the window, sensing Alex's eyes on me, and pull the last out of the cigarette before flicking it in a Catherine wheel of sparks into the garden. If the grass and trees outside were as dry as they were in the summer, a blazing fire could start and engulf the lot of us. I return to the table. Jane pulls her shawl round her shoulders, and David tries to refill the glasses, but both the guests insist they've had enough. David serves the two of us water. 'Why don't you get the dessert, darling?' he says.

The wine mixed with all the pills I've taken has gone to my head, and I cash in on David's unexpected vulnerability. Before the accident I never would have goaded him like this. What will it be later, what punishment fits this particular crime?

'Oh, I need another drink first,' I say. 'I've got some catching up to do.'

I swing my legs round to face Alex and cross one limb over the other. The slit in my skirt falls apart to show the top of my thigh, stopping a couple of centimetres short of my knickers. Alex leans back, louche in his chair with his legs wide and the napkin in his lap. He keeps his eyes on the top-most V in my skirt for a second too long before he closes his legs and glides them back under the table. As he does so he lifts the napkin to dust his lips, and exposes the line of his erect penis in his trousers. His groin is hidden from the others, but I can't tell whether he's meant me to see, though there's a small smile on his face. I spin round to David who's watching me with a wooden glare. My stomach bubbles. Would it be too soon to go to the bathroom and bring up the food?

Jane scans the pictures in the room with pigeon darts of her head.

'Pudding?' Her voice has raised a degree. 'I'm not sure I could fit in another thing. That was absolutely delicious, Rachel.' She folds her napkin into a small rectangle and places it next to her plate, giving it a little pat, as if I would want to use it again. 'We have an early start in the morning,' she says. 'The horses don't care if you've had a late night, and we planned to go for a ride before breakfast tomorrow. Didn't we, darling?' She stares at her husband, who takes a moment to jerk into action.

'Yes, yes, that's right,' he replies, 'we did.'

I tip my water into David's glass and top mine up with wine.

'No, we insist,' David says. 'It's no trouble, is it, Rachel?' He clasps his hands on the table in front of him and bends his torso across his knuckles to address Alex. Jane flashes panic at her husband but he's snared now. 'You haven't finished telling me about your new business venture.'

I recognize the tone in David's voice: his restlessness to win, to find new arenas in which to compete and succeed. Our production company has become formulaic in its success and David needs a new challenge. As if we don't already have enough. Perhaps if there was more between us as a couple, David's need to look outward would be less. But then again, I doubt it.

'Where's the land you're developing?' he says, fixing his eyes on to Alex – there's no chance now that our guests will be allowed to leave without rewarding David's attention. 'How far into the planning process are you? I might be interested in coming on board. I've got a fair bit sloshing round the accounts, and I'd rather it made a real profit than the paltry interest the bank pays.' He loosens one hand from his grip on the table and leans across to me, stroking my arm which lies on the tablecloth. 'Go and get the dessert for our guests, please, darling.' He lifts my hand and kisses it, looking long and slow into my eyes; a threat that only I can read.

The kitchen's hard halogen light smarts my eyes and magnifies the mess of dishes and saucepans covering the worktops – I'll leave them for the cleaner in the morning. From the fridge I take a pear tart and remove it from its packaging, then pour cream into a jug, holding the pot high so the strand of cream glugs and ripples into the pool at the bottom. I tip it between the two containers a couple of times.

'How are we doing, Rachel?' David is standing behind me. I freeze. I hadn't heard him come in. He comes up close but I don't turn, his proximity a noose of static between us. 'Is there a problem?' he says. His lips brush my neck. The hand I hold the jug with starts to shake. He moves his mouth close to my ear and whispers, 'I need you to stop this. Now.'

His steps retreat and I turn to watch the last of him exit the room. Next door I hear him continue his conversation with Alex, and I turn off the extractor fan so I can listen more clearly.

'So, it's Bill Briggs's land, is it?' says David. 'Around Blackthorn Lane? I never thought he'd sell. That farm's been in his family for centuries.'

Blackthorn Lane. The road where the accident happened.

In my lower back, the parasite of pain I've had since the accident burns and expands into my gut. I grip my stomach.

Alex replies, 'Well, we've known the Briggs family for generations. My father tried to get a project going on the land years ago – back in the seventies he was going to build some flats – but there was too much red tape involved.' I bend over the sink. 'This time we're only taking a section of the woods close to the road. It's mostly a brownfield site, though you wouldn't know it. The vegetation has completely swamped what buildings were there as the place has been idle so long. Bill will get to keep most of his arable land. He's up for selling more in the future though. It could be a real money-spinner.' The voices have relaxed again, the filter of business soothing the stilted evening. 'My man at the council's assured me the planning's nearly gone through. Bit of local resistance to public rights of way and whatnot, protected species claptrap. They're threatening to set up camp. Load of work-shy pikeys if you ask me. But we know how to get round these things – it pays to be a member of the same golf club as the councillors, if you know what I mean – and we're about ready to start digging. There are a few transients around there, some old vagrant who lives in a caravan. A lunatic by all accounts. Dug his heels in years ago when my father was trying to develop the area, but all he does now is walk everywhere with a bloody briefcase. So there's no one really to kick up much of a fuss, and nothing the bulldozers can't handle.'

A white-wine bile creeps up my throat. The walking man. I didn't know he had a home. A caravan in the woods. He must have been on his way home to shelter from the rain when I hit him. Almost there, then never home again.

'And on the subject of funding,' Alex continues, 'one of our investors is looking a bit shaky. We'd love to have you on board but you'll need to step on it. I know it's a different avenue from your normal line of business, but we'd only be asking for your investment at this stage, unless of course you wanted to be more involved. I'm sure you understand the politics of a new project, how sometimes we need to push through the formalities sharp-ish, and not all the paperwork ends up going through the formal channels. One or two members of the planning committee may need some guidance casting their votes in our favour.' I hear him slurp his drink. 'It's impossible to get these deals passed without a bit of persuasive currency changing hands. I should know, I've worked on enough of them.' A wine glass chinks. 'No wire taps in here, are there?' he adds with a guffaw.

I peel off my cardigan and hold on to the edge of the sink. Freezing air blasts through the open window, but the cold does little to help the sweat. The pain is a lump in my stomach. I retch.

'Do you need a hand?' Jane's voice is close. I turn to see her holding a pile of plates. She puts them on the side and rushes forward. A knife falls from the stack and jangles on the floor. Jane's fingers are chill against my flushed skin. 'Good Lord, are you all right?'

'Would you mind leaving me alone?' I say. 'Please.'

But she continues pulling at my arm and calls out, 'David, David, your wife! Come quick. She needs you.'

I shudder at the thought of what it is I need from David.

The two men join us in the kitchen. David comes up behind me and picks up my cardigan, throwing it over my shoulders while prising my fingers from the sink. Alex fills a glass with water and tries to get me to drink, but the water splashes down my front. A surge of vomit comes into my throat. I swallow it down. Jane fiddles with my arm and it's the tickle of her touch next to the tugging and pulling that finally breaks me.

'Get off me!' I shout. Everyone pauses in their effort but no one takes their hands away. 'All of you.'

There's a flurry of activity and hushed voices. Alex and Jane leave the room and David follows them with 'sorry' and 'not been herself recently'.

'Do get in touch if there's anything we can do,' I hear Jane say from the hallway. 'Of course, of course,' David replies. Even an emergency has its etiquette, a polite pseudo-concern, but everyone knows the most that will happen is a follow-up call. I want to rush into the hallway and punch Jane in the face, though all I can do is slide to the floor. With a clatter of footsteps and banging doors they're gone.

David comes back into the kitchen. From my position on the floor, I see only his feet. He stands next to me, motionless. Spotlights on the ceiling reflect elongated white shapes on the polished leather of his shoes, but the pattern is interrupted by a splash of gravy from the meal. Seconds pass. Slowly, David bends down on to his haunches with clicking knees, and uses a tissue to wipe the small imperfection from his shoe. He stays in this position to deliver the speech that I know is coming.

'We have a business to run,' he says. 'We're partners. There are meetings on Monday and projects that need your input.' His voice is soft and he spreads out his words as if he's talking to a toddler. 'Take a good look at yourself, Rachel. What do you see? Where has my wife gone? You've had a week now, and I'm relying on you to pull yourself together and get back to business. If you don't get this hysteria in check, I'll take everything away: this house, your car, your nice clothes. You try and stand up to my army of lawyers. And as for your little detour in the woods, I won't protect you any more.'

'But what about the man?' I say. 'His body. If they bulldoze the area they'll find him.'

'You don't even know if they're building in the same part of the woods where you left him.'

'How do we find out?'

'There is no "we", Rachel. You need to move on. You left no traces? All your things were accounted for?'

'Yes,' I rub the floor with my palm, 'but it'll be obvious he didn't die from natural causes.'

'It's safer to leave him where he is. He was a drunk. A loser. Bad things happen to bad people. If someone discovers the body, there's nothing to lead them to you, and no one will bother to look too closely into the death of a homeless man.'

'But I'm scared.'

'Deal with it.'

'But, David—'

'Enough.' He pinches my nose and the force of it snaps my head back, cracking my skull against a drawer handle. My mouth opens in a silent gasp. With his other hand David pushes the dirty tissue into my mouth. The gravy is a cold slime on my tongue, and the paper hits the back of my throat. I struggle between breath and vomit.

David stands and his shoes swivel, taking him from the room. Before he leaves, he opens the boot-room door.

I lean forward and retch, spitting the tissue into my hand. It's brown with the watery sauce and soaked in saliva bubbles. From the hallway I hear David's footsteps. He whistles to the dogs. Leads jangle, barking, a door opens and shuts, then silence. I pull myself up and run the tap to swill out my mouth. It takes several goes, leaning my face into the stream, water splashing over my face and soaking the front of my dress, before my mouth is clean. My tongue holds the memory of the pressure from the tissue.

Would Will still want me if he saw me like this? Would he chase after David and smash him to the ground? Or perhaps he'd think, like I do, that I deserve all I get.

On the worktop, the carcass from dinner is split and flayed. A dozy fly buzzes round the meat. I take a fresh bottle of wine from the fridge, pressing the cold glass on my forehead and cheeks before pouring myself another. With the bottle and glass in hand, I go up to our bedroom where I change into nightclothes and jump into bed, wrapping the duvet close round me to stuff up any shafts of air.

In the ceiling above the bed is a large glass apex with no blinds or curtains to hide the stars. David and I had ideas that we'd lie here watching the turning of the heavens, and it makes me laugh that we ever had conversations like that. But there must have been a love of sorts once, or at least I believed there was; fear and control won out in the end, but for a while the fresh brilliance of being held convinced me it was love. In reality we rarely spend waking time together in here, this place which was designed as the energetic centre of the house; after David has sex with me, we turn away from each other in silence and sleep with eye-masks.

I drink some wine and put my laptop on my knees. The battery is dead. From my bed I scan the room for the charger, looking across the furniture and mirrors carefully placed to create the maximum positive chi. David's self-help and NLP books have their own built-in bookcase for easy bedtime reference, and some of the other shelves are given over to books on movies, art and music: *100 Books You Should Read Before You Die*. Even though I've never seen David read any fiction, I've often heard him quote from Dickens or Kerouac, the text chosen depending on who he's talking to; his ability to sum up the person in front of him and mirror back what they most want to hear has never ceased to amaze me. Currently on his bed-side table is *Meditation for Dummies*.

The charger isn't here so I get up and walk into the adjacent dressing room where David and I have a ward-robe each, divided in the middle by a mirror. My work bag is on the floor next to the cupboard but the bag is empty. The drawers inside my wardrobe are open and I push them shut, checking first that the old McVitie's biscuit tin from Mum's house is still safe in the bottom drawer underneath my scarves and belts. Inside this tin are all my precious things: ticket stubs from a gig I went to see with a friend at uni, dried flowers from Mum's garden, some old textbooks marked up by a teacher who was kind to me. Dad's letters. The only other items I brought from Mum's house were the few pieces of Dad's clothing he left or forgot when he moved out. I kept them in a bag because they smelt, but when we moved to this house, David put them out for the bin men. 'What are you doing carting around those old rags?' he said. 'You hardly knew your father anyway. Time to let go of the past, Rachel.' I rescued the clothes and hid them in a cardboard box in the garage. There's a shirt with a tear, some gardening trousers and a large woollen overcoat.

All the things that matter to me are concealed. Every-thing of David's is on display.

I give up on the charger and go back to bed, taking

another gulp of wine as I sit on the edge of the mattress, then deciding to finish the glass. The liquid settles my stomach, like a blanket over fire, but it doesn't take away the pain. Lying down, the duvet tightens round me as I squirm to get more comfortable, and I drift into thoughts which cross over with dreams and back again so that I can't tell what's real: an endless tarmac lit by car headlights, rolling and rolling, the edges of my vision falling to black. The man in the woods, his body in time-lapse, maggots and worms eating him in frenzied circles until all that's left are white bones.

I raise myself from the pillow and check the time: 10.58. David is still out. Perhaps I've got away with it tonight, the dirty tissue message enough. Or maybe I'll wake tomorrow, as I have before, to find the bedcovers trailed in paw marks and the bloodied end of a rabbit on my pillow. The dry-cleaners couldn't save the antique throw that used to belong to my mother – she used it to cover our sofa at home – so now the dogs have it as their bedding. I click my mobile on to Will's number. He's listed as the out-of-hours doctor; that way David can't find him. I start the call but press the end button after it rings once. As soon as I hang up I delete the call from my phone history. Will knows not to call me back.

Again I slip into a half-sleep and see the dead man sitting on the steps of a caravan, drinking from a can. He wears the scruffy blue coat he died in and oversized trainers with the laces undone. Dressed as I remember him. I'm at the caravan too, we laugh together like old friends. My mother is inside. She collects his things into a pile and pours ink over them. I ask the man if I should let anyone know he's dead or if, like me, he wants to disappear. He doesn't answer but carries on drinking, watching me over the top of the can.

Next time when I wake, I sit up and turn the light on, and rifle through my bedside drawer for some more codeine which I press out of their foil pouches. I wash the pills down with wine from the now half-full bottle. This bed is where I came the day of the accident, to this same cocoon of warmth where the universe shrinks to the clutter of my mind, like the small dark spaces I would seek out as a child when I fantasized I was a cat finding somewhere safe and secret, pretending to go through a hole the size of my whiskers. The hiding place would help to block out the noise in my head, and make the memories go away. But I've forgotten the old ways of fooling myself that nothing can touch me. Instead I've cultivated a blank space.

I remember the smells and sounds in the bedroom the night after the accident: the smoke seeping into the room even though the windows were shut, footsteps outside on gravel, the sound of the engine firing up filtering into my dream as my car was driven away. What surprised me – apart from David involving someone else in the equation – was that he knew who to call to make something as big as a car disappear. He knew the routine in an instant: to clean everything, and burn what couldn't be restored. No mean feat for a mere businessman. Knowing David as I do, I imagine this new avenue for his talents has yet to be exhausted.

At the time it had been something of a relief to know that David was dealing with the aftermath of the accident, and that he approved of my hiding the body; no dysfunctional marriage exposed by an unhappy businesswoman, no messy drink-driving manslaughter case. We don't do scandals in this house. Nothing to interfere with business.

We have a crime number from the police after we reported the vehicle stolen. They found the car near London and informed us it had been torched. David likes certainty, he takes pride in being able to plot my mood and actions, and in the past that's always worked; he's set upon my emotional blips with a keen, clinical force, and I relied on his ability to give me boundaries and shut me down. It made me safe. Now something new has passed between us, a mistrust. What's occurred is bigger than anything we've encountered before: a death, plus tonight's public humiliation in front of the kind of people David cares about impressing the most. These are errors I've seemingly courted. He'll be wary of me now, unable to compute the future he's so painstakingly nurtured over the years. I'm a malfunctioning satellite spiralling away from the mother ship. If he can't turn me around, he'll switch off and cut me loose. I sense the looming threat of David's distrust. If he can't bring me into line there is nowhere I can disappear to that will be far enough away. Before, the penalties were only ever emotional, but it feels like something in me has broken and the old ways of settling things will no longer work.

I light another cigarette and roll the burning tip up and down my arm, seeing how long I can hold it in place before it singes my skin.

PART TWO

6

TEN WRAPS

David's supply is running low. He wouldn't call himself an addict, that would be below someone of his stature – dirty – but he uses nearly every day, apart from the small coke holidays of a week or two here and there to prove to himself he can take it or leave it. He keeps his habit hidden, therefore tidy, therefore respectable. In his eyes, the line he snorts in the morning gets him ready for the day and sharpens his wits, and the little and often he takes until close of business maintains this tempo. The paraphernalia of his habit – mirror, vial, silver coke straw, fine metal razor blade – are locked in a drawer of his desk at the office, and I've never known him, since the days he started to dabble at university, to share his supply or to admit to anyone other than me that he uses. That would be a defeat. Drugs are not recreational, they are business.

I buy for David. It's always been that way, right from the early days when I knew someone in student halls who supplied, and since then we haven't found a system that better maintains his privacy. David wouldn't sully himself to transact with persons of a lesser financial status, but it's OK for me. The higher up the food chain we go, the more risk I take, but if David is ever concerned, I insist the job is better done this way – with fewer levels involved in the process, it's safer. Besides, I tell him I meet a man who knows a man. He doesn't know I go to the source. David won't ask for names, he wants to know as little about the process as is necessary, and that way he maintains his elevation above the grime. If I got caught in the wrong company, David's inspector friend in the force ought to be able to pull a few strings. I suspect David has other contacts now who could easily hook him up with a regular supply, but he likes to keep his personal tastes concealed; a need is the same as a flaw, and you never know who might want to trade on that weakness at a later date. And anyway, I've always had a talent for sniffing out scumbags. Each time a source gets arrested, goes underground or joins NA, I slum it in the pubs of a different town: car parked round the corner, dress code trashy, hang out long enough on a bar stool – it's amazing what you get offered. The irony is I've only ever tried the stuff once, and the result was a teeming paranoia instead of the expected exhilaration; an outpouring of all I keep wrapped up inside. Never again. Booze, and lots of it, is good enough for me.

It's a once-a-month trip to the dealer, to Will on the coast, to top up David's supply. I've been buying from Will for a couple of years and sleeping with him for most of that time. Even though we usually do the deal at his house, last night was only the second time I'd stayed over, the first being the night before the accident four weeks ago. That all-nighter ended in such calamity it's incredible I decided to chance it again, but these days I seem to attract chaos, or perhaps it's a courtship, and since the accident a part of me has given up and is throwing itself over to fate. Plus, more recently, there are only a couple of things that settle the constant buzz of dread that circulates my body: one of them is alcohol and the other is Will.

It's 9.00 a.m. when I wake and I should have left hours ago, before dawn, before David realized I wasn't in our bed at home. I've been on my best behaviour since the dinner party, and have been back to my usual self at the office so David believes his authoritarian regime is working, but my absence last night will reverse all of that. I have a loose excuse – a meeting I'd engineered at the Grand yesterday afternoon, and a room on my credit card with a receipt to show – but I should have called to let him know. If I'd heard his voice it would have panicked me home so I chanced it, the alcohol fuelling my bravado, and now I'll have to pay.

I settle into an armchair in Will's front room – my head thick with sleep and last night's whisky – as the figure of the man pacing the country lane replays in my brain. *Crash* against my windscreen. I no longer squeeze my eyes shut or hold my head in my hands; the images will keep coming no matter what I do. Sometimes, if I'm lucky and I wake from a dreamless sleep, it takes a few seconds to recall the source of the disquiet, and then *boom*, back it comes, barrelling into me. From my bag I take the packet of diazepam and knock back a pill with some water from a half-finished glass on the floor. A noise of clanking cups and cutlery comes from the kitchen, plus Will whistling through his teeth to the buzz of the radio, but I'm not ready to face him yet.

This room is full of furniture, so many pieces it's hard to manoeuvre in the space. Mostly they are finds from skips and junk shops, pieces that other people have done away with, and for good reason. But to Will they are special: mismatched chairs in swirly granny fabrics, a 1960s sideboard with chunky knobs, a coffee table made of orange wood and glass – items that are vaguely kitsch, but not vintage enough for good taste. An old jukebox sits in one corner, not the cool American diner variety with curved edges and illuminated plastic, but late 1970s with sides of tan plastic and a playlist featuring the Darts and Showaddywaddy. The paper song-listing is crinkled with mildew. By the time Will found the machine the rain had already got in and it didn't work – it never will – but he doesn't mind or even want to fix the thing. He's saved it to give it a place to while out the years, like a horse gone to pasture.

In pride of place on the mantelpiece is an antique clock: dark wood, ugly pre-deco glass face that opens for winding; a job Will never forgets even when hung-over. His grandmother left it to him and he believes it's valuable, but there are heaps of these same timepieces clogging up the windows of charity shops. The heavy clunk of the clock's tick fills the room with stasis, but the feeling is one of containment and safety. As long as I don't think about leaving. And as long as I don't have to stay.

Wind launches itself at the building. The walls shudder with each blast, like a cheap stage set, and the cold seeps through the near-useless membrane of the single-glazed window. My hands and feet are yellow, and I wrap Will's dressing gown tight round me and rub my fingers and toes, but the blood won't come back. From the tatty armchair where I sit, I look through the window of his two-bed bungalow, set up on a hill on the outskirts of town. A camera flash of winter sun bounces from windows across the road, the light too thin to take the chill from the air. Tiers of houses on sloping streets give the impression of teetering down the hill, like a brickwork glacier, and in the valley below they are met by a dam of factories in an over-stuffed industrial park. Beyond that is Will's own personal fragment of sea. From his vantage point up here on the hill, he can watch the boats and trawlers slide in and out of port, big rusty hunks of metal and rigging which for Will transform into vessels of magnificence and beauty. For that view alone it is worth living here.

This house used to belong to Will's gran and he spent most of his boyhood here. One drunken night he told me the story of his mum, how she'd had him when she was a teenager. He remembers her popping in from time to time to bring him sweets from her job at Woolworths. Later she got a boyfriend, and as Will grew older he saw her less and less, so it was his gran who brought him up. I get the impression the old woman had had enough of child-rearing by the time Will came along, but some care is better than none at all. Will has never met his dad. He thinks he was, or is, a fisherman, and Will's obsession with the pubs around his town, striking up conversation with anyone who works on the water or in the port, is part of the myth he's created for himself that the sea is in his blood.

'If I ever bump into my old man,' he says, 'reckon he owes me a pint.'

I wonder why his dad is the hero and his mum the demon. They both left.

Will is hidden behind the open kitchen door. His shadow casts a fuzzy shape on the lino, and the outline vibrates as he works at the pots and pans. A back door leads from the kitchen on to a small concrete courtyard, north-facing, and this door clicks open and shut, the noise followed by a scatter of paws on the slippery floor signal-ling Bessie, Will's little dog, coming in from the yard.

Bessie lies down on the floor next to my chair and I stroke her sweat-damp coat. She's old and smells doggy. Skinny ribs rise and fall with each puffy wheeze and my fingers sense what little fat there is between her fur and the bones underneath. Her body is winding down. 'You're not long for this world, are you, my sweet Bess?' Will said last night as he stroked the little dog on his lap.

Lying back into the cushions, I know I need to get dressed, find my mobile, connect with the day, but I allow myself a few moments as I wait for my head to clear. If I wasn't here, what would I be doing now?

It's a Saturday. David is at the gym or walking the dogs and I'd be at home no doubt, tiptoeing around the empty house like an unwanted guest who's outstayed their welcome. I picture myself walking through our immaculate rooms, the walls and furniture colour coordinated, and my stockinged feet testing the spring of the carpet under my toes. The fabric's quality thrills me, and the vacuum lines left on the wool by the cleaner look like a manicured lawn. I'm always afraid of spoiling the pattern. The luxury and perfection of the house are my roots, keeping me grounded and sane, and with no clutter or mess I can half believe that state exists within me as well.

If I was there, what would I be doing? I'd be planning to go out.

'Do you want a tea, angel?' Will calls from the kitchen. He's been scrabbling through his repertoire of cutesy names, trying to find one that fits.

'Rachel? Are you there?' He turns the radio down and pops his head round the door. I smile – a small smile. 'Tea?' he says with a big grin. His nose is on the large side, his lips uneven and flat, and his eyes are squinty with one black socket from last night's drunken fight, but when all these features are arranged as a whole, some magic of nature creates the sum of a good-looking man.

As he smiles, lines ripple from his mouth through to his cheek, and even though his skin holds the wear-and-tear of over twenty years of drinking, underneath is a warm boyish face.

'OK.' I raise myself from the creaky chair and follow him into the kitchen, to sit at the yellow Formica table. The surface is speckled like a bird's egg and scarred by years of cutlery.

Will turns his back to me and resumes the washing-up. He leans across to put the kettle on with a confident flick. It's his house now, not the pub or the bedroom with the lights off. We've explored secret parts of each other's bodies, but today is only the second time we've been together the next morning, and this everyday world of Will embarrasses and shocks me, more so than if he'd stood in front of me naked; there's greater intimacy and more to reveal from the minutiae of his domestic rituals than in the sex we have. He looks different in daylight and in his own home, away from the protective cloak of the dimly lit pub, and his actions are more mobile though touched with self-consciousness. I get the sense the kitchen hasn't been cleaned for a while and it's being done in my honour, or even more worrying, out of some kind of proof to me that he can do it, that he is a viable human who functions on the same level as everyone else, that we could have a future. My hangover helps me resist the temptation to join in and pretty up what is essentially a grown man's den.

My coat hangs on a hook in front of the glass panel on

the back door, blocking out the daylight and throwing a shadow over the table. The fabric was smoky from the pub and I'd dropped it on the floor, so Will must have hung it up this morning. On top of the table, folded in a pile for each of us, are the rest of our clothes. Last night they'd been scattered in a line towards the bedroom, like Hansel and Gretel breadcrumbs.

After sex, Will had buried his face in my hair. 'We could go away, you and me,' he'd said. 'I could arrange a boat, no one would know, we could disappear.' I lay on his stripy nylon sheets and stared at the ceiling, tracing the damp spots in the plaster above my head and joining up the dots, thinking how true it is that without women most men fall apart; they eat crap, they die young – there's no one to tell them to go to the doctor's. And so I stroked his head, kissed him, told him I'd consider it, slipping into role and making myself real to him because it felt good to be needed, all the while resisting the realization that he mattered to me. With the worst of what I throw at him, Will keeps letting me back; he remains consistent, his feelings unconditional. The sense that I don't deserve his attention overrides the strong temptation to jump in, and of course there is always the background hum of David, my loyalty to him more of an addiction. After all these years of being guided through my life, without him I would be rudderless.

In the kitchen, a mug of hot tea is plonked on the table in front of me. Spills lap over the sides and Will mops them up immediately then returns to his washing-up. He wears tracksuit bottoms covered in splashes of paint, and on his feet are a trodden-down pair of slippers. The radio plays music. He turns it up, swaying his hips to an old Smiths song, then turns to face me with a soapy washing-up brush in one rubber-gloved hand and a cigarette in the other, smiling his huge smile. He sings along to the track.

The butt end of his fag is soggy. He drags sharply on it then raises his hands in the air as if this is a connecting moment for us, hauling us back to some utopian youth where the world was at our feet. His youth may have been like that, but mine passed me by.

The kitchen clock reads 9.30. Through the window, thick clouds steal up the last of the blue sky, and the sun dims like a switch. Will turns on the kitchen light. The unshaded bulb has little effect.

'D'you remember this one?' he says, taking a swig of his tea, still swaying to the music. Even at uni I'd never really liked The Smiths – all that sleeve-wearing emotion – and I pretend I don't know the song. Will laughs and sings, muffled with the cigarette still in his mouth. 'I used to play this one with the band.'

He turns his back to resume his sink duties, dancing at the worktop, the baggy movement of his muscles pressing through the fabric of his trousers, and I question why it is that I like him. With David there was no choice; it never felt like a romance, more a togetherness with no question of it being other; we were a given, he made me his. With Will, I shouldn't keep coming back – there's no practical future here, and it would be dangerous for both of us if

David found out – but each time I see Will the sensation of *us* grows stronger. It comes from nowhere I know how to control. I gulp down my tea, and with it any desire to make this a reality. As the liquid hits the dregs of last night's spirits in my stomach, nausea rises up.

A text-ping comes from inside my coat. I stand, giddy for a moment, the alcohol still thick in my blood, and walk to the door to fish my mobile from the pocket. Scrolling through the messages I notice missed calls as well, all from David. The texts start with a brusque, 'Where are you?' at midnight, and end with the most recent, 'I will find you both.'

His presence looms through the phone. What he would do if he found us makes me more afraid for Will than for myself.

'I need to go,' I say. I'd hoped to drink less last night, to give it more time before I drove home, but the panic of knowing that David is waiting has set in. 'I've stayed too long.' I'll drive more slowly this time, I'll pay attention. Get a strong coffee on the way home.

Will stops moving but doesn't turn round. The radio crackles as the tuning slips and a burst of voices from a local taxi firm hisses across the ether. 'Fine,' he says. 'Off you go.'

With my pile of clothes in hand, I push the chair aside. One of the rubber feet has worn away and the bare metal screeches across the lino. In the lounge I gather the rest of my things: my bag, my shoes, the cashmere sweater which Will missed, now covered in dog hair. Bessie's eyes follow my movements, the useless guard dog and the dispassionate burglar. Will turns off the radio and I hear his feet scuffle the carpet as he comes up behind me. He kisses my neck. His breath holds the tang of last night's alcohol.

'We can't meet in the pub any more. In fact, we can't do this again,' I say in a small voice.

'Please don't leave,' he says. I relax inside the fold of his arms. 'Stay a bit longer.'

Light wisps of rain have begun to fall and the morning appears closer to dusk. Across the street my new Mercedes is parked with rusty vehicles on either side. David insisted I have a duplicate of my last car so that only the discerning would notice the change. It's also a demonstration that nothing is irreplaceable – with enough money you can do almost anything you want.

The vehicle in front of my car is Will's other business opportunity. MAN PLUS VAN is etched on the side of the grubby transit, with his mobile number outdated by one digit. Between the occasional trip to the tip and the cocaine profits which he doesn't snort himself, he has just about enough money to scrape by. Occasionally he has a windfall, a new leather jacket or a guitar – I never ask where the money came from – and when we meet at the pub, I always pick up the tab; the etiquette is that the dealer never pays. That way we get round the shame of his poverty.

Will turns me to him in the circle of his arms. A scruffy quiff flops over his right eye. Once he showed me a photo of himself in his band from twenty years ago, and nothing much has changed: his style, his clothes, the drinking habit and the fighting – all serve as a homage to his adolescence, the glory days from which he's been unable to evolve. Without the advantage of youth, his image has lost some of its glamour. I twitch a smile and think about the man he should have been, and where it all went wrong for him. At what point did he realize, like me, that he was totally alone?

'We could go back to bed,' he says.

The fresh bruise on his eye socket is taking on a purple tint. In the pub last night, insults were spat, old lines of territory tested, then a firework of fists erupted from Will and the other man, over in seconds. I watched with thrill and terror as Will punched the man with less effort than it took him to lift his pint. He was very good, as if he'd been fighting all his life. The man on the floor didn't get off as lightly; blood spilled from his nose and poured into the barmaid's beer towel as she hollered at the retreating Will. The wounded man got up and chased us to the door, shouting, 'I'm not done. Come back, you and your fucking slag.' I had to pull Will to the car, the fear and excitement giving me the same strength I'd once used to drag a body. On the journey home, all I thought about was how easy it would be for David to find us if he really wanted to.

Gran's clock chimes ten. Seconds waste into rapid minutes. 'I have to go,' I say, taking Will's hand in mine with a light pat before I move apart from him. 'It's late and I've got things to do.'

'What things?' He glares at me, snatching away his hand, an alcohol temper rising in his face. 'See that fuck-wit of a husband of yours? Spend loads of money on crap at the shops?'

I shake my head. His eyes glisten. I want to tell him that I don't like shopping, that my husband's touch chills me, and that even with all the imperfections I've never had anything as close to happiness as this. Instead I move close again and nuzzle into his shoulder, wishing that everything were more simple. 'I'm sorry. You should forget about me. I'm bad news.'

'Rachel, we can work this out.' Will strokes the back of my head. 'What I said last night about getting out of here – I know I was pissed and I know it probably sounded nuts, but I meant it. We could leave. We could go somewhere where David couldn't find you.'

'You don't know David. If you did you'd know there is no getting away.' With my logic setting in again, I'm itching to leave and get back home before any more time passes.

'Well, I'm not scared of Mr Big, chucking his money around to get everything he wants.'

My impatience turns to panic. 'Tough talk, you with your shabby little house and cash under the mattress. Leave problems you can't handle alone.'

'Fuck you, Rachel.'

'Yeah, fuck you too.'

'You're a bitch.'

'Well, you're a bitch's whore.'

Will grabs an empty can and hurls it into a wastepaper basket, the bin frayed with spikes of wicker. As he picks up an ashtray and dumps its contents into the basket, clouds of ash plume through gaps in the weaving, covering his hand with speckles of grey. He circumnavigates the room, careful not to come too close to me, punching cushions and hurling them on the sofa. A mist of dust disturbed after a long time is suspended in the air. I watch him for a moment then go to the bathroom, locking myself in and speed-dressing. In my bag, next to the walking man's watch which I carry with me at all times, I check I have the receipt for the hotel – the evidence that David will probably ignore – plus the wraps of coke I bought last night. Ten. Ten grams. Enough to last David about a month. A month until I have to see Will again. I wonder if it will be hard to stay away or hard to come back.

I wait to hear Will go back into the kitchen before I come out, then I walk through the lounge to the small porch. As I twist the latch, the front door bursts open with a gust of wind from outside and the latch bangs into my shoulder. From behind me comes the click and fizz of a can being opened. I close the door quietly behind me and cross the road to my car.

Having greeted the day, my hangover is worse than I'd expected and the keys shake in my hand. I slide into the incubated heat of the vehicle, the sun on the windscreen warmer without the wind. The temperature tops up my blood. Here in my private enclave it's safe, the only place that's mine and mine alone. The engine starts and I drive away.

In the rear-view mirror I see a reflection of Will standing at his window holding a can of Special Brew. He doesn't drink. He is statue-still and looks small, like a little boy, and even though I don't want to stay, I want to go home even less, and I wish I didn't always have to start a fight to make it easier to leave.

7

DIRTY FOOTPRINTS

I pull up in our drive and expect to see David in his favourite position inside the house: sitting on the long red sofa and looking out from the floor-to-ceiling window of our main lounge. He likes to sit with one foot hooked over his opposing knee, arms stretched along the back of the settee as he surveys his manor. From this position he has the added benefit of announcing his presence to whomever approaches. But today the sofa is empty, his car gone. No scrambled barks reach through the front door, so he's taken his babies. The empty building holds its breath. David's angry texts lassoed me home, and now I'm here my punishment is his absence, leaving me guessing and worrying. Two wrongs do make a right in this house but I don't mind; it's better this way, gives me time to tidy myself up, to regroup before the showdown and to polish my excuse. First there'll be David's loving concern, the caresses and whispers that deliver the hidden threats. Then the silence – a tricky monosyllabic detour of hours or days depending on our resolve – and finally the point at which I fold and explain my behaviour. When this comes, when I finally repent – which I always do – he'll let me know he doesn't care anyway. Games. We've become very good at them. We have little else.

I head for the kitchen, fill a glass of water and stand with my back to the sink in the immaculate room. Cabinets run in long undisturbed lines, and the worktops exude a show-home sheen of sanitized happiness, a fantasy that David's worked hard to mimic, so much so that he actually believes it's true; we have arrived therefore we are happy. The few things on display in the kitchen – the cappuccino maker that's been taken apart for cleaning, plus the maple knife block – are there for a reason: they speak of success and privilege, attributes that David has spent his life attempting to acquire.

David's broadsheet is spread across the marble kitchen table. Next to the newspaper is a cup of mint tea, half finished, still warm – half-an-hour warm. He prefers coffee, but allows it only as his good-boy treat. The phantom of David's action is held in the mug and newspaper – the *Financial Times* – the pages spewed apart where he's flicked them over, standing as he does with one hand splayed on the table for support, his other hand hauling the sheets across and wafting air in his face. If I dusted the table for prints, there would be one complete palm next to the paper, fat and solid, pressed on to the table, his presence vast and close even in his absence.

I open the fridge, look inside, close the door. Everything is packaged, bottled or sealed. Nothing leaks or breathes. When was the last time I'd cooked? Probably that fateful dinner, three weeks ago. After the cleaner surmounted that chaos, the house has stayed clean. She comes twice weekly, but there's no need really; nothing is used or gets dirty. I work late and can't be bothered with food, snacking on whatever's available: bits of cheese, supermarket soup, stuff that doesn't need putting together. Even opening a tin is an effort too far, and I buy ready meals with only a film of plastic to puncture before the microwave. With my back to the sink I stand as I do now, spooning the food straight from the hot plastic tray into my mouth. A few mouthfuls before I'm nauseous. David dines out mostly – supper at the club, power bars at the gym – so long as when it matters, when clients come round, there's something of value on the table; a meal that looks expensive and has been cooked by a wife who cares. Though we'll be using caterers from now on.

Next to our kitchen is the large open-plan dining room set inside a glass annex. Doors concertina the length of a whole wall, so that we have an uninterrupted view of the garden. 'Where your home and nature combine, bringing the outside in,' the house particulars said. We've opened the doors only once, to air the paint when we redecorated. This room has tall ceilings and the table is overlooked by the guest-bedroom mezzanine and en suite. Marble tiles, heated from underneath like an emperor's palace, spread throughout the whole ground floor so that each room flows into the next. A space big enough to house a small car showroom, furnished only with a telephone table, chaise longue and modern grandfather clock, is the central entrance, and on the opposite side to this is another reception room with standard Eames chair and Noguchi coffee table, making the house perfectly balanced. 'A modern take on the double-fronter,' the estate agent said as if reading off an autocue. 'A symmetry of windows and doors and a lawn that rolls out on all sides around the building making a grand family home, a perfect vision of domestic happiness.'

At the viewing, the agent opened built-in cupboards, smiling into the pristine spaces with his porcelain teeth. 'Top-end developers,' he said, 'they only touch the million-plus.' Upstairs he fiddled with the remote control for the lighting and in-house sound system. 'The children's den has its own separate entrance,' he said, 'good for when they're teenagers.'

'Better get on with it then,' David whispered, standing behind me with his arms hugging tight round my waist as the agent demonstrated the lighting system. I thought he was teasing me, but after nearly twenty years together I know better now; neither one of us wanted children, he just liked to make me feel bad.

David fielded another call, and I moved past the agent into an adjacent room. Up here on the first floor at least the rooms had walls, lower ceilings and the potential for comfort and privacy. Another large window looked down on to tiered decking and an expanse of fluorescent, newly laid turf. Long fingers of virgin grass reached towards the sky.

'That'll need scalping,' David said. At the far end of the garden was a line of trees: an oak, horse chestnuts, a floppy willow, all mature, their foliage broken up by a glimpse of our neighbours' roof at least a hundred metres away. Aside from that, we could have been in the middle of nowhere.

'There's Sommerton College, which is close,' the agent said, standing in the doorway and smoothing his shiny pink tie inside his jacket, 'but most of the buyers at your end of the market – mostly Russian money these days – choose Charlton School. We have all the phone numbers at the office, may even have a prospectus or two – it's one of our most frequently asked questions. How many children do you have?'

A blush crept up my neck as I walked into the en suite, leaving David to answer. I tested the shower, turning it by accident to full blast, and my fringe and sleeves caught the edge of the spray. David came in as I was shaking off the drips. He stood watching me, rocking back and forth on his feet, then turned and left the room, shutting the door hard behind him. The conversation muffled through the walls. 'I'm interested but it's been over-valued,' David said. 'We can talk when it's come down by fifty K. Does Michael still run your office? I play tennis with his brother.'

The house was alien to me from the beginning, the choice to buy it never mine, but the comfort of being able to afford it filled part of the hole left by a childhood of going without. For me the building has no soul, but then it's people that turn the house into a home.

We've been in the place for five years now. Everything is treated with the utmost care and still looks new, as if we don't have the money to replace it, only there's more than enough cash to do what we want. Like ghosts, we waft through the rooms, leaving no dent or stain. David's pathological fear of damage is one of the well-managed traces of his sour and frugal beginnings: the two-up two-down terrace and his comprehensive education, the tins of marrow-fat peas, and parents who settled for whatever came their way. He's closer to recreating the mood of his childhood than he knows with our structured emotional void, but money is the cushion and the mask. Having purchased the outer basting of class – the uniform of his desired pack, a colour-by-numbers chic – he only loosely covers the truth; up close, he reeks of bad breeding.

From the boot room next to the kitchen I hear a scuffle. My skin bristles as I imagine David standing on the other side of the door, spying on me all this time through the glass panel. I turn slowly expecting to see his face, but there's nothing. Then there's a whine. I walk towards the door and open it to see one of the dogs tied up close to the wall on the dog hook. She's been fitted with a tight muzzle and her head pulls on the lead that's been looped too short for her to lie down. A full bowl of food has been left next to the back door, too far for her to reach – though even if she could, the muzzle would stop her eating. A meaty smell loiters in the air. The dog whimpers but the muzzle stops her barking. Only last week she was David's favourite. He's switched allegiance again. I wonder what she did to deserve this; probably gnawed a precious shoe or book of David's, even though it's his fault if he left the door open and she got into the house. As I reach in to loosen the lead she jumps at me, pawing and scratching my arm, making it bleed.

'Stupid bitch,' I say, and stand back against the wall. Her eyes drill into me. She stills and I move more slowly this time, unclasping her lead so she can move around. She shakes her head then hangs it low with a rumbling growl. I remove her muzzle and she runs to the food, eating in manic gulps and finishing in seconds, then she trots to her bed in the corner and lays her head on her paws, looking at me with suspicious eyes.

I shower and put last night's outfit straight into the washing machine. Before I close the machine, the smell of Will's house lifts from my clothes – Bessie, tobacco, bacon – and I sit with the ache it gives me for more than a beat, breathing in the memory. I can't name the sensation, it's not pleasure or pain, perhaps both, but it's strong enough for me to hold the air in my lungs for as long as I can.

Back in my bedroom, I walk into the adjacent dressing room where David and I have our own built-in wardrobes. The door to my closet is open and the floor is scuffed with footprints. The cleaner's day was yesterday and I know I left my cupboard tidy. As I open the doors I see that most of my clothes have been removed. A skirt, a pair of jeans, a jacket and a couple of work blouses remain. My eyes lift to the shelves above the clothes rail to see that all the shoe boxes have gone, apart from one with a pair of boots inside. I check my drawers. There's one T-shirt, two pairs of knickers and tights, plus one pair of socks. All the scarves, belts and accessories have been taken, and only the red biscuit tin from Mum's house remains in the bottom drawer. I open the lid. Inside is ash. I sink to the floor in my dressing gown and double up with the pain in my back and stomach.

All my special things.

8

INK STAINS

When I wake it's gone lunchtime, and even though I'm still groggy from the extra dose of sedatives I took earlier, I remember I have a meeting this afternoon with the estate agent at my mother's old house; the place I grew up and the home where she lived until her death a year ago. We put the house on the market immediately after she died – we knew she was going, and I was more than ready to move on – but the place hasn't sold. The agent suggested some weeks ago that we meet at the property to discuss tactics, and I reluctantly agreed; going back there means hooking into events from which I've disconnected and had hoped to leave that way. This day has already proved too much, and it would be far easier to cancel the meeting, but I've put off the appointment several times before now. Besides, I have a need to be shot of this weighty piece of history.

Before I leave home, I take the tin of ash and stand in front of David's toy collection – the most expensive ones

– and throw. Dust plumes out and settles on the glass shelves of toy robots and Matchbox cars. The minute particles will be working their way into each tiny hinge and screw, and the fur on David's Steiff teddy bear turns from golden to grey. David won't trust the cleaner with this mess, and it will take him hours to rectify, if it's even possible to return his precious things to their prime. These toys that have for years been fiercely guarded against sticky toddlers, locked away from their natural purpose and passed on from collector to collector, now ruined in seconds. Outside, I dump the tin into the wheelie bin, and in the garage I root around until I find the box of my father's discarded clothes; these rags are the last items of his that I own, and I don't want to chance David finding them. The gardening trousers and big overcoat reek of damp, and mildew has bloomed on the old shirt. I put the clothes in the boot of my car, removing the spare tyre first and storing the items under the moulded cover, then place the tyre in the box where the clothes have been.

My mother's house is half an hour from mine, in another village outside of Brighton, and as I drive the tears come; my inability to leave David means I deserve to stay even more, but part of me has split away from the mainframe and is knocking the rest into chaos.

For the remainder of the journey I don't notice the distance or the time until my surprise as I autopilot into the driveway of the 1930s semi. The car door opens directly on to high grass in the front garden where weeds and flowers have made a temporary meadow. Next door, the pristine face of the neighbour's house averts its gaze from its ugly twin, with a tall line of conifers growing along the dividing path. If that house had a nose, it would point in the air. As a child, before the trees had been planted, I used to see our neighbour on his hands and knees on the lawn, pulling up daisies by their roots; he wanted no moss, no clovers, only grass. At the time he looked so old with his bald head, heavy-framed glasses and paunch popping through the buttons of his shirt, but he was probably younger than I am now. It was as if he'd reached a point in his life where he'd decided he was a grown-up – he was done, cooked – and he'd taken on the mantle of age. At least my mother refused to fit the expected conventions, even if it was to the detriment of all those around her. Curls of paint fur the windows of Mum's house, pebble-dash has fallen off in chunks and the roof sags, but it was ever thus. No wonder no one spoke to us. No wonder no one wants to buy the place.

I open the front door. A layer of post snags on the floor as I walk into the hallway with its familiar smell of damp wood. The odour is stronger than usual, the air holed up inside the gloom of walls. All the internal doors are shut so I open them one by one – first the lounge, then the dining room, next the kitchen at the back – and each space in turn startles me with the reality of absence. This is the first time I've been here since the house was cleared, and everything's been taken apart from the light bulbs. Only the thin carpet retains the impressions of Mum's old

furniture; years of heavy wood weighing down the fabric.
Butting up to the wall in the lounge is a rectangular dent
made by the pine dresser. The piece used to lean forward
slightly, its shelves designed for a plate collection, but
Mum stacked it with papers and boxes of knick-knacks
that she never got round to displaying. Four round dimples show the past position of the velour chesterfield – my
parents' first grand purchase for the house. The sofa was
too big for the room, and after Dad left, the fabric was
damaged and the sofa began to smell of old food. Dust
collected in the dimpled buttonholes so Mum covered it
with a throw. She couldn't afford to reupholster. We were
always broke.

The thought of what I have already lost today, and
the silent threat that came with the elimination of all that
was personal to me, makes it hard to focus. Simon the
agent is due in half an hour, time enough I hope for me
to put a lid on what Mum's house holds, although there
are few significant events I recall. I don't know to who or
what I'm saying goodbye. In Mum's kitchen I slide open
cabinets, remembering how I used to stand on a chair to
reach inside, but the image of me as a child is more like a
photo, a memory of a memory. The little girl I used to be
has become just another character I played, but somehow
I've forgotten the lines of the script. At the back of one of
the cupboards is a lone packet of jelly, sell-by date 1979,
with a picture on the outer cardboard of a woman and a
small boy, smiling and making the jelly together. The
colour has seeped from the packaging and if it wasn't for

the sell-by date I'd think that the carton was from another lifetime. The seventies seem like only yesterday, but already my past has become vintage.

Stains and scrapes on the walls and floors mostly belong to Mum, but they trace my childhood like a map of experience. There's a dark-brown circle on the lounge carpet from a bottle of red wine. In the dining room, the bottom half of the wallpaper has been torn off, and the remaining edge is a layer-cake of paint and paper plastered on by previous occupants. Mum once tried to steam off the slices of wallpaper, and I watched with excitement as she attempted to obliterate the past, my small hands ripping at the walls until my nails were filled with gluey paper. 'Come on, Cinders,' she said. 'Put some welly into it.' We laughed as a long sheet I was pulling broke free from the wall and I fell backwards on to the floor. As with most of Mum's passions, the redecorating began with great energy but was never finished. Even as a child I knew this wasn't how people should live but I got used to it. Now these imperfections remind me of what's for ever gone and can never be made good.

Upstairs I pace through the bedrooms, avoiding my old room. The air is colder up here, and I run my hands over the freezing walls. In every room the recollection of my childhood is slight, and fireflies of memory disappear as soon as I turn my mind to them. I passed through my past, I didn't or couldn't savour the time, and now my history is huge and vacant, like a film I never finished watching.

Back downstairs I bundle the post together and sit on the carpet in the bay window of the front room, leaning against the cold radiator. The nets are still up and as I sink to the floor the grey material ghosts out. For a moment I smell Mum, or Mum as she ended up; the boiled peas and rubbed nylon tights of old age. As a younger woman she joked that she couldn't wait to clock up the years and have good reason to be a cantankerous old bag, and when it finally came to her, she played the part as well as any other she'd inhabited.

The letters are mostly circulars for double glazing, some holiday brochures and credit-card invitations. Mum only ever used cash, of which there was never enough. It wasn't that she was scared of debt, in fact if she'd had a credit card she would have maxed it out within days, it's more that she wasn't able to function in the world of banks and mortgages. She pretended such things were beneath her, that money was part of some global conspiracy towards materialism, but really she was terrified that the real people would find her out and reveal the absence of capability she professed to hold in abundance. For all her blather about free spirits and open marriages, she was a woman of her time. Dad grumbled to me once, on one of the few occasions I spent the weekend with him after he left, about how he still had to pay the mortgage. After she died and I read the deeds, I saw that he'd never signed the house over to her, it had always been in my name, so he'd had as much of a hand in keeping her in her place as she did herself through her own inability to grow up.

I sift through the post: a birthday card to Mum from Australia from someone called Daniel. 'Always in my heart,' he writes. I have no idea who he is but that doesn't surprise me. The rest is junk mail and several free local papers, one of which lies open on the carpet. We don't get the local news at home as David has put a sign on our letter box to forbid delivery of anything not directly addressed to us, and since the accident he's been even more guarded with what I see. The few times I've gone to watch TV, I've not been able to find the remote control. But really I'm a coward, I could go online and check the news but I choose not to. On the floor at Mum's house, I flick through the pages of news and community trivia. It surprises me that all this living goes on without me. Trapped cats, fights in the High Street, a vandalized bus shelter. Names: Marjorie Staples, Brian Cahoon, Anita Brand. Is it they who are invisible or me? A large section of the paper is dedicated to the campaign against Alex's development off Blackthorn Lane, and there are several pages of protest letters alongside photos of old women in anoraks holding banners. The centrefold shows a group of activists dressed in blends of khaki, as if they've all shared a giant washing machine on a hot wash. Hairstyles are matted, scarves and piercings feature large. They stand at the entrance to the woods and in the forefront is their leader, a man captioned as 'Tyrone Aldridge'. He's tall and muscular, and in one hand he holds a chain. His other arm crosses the shoulder of a pregnant woman with a small baby. The caption reads, 'We shall not be moved.'

Folding the paper shut, I catch the front-page headline: MYSTERY BODY FOUND NEAR CONTROVERSIAL DEVELOPMENT. A picture of a road – the road I drove down, Blackthorn Lane – and an aerial map pinpoints the location of the body, some way from the development site but in the same woods. The article talks of 'levels of decay consistent with a month' and 'police treating the death as suspicious'.

There are voices and then keys in the door. Simon enters, followed by a young couple flapping the house details in their hands. Two children lunge after them, leaving wet footprints on the carpet, and they scatter into the rooms. Simon's eyes search the space and settle on me on the floor, my legs splayed out and surrounded by papers.

'Good God, Rachel, are you OK?' He moves to help me but I wave him away. 'Sorry to barge in on you like this. What on earth are you doing down there?'

Pushing myself up, I stand with a small sway.

'This is Sally and Clive,' he says, 'they had a viewing only yesterday, and they love the house.' Simon extends his arm behind the two people standing on the other side of the lounge door. He prods them gently forward from the comfort of the doorway. 'They rang on the off-chance of a second viewing today and, as I knew I was meeting you here . . . I hope you don't mind. I tried calling but your mobile was switched off.'

'No, it's fine,' I say, stroking down my rumpled clothes.

Sally bounds forward and stretches her arm out to me. I shake her hand.

'So nice to meet you,' she says. 'I was just saying to Clive, it's always good to meet the former owners. Get the vibes and all. Check out they're not murderers or anything.'

The couple look at each other and laugh. Simon joins in with a bellow.

'How long did you live here?' Clive asks.

After a pause I realize he's talking to me. 'Oh, when I was a child.' I shift my feet. 'It was my mother's house. I left years ago.'

'I love the way you've kept all the original features,' Sally says. 'So many people ripped these houses to pieces. I mean, you have the old Bakelite door handles and everything. Your mum had a real eye for quality.'

'Um, yes.' I smile. Mum hated all this old stuff, but if you wait long enough everything comes back into fashion. Sally laughs a small laugh. We all stare at each other.

'Do you mind if I start the tour, Rachel?' Simon asks, then turns to the couple. 'Or would you rather show yourselves round this time? Get a proper feel for the place.'

The children's footsteps thump up the stairs and they go into one of the rooms and shout. It sounds like a fight. There's crying.

'Yes, that's a great idea,' Clive says and nudges his wife towards the stairs. 'See you in a mo.'

They follow the children up and their voices filter

through the threadbare carpet and floorboards above my head. More screams, shouting from the mum, then quiet.

'Are you OK, Rachel?' Simon says.

'I'm fine. I wasn't expecting anyone apart from you, that's all.'

'Yes, I'm sorry about that. Bit of a surprise for me too, but you have to strike while the iron's hot. They're the only people who've asked for a second viewing since the property went on the market, and I know you're keen to sell. After all, if the Sandersons take the bait then we're all done and dusted, and our change of tactics meeting is null and void.'

I hold my hands together in a tight grip to stop them from shaking and look out the window.

'It's always sad leaving the family home,' he says. 'Would you like to be alone for a bit?'

I turn to him. 'Yes, thank you, that would be good.'

He follows the Sandersons upstairs and I pick up the paper again, reading the article in more depth. 'Police not ruling out foul play . . . searching the UK Missing Persons register . . . appealing for witnesses . . . building work for new estate on hold.' The whole newspaper is too big to fit in my bag but the front two pages will, so I fold them into a small square and zip them inside a pocket, the same place I keep the man's watch.

Footsteps move slowly in and out of the rooms upstairs. Doors squeak. 'I want this room,' I hear one of the children say. 'No, I want it,' from the other. 'She always gets what she wants, it's not fair.' Relaxed laughter from the parents, no more scolding, already at ease in the house, and I sense that they will buy. Simon bounds down the stairs and from his speed I can tell he's taking two at a time. He launches himself through the lounge door, cheeks blazing with the possibility of a sale.

'Rachel, if you wouldn't mind . . .' He takes a moment to catch his breath. 'I know it's something the surveyors will pick up on, but as you're here, we could really speed this thing along.'

'What is it?'

'The Sandersons, they have a question about a wall. I wonder if you could help?'

I follow Simon up the stairs. With each step, his trousers lever up and reveal an inch of stripy sock at his ankle. There's mud on the heels of his shoes and the dirt has bled into the hem of his trousers, but all he'll see is the polished leather on the toes of his shoes and the neat line of his trousers as they drop across the laces.

Upstairs the viewers are huddled in my old bedroom and the children bounce on a bed frame that's been left by the house clearers. Sally and Clive are tapping walls and listening to the dull knocks, opening a tall floor-to-ceiling cupboard in the far corner next to the window. Inside the cupboard is an immersion tank, and above this are slatted pine shelves. When I was a child, after I'd brought the washing in from the line, I'd fold the clothes on to these shelves. The system involved making three piles: one for me, one for Mum and one for towels and bedding. They would dry beautifully in the warm space. The lagging round the tank is trussed up with thin leather belts and buckles, like a series of Victorian waists. Fibrous fluff, probably asbestos, puffs out from slits in the material, and underneath is a rust-red tank through which has passed the water of so many of my baths.

'We were wondering,' says Sally, 'if you knew when this was put in? The cupboard, I mean. Whether it was an addition to the house or if this wall's meant to be here? You know, if it's a supporting wall?'

The couple keep their eyes on me.

'You see,' says Clive, 'we'd have to take this out and knock through. The room's far too small, and if we opened it up we could make a proper bedroom for the kids.'

Underneath my clothes it's as if a blow heater's been turned on. I look past the couple's shoulders to the window, wishing I could open it and fill the room with freezing air, but Sally and Clive already have their coats pulled tight round them. Outside, a tree close to the house sways in the wind. Once I'd tried to jump on to a branch from the window, but looking at it now, I never would have made it. Mum caught me before I made the leap and smacked me. Years later, when she recounted this story, she told me, 'You were always trying to run before you could walk. You never had any sense.' I'd wanted to shout, 'I was a child. You were the adult. Where were the lessons?'

'Clive's a bit of a DIY nut,' Sally says. 'Likes nothing better than to strip a place bare and start again. Obviously if this is a supporting wall and we've got to put in steels it's more expensive, and we may have to put in a lower offer.'

The cupboard is thin, like a larder, and it goes back a long way. The immersion tank sits at the end and in front is space for more shelves, but they've been taken out and stacked down the side, the brackets left on the walls. I kneel down and squeeze into the small space. A smell lifts up: dust mixed with something sharp, ammonia, but it's faint. There are stains on the carpet, big plumes of dark colour, like ink. On the wall inside is a quote I wrote in pen – some hippy thing Mum'd said after being dumped by one of her boyfriends, about letting the one you love go free.

I straighten up and bang my head in the small space as I try to catch my breath.

'And we wanted to know what this was for,' Sally says, prodding a hinge and rusty padlock hanging on the inside of the door. 'What d'you think your mum kept in there? A family of pixies?' She laughs. 'So strange to have a lock on the inside, don't you think?'

I pull off my jacket to try and get some air as I lean against the wall. A slick of wet is left on my hand after I wipe my forehead. The Sandersons look at each other with concern, and Simon moves towards me.

'Is everything all right, Rachel?' he says. 'Would you like to sit down?'

'No, I'm fine, just getting over the flu, that's all.'

'Oh, I'm sorry,' says Sally. 'Look at us keeping you here when you're not well.'

'Yes, I have to go. Please excuse me.' And I walk towards the door, my footsteps out of kilter.

'Did you . . . I mean, if it's possible before you go,' Simon calls to my back, 'have any thoughts about this wall?'

I turn to see the trio lit up for my answer, the sale more important than any health issues I might have, though they'd fall over backwards to disagree.

'The cupboard was built when we had the heating put in,' I say. 'You can rip the whole thing out. Take it all down. Get rid of everything.'

I hurry back downstairs, not bothering to say good-bye, and close the front door behind me. The garden path is a chequerboard pattern and some of the tiles are broken where the frost has got in. In the centre the tiles dip a couple of millimetres, worn down by each person who walked the path: Mum, Dad, a smaller me, past owners, generations of postmen and milkmen chipping away a few atoms at a time. New tiles are expensive, so the Sandersons will probably skim over the top with concrete and fossilize the pattern. I think of the new family coming into this house, Sally and Clive, their two kids running to the door after school, and I hope for them that the walls give up the old so that the family can start anew.

9

1979

Our house is on a road where all the houses look the same. Upstairs above the main bedroom the pointy bit of roof has beams outside to make it look like a Tudor house, but it's stupid because the houses here aren't that old. Some people have painted the bits of wood different colours but it annoys me as they would look better if they were all the same. The government should make them all be the same.

It's nearly spring and, even though the air is chilly, if I stand in the sun it's like summer will come soon. I open our front gate and the metal scrapes a quarter circle, a 90-degree right angle on the path. My feet have got big so I have to tread across the lines on the path, but later I'll do ten laps of the garden to make up for the bad luck.

Next to our house is the Masons' house, and our middle walls are joined. If I'm ever in Mum's room I can hear the Masons opening and shutting their cupboards, and it makes me embarrassed about what they hear us doing. Both our front paths run alongside each other, so that if Mr and Mrs Mason are walking to their door at the same time as us it's hard to ignore them, especially as I used to be allowed to say 'Hi'. They've stopped saying hello to us now anyway, so that makes it easier. Mr Mason has planted some Christmas trees in the middle of the two paths, but they're not tall enough yet and I can still see over the top to his boiled-egg head. Our front lawn is surrounded by daffodil beds. Mr Mason only has grass. When he mows it, the lines look like a cricket pitch. The flowers in our garden have gone crispy and they bend forward and kiss the ground. Grass has grown over where the lawn and earth meet, but when Daddy lived here the line used to be straight, like a new fringe. I have a fringe too. I cut it myself. I want to look like Blondie.

After school I let myself in round at the back door. Normally Mum comes home after tea, probably from Uncle Peter's, although she always says she's been to her evening class. Today it's a surprise and she's home. The back door is wide open and I can hear her inside chatting. Mum likes to air the house, even when it's cold, 'to get rid of the food smells' she says. I like cooking smells and wish we could have a home that smells like other people's, even if it is boiled cabbage. In the back garden there are small piles of freshly pulled weeds, so I know Mum'll be in a good mood – she likes to get busy when she's happy. She does the gardening in bare feet so she can feel the earth's vibrations, and she hitches her skirt into a knot at the side. I'm glad she didn't get round to doing the front garden this time.

Stone steps lead up to the back door. I go quietly into the kitchen where the table is laid for supper and there's the smell of a cake in the oven. In the next room, Mum is humming and beating the cushions. She walks into the kitchen and then runs to me, putting her arms round me and kissing my face. I'm too big, and if anyone could see us I wouldn't let her do it, but there's no one else here so it's OK.

'Oh, my beautiful, fantastic princess,' she says, stroking my hair, 'let me get a proper look at you.' She sits on a kitchen chair and pulls me onto her knee, then holds me by the shoulders with her arms stretched out. I lean back to make a distance between us, and she studies my face and smiles. Then she pulls me to her again and squeezes. I wobble on her small knee. 'Oh, your bottom's so bony,' she says as she laughs. 'When did you get so big?' She jiggles my weight around to find a more comfortable position, and when she stops I rest my body into her a fraction.

'I thought we'd have an early supper,' she says, 'and then maybe go for a walk.' I put my head on her shoulder. 'The lane is looking so beautiful today. I came down it on the bus this morning on my way back from the shops, and I thought, my little Rachel would love this. She's always dreaming of far-off places but she doesn't know what we have here on our doorstep. After that we could come home and play a board game or something.'

She holds me away from her again and cups my face in one of her hands, looking into my eyes. 'If you like?'

The Monopoly box is sealed with Sellotape and stuffed on to a shelf of the dresser. Last time we'd played it was at Christmas, when Uncle Ralph had been Mum's friend. Most of the pieces were missing so we'd made it up with thimbles and matchsticks instead of houses and hotels. It was fun. The new pieces were too big for the board and the game got muddled, and we laughed so much that I spilled Mum's drink over everything. Ralph poured her another anyway so it didn't matter, apart from the board. I'm not sure if it was dry before we put it away. It might be stuck and tear when we open it today.

Mum had a big party that New Year's Eve, and it was the first time she met Uncle Peter. Ralph and Peter had a fight while Mum was giggling in the kitchen. She said Peter could be her Sugar Daddy as he's older than her, about ten years I think, but all grown-up men look like turtles to me. I mixed the drinks for Mum's friends. Peter asked for whisky on the rocks. They all thought it was funny when I had quite a few sips too. It made me cough but I liked the taste. Mum said she didn't believe in any of that old codswallop telling you what you can and can't do with your kids. 'A hundred years ago she'd have been married with her own children at this age,' she said. Mum's friend Jeanie had to put me to bed after I fell over. I woke up the next day heavy from all the layers she'd put on the bed to keep me warm. She must have got the covers from the airing cupboard in my room as there were towels and all sorts on top.

The kitchen clock reads half past four. I'm desperate for the toilet and I wriggle on Mum's lap to get more comfortable but I don't want to leave yet. I want to curl into her shoulder and sleep.

'What do you think then, Rachel? Good idea?'

I mumble into her shoulder. 'Yes, Mum, I'd love to.'

She holds her arms round my middle and squeezes my bladder tight. I jump up and stand in front of her with my legs crossed.

'Please don't go, Mummy. I need the loo. I'll be back as quick as I can.'

'You silly thing, Rachel,' she says, laughing and shaking her hair with big flicks of her head. 'Where would I go?'

I speed to the bathroom and when I come back down she's on the hallway phone. She's taken it into the living room, and the phone's spiral cord is jammed in the door frame so the door won't shut properly. The coil jiggles as she moves on the other side. I put my ear on the wooden panel and listen.

'No, I've told you already,' she says, 'I'm not standing for it any more. I have a child to think of as well, if you hadn't noticed.' The curls of the cable stretch and wiggle.

From the kitchen comes the smell of burning. I run to the oven and with a tea towel I pull out the hot baking tin. The cake is my favourite – pineapple upside-down. I love the way the gooey syrup from the fruit soaks into the dough and oozes down the sides when it's turned out of its tin. It's even better a little burnt like this, as the edges of the cake go crispy and chewy. I get a plate and try to turn the tin over, but the towel's too thin and the cake and plate slide around. Some of the hot juice dribbles over my hand.

In the other room the receiver slams down, and through the walls I hear Mum say, 'Well, we're not going to let that man spoil our day now, are we, princess!' She comes back into the kitchen and I freeze with the plate in one hand and the tin in the other. The metal burns through the towel.

'I'm really sorry, Mummy,' I say. 'I was trying to help but I think I got it wrong. Please don't be cross.'

'Oh, let's not worry about that, shall we?' she says, and takes the plate from me. 'Old butterfingers Rachel never could do these things, could she? What a princess she is!'

At the sink I wash my burn in cold water and wipe some tears on my sleeve, thinking about the eggs on toast I cook myself most evenings without making a mistake.

She laughs and sets the cake in the middle of the plate and wipes the messy bits from the edge of the china with a cloth. The juice is the best bit and I almost ask her to leave it but decide it's better we have a nice time.

'Right then,' Mum says, 'let's get on with our lovely day, shall we?' She pats a chair for me to sit on and then sits herself down opposite. The side flaps of the yellow table have been pulled up to make it big enough to fit everything on. Mum takes a tea towel from a plate of sandwiches, like a magician pulling a rabbit from a hat, then she puts the cake plate down next to it and does little hand claps in front of her face. There are egg, ham and fish-paste sandwiches, with slices of tomato and cucumber in a green and red pattern round the edge of the plate. In the middle of the sandwiches is a sprinkle of cress. Her head dips to watch my face. 'Well, go on then,' she says, 'help yourself.'

I tuck into the food – it's really lovely – and for afters we have cups of tea and the cake, still warm and eggy from the oven. The slice crumbles in my hands so I make a ball of the bits on my plate, sticking it together with little dabs, and I hold the plate up to my face to get the food in my mouth without spilling. I've seen Chinese people on TV eating bowls of rice like this. Mum does the same and we giggle, our faces close across the table. When we're finished we leave all the mess on the table apart from the leftover cake, which I don't want to go stale. I put it in the empty red biscuit tin. Mum puts on her shoes and brushes her hair in big sweeps in front of the mirror by the back door. Most weeks the hairdressers do her a style: a puffy round bun with tassels of hair round her face. Today though she wears it down past her shoulders. I hadn't realized it was so long. Her dark roots are beginning to show where she hasn't had it dyed recently, and a few really blonde strands float down and stick to her cardigan.

She grabs my hand and leads me outside. The back

door is open and I pull away from her, getting the key from my pocket to lock it. 'Oh, don't worry about that,' she says. 'You can leave it wide open for all I care.' She laughs with a big open mouth and her head turned up to the sun. 'We're perfectly safe. I've decided that today we're untouchable.' I leave the door and catch up with her, taking her hand again, and she swings our two arms forward and back in the air.

We go left into the lane at the end of our road. This is the way the bus goes, past fields and to the next big town. The other direction is my school and our village. Mum says it's the perfect place to live and that we're lucky to have the best of both worlds, 'Countryside and community.' It's getting late and the sun makes golden spots on the trees. Tiny buds dot the branches and there's the smell of wet mud. I hold the air inside my lungs until I think I might burst.

A car passes at speed and we have to stand back quickly.

'Silly old so-and-so,' Mum says in a sing-song voice.

I breathe out. 'Is Uncle Peter coming over tonight, Mummy?'

She steps into the road and pulls me after her. 'You should call me Patty, like my friends do. After all, we're always being mistaken for sisters.'

Mum's name is Patricia. She shortened it after Dad left. We're almost the same height now and I no longer have to bend my neck to look at her. Her skin shines and bounces in the sunlight. Long lashes flap against her cheeks, like mascara butterflies, and when she smiles there are small creases at the edges of her eyes. I've never seen anyone so beautiful. We chat about boys and school and what we could do in the summer. She says maybe I won't have to go to Daddy's and we could go bike riding instead and swim in the sea. I think she's forgotten that Daddy's last letter said he was too busy this summer to have me anyway, but it's fun making plans so I don't say anything.

A few more cars pass and we pull back into the verge, getting tiny twigs and mud in our shoes. We empty them out and walk in our tights and socks. Mum smiles and waves at all of the cars with big sweeps of her arm. Some of the drivers wave back. Some don't. The last car that passes speeds up as it rounds to the other side of the road to avoid us. Mum holds her arm high in the air and waves it to and fro, as if she's calling a ship, but the driver keeps her eyes on the road. The red tail lights vanish round the darkening corner. 'Yes, and you're not so perfect yourself, Mrs Pierce,' she shouts at the car which has already disappeared. 'Interfering old cow!' Mum's voice echoes against the steep banks of the lane. 'You're just jealous of other people having fun.'

Mum turns swiftly round, as if we've reached the end of the track, like at school when we race up and down the field, circling a traffic cone. 'Come on then, spoilsport,' she says more quietly, but walking fast. 'You should have brought your coat. I guess we'll have to go back.'

My jumper is thin and my hands are cold, but I'm

trying really hard not to shiver. 'I don't mind,' I say, 'let's keep on going.' I tug her arm back towards the way we were walking even though she's already built up speed in the direction of home. 'We can always get the bus back from town.' I grasp her hand with both of mine.

'Don't be daft, old silly-pants.' She pulls her hand out of my grip. 'Mummy's got things to do.'

On the way back, if a car passes, Mum looks to the side of the road, commenting on a tree and touching its leaves, and after the car has gone Mum rejoins the road with a fast walk. I try to talk about the school holidays again but instead she asks what homework I have to do this evening.

As we turn the corner into our street, we see Uncle Peter's car is parked in our driveway. He leans against the bonnet with straight legs crossed in front of him and his pipe hanging from his mouth. In his arms is an enormous bunch of flowers. Mum strides ahead of me and past him, up the path to the front door. He runs after her and grabs her round the waist.

'Pat, please, Patty, hear me out,' he says.

She struggles away from him and reaches for the door handle. I walk round to the back, run up the stairs and peep from an upstairs window. Mum and Peter are standing in the front garden near the door, and the tops of their heads are stuck together. Mum's long hair mixes with his as Peter grasps it in his hands. I think about what their tongues are doing and whether it feels different to the back of my hand. Across the road, there's an eye-sized gap in Mrs Simpson's net curtains.

I lie on my bed watching the light fade from blue to black. The pipes in the wall hiss when a tap is turned on and from downstairs there's a chink of metal on glass. I guess Mum is filling a vase. Peter's smoke creeps up the stairs and curls round my door. I open the window to let out the smell and the room turns to ice.

10

PENCIL POINT

Less than a week has passed since I came back from Will's, and the stand-off between David and myself remains unbroken. The ash I threw over his toy collection was cleaned up by the time I woke the next day, and nothing was said about the mess, as if it never happened, as if I'd gone mad and imagined everything. I showed David the receipt from the Grand but he ripped it up without looking at the date. When we're together now, David's eyes follow my every move, and most of his phone calls are taken in private. He leaves small clues around the house to remind me that he hasn't forgotten, that his silence is merely a mask for intention. A jugged hare has been in the fridge for days, uncovered, so everything including the milk has taken on the flavour of the gamey meat. I've had to throw all the food away.

Each day I wake before dawn to a quick pulse in my chest and a dream-replay of the man on the road, now a truncated version of the main events: wide eyes, thud, flip, blood, drag, dead. At times it seems like this same vision has been the recurrent theme of my whole night's sleep, and I'm more tired when I wake than when I go to sleep. The pain in my stomach grows daily, and I choke down tablets the size of horse pills. I finally made it to my GP. She's concerned I'll get woozy with anything stronger, but the meds only knock off the edge. Sometimes I experiment with an unsafe dose, or take nothing at all and let the sensation in my body remind me that I'm still alive. The doctor has sent my blood for tests and has requested an ultrasound of my abdomen, but at the last appointment she prodded and pressed and said she could feel nothing alarming. 'Have you been anxious at all lately?' she asked when I said the pain sometimes travels to my legs. I didn't tell her about the times I go numb and feel like I've shrunk to the size of a pinhead inside my body.

This morning I creep from under the covers, and my husband's sleeping body rolls into the warm space I've left behind. The bed looks full, as if there was never enough room. In the bathroom I wash the crust from my eyes, dress, then take the watch I found at the roadside from my tampon box – its overnight hiding place – and wind the piece before putting it in my bag. The tick is old-fashioned and loud, and in the morning quiet I think I can hear it through the leather of my bag, so I muffle it with tissues, holding the pulse for a moment before it goes silent. Downstairs I grab a coffee then leave, driving through unlit streets and past hibernating houses, willing the new morning to arrive and with it the offer of a day. Any day will do, only better than the last. Instead I feel like a trespasser.

My plan is to get to the office early to prepare for my public persona of work Rachel, the authoritative and decisive manager who oversees the rivers of finance flowing in and out of our current productions. It's becoming harder these days to summon up this character, and as soon as I return home she scuttles away and hides for the rest of the night. Today, on my way to work, I decide to make a detour down the road where the accident took place, to witness the size of the police operation, and calculate the impact of one man's death.

I drive to where the lane bends sharply at the tree. My car slows to a standstill in the centre of the road. Tarmac sucks at the tyres.

This is the place.

All that's left of the investigation are car tread marks on the muddy verge and a flapping strand of blue and white police tape. There's nothing else here; the evidence transferred to the lab now and the body in deep freeze. I'm sorry they took the man away. There was some comfort in knowing he lay close to where he'd lived, his body returning to the woods atom by atom. I wonder what else the police found, if anything of mine was discovered. A small part of me wishes they'd come and get me so I could be done with all of this.

My car engine murmurs in the background of my thoughts. I press the accelerator and the vehicle jolts forward, carrying me further down the lane, and again I pass the horse-box house I saw on the day of the accident. It's joined now by two other vehicles, both in the same ramshackle state. One looks like an ex-post-office truck, the writing on the side painted over with a darker shade of red, and the other vehicle was probably once a police van, the type that would have ferried officers with riot shields to a demonstration. In its previous incarnation, the van could have been used against these activists whose camp of tepees and tree houses has spilled into the woods. Smoke drifts across the road from a camp fire.

About half a mile further along the lane I catch a glimpse of something through the bare trees: a flash of colour in the distance, a structure on a small incline. A roof and a window, the glass filling up with the grey dawn. It must be the caravan Alex spoke of. The home of the man I killed. Cold fear creeps up my spine and I speed up towards Brighton.

Teller Productions is situated on the main route into town, about a twenty-minute drive from the woods. When I arrive, I park in the forecourt and turn off the engine. Reflected in the gloss of the windows, a pale sun bleeds into the dark sky, the image broken by a polka-dot of rain on the glass. I run to the entrance and fumble with the keys in the lock, and once inside a single tone counts down the thirty seconds before the alarm proper goes off.

I input the code twice before getting it right. Then silence. The hush expands through the still air.

The heating hasn't come on, but even when it does the office will still be cold. David goes to the gym every morning and comes to work pink and sweaty, ordering Kelly the receptionist to open windows. She brings extra layers of clothes which she keeps in a bag under her desk. 'Good temperature for mental agility,' David says. He'll shower again in his office en suite even though he's already washed at the gym; if David had a choice, he'd deny his body the filth of natural secretions.

Here in this early dark the chill is almost solid, and the room is paused, waiting for the labour that will lift it from sleep. I pace between the desks and mute phones, gathering my jacket and scarf round me. My breath dusts the air for seconds before melting away. In the middle of the room a chair is slung out from its desk; a witness to a rushed exit last night. The standby light on the copier flashes in the corner like a distant satellite. I'm careful not to disturb anything, as if I'm a time-traveller passing through, and only the persistent rain ticking on the windows lets me know the world is still turning.

This empire has taken David and myself fifteen years to build, and we moved to these premises about five years ago when our old offices had reached bursting point. David spotted this run-down warehouse in the right part of town, the building next to a nursing home, and he made enquiries with the owner, convincing them to sell at a knock-down price – 'Take it off your hands, smarten the place up. It'll increase the value of your adjoining business.' The place was gutted, internal walls were pulled down and a suspended steel mezzanine cut the space in two – upper and lower. Where once stood a brick wall with a few small windows, huge sheets of tinted glass now front the open-plan layout looking out over the car park and road.

We have desks for about twenty staff, and each of their workstations is cluttered with the minor debris of their outside lives – family photos, kids' drawings, snow domes from Florida and the Canaries – set there as small acts of defiance; a retreat to better times. David hates the way these knick-knacks ruin the lines of symmetry made by the desks, but in order to appear the tolerant, benevolent boss he allows the clutter. Our people are expected to check in to work at least once a day, preferably in person even if they've been on location, and their broad desks and ergonomic chairs are a declaration of the company's investment in each individual. David is in by 8.00 a.m. and leaves twelve hours later so 'there are no excuses for shoddy work, only poor time management'. In our line of business you stay until the job is done – contracts are only given to mothers willing to dose up their kids on Calpol and send them to school with a fever – and most of our staff and freelancers know that the boss's expectations are a small price to pay for the chance of almost constant work, plus the golden ticket of a future reference from David Teller himself.

I walk up the metal stairs to the suspended floor where

a glass balcony runs the entire width of the building. Standing at the bar it's possible to survey most of the office. It's David's favourite spot. The only rooms in the building with a door, apart from the toilets, are on this floor, and they are the meeting room and mine and David's offices. David insists I keep my door open so I am present to all incoming traffic; I'm the gatekeeper of his day, a stronghold reinforced by the austerity of my welcome through which nothing and no one can pass. His door remains shut at all times.

My diary is open on my desk on today's page, the computer pushed to one side. I sit and shut my eyes as the day rolls out in front of me: meetings and lunches and the constant drill of phones that signal incoming shuttles of work. A day like most other days at Teller Productions, but it wasn't always this way. 'Luck is a residue of hard work,' David says, even though this phrase contradicts his modus operandi – 'Ask and the universe shall supply' – but all are variations on control, so whatever works best at the time, works for David.

Our success is, though, very much the result of mine and David's determination and vision. These last fifteen years have seen us expand from small corporate videos to long-form commissions for cable channels and several for the BBC and other terrestrials. We specialize in pro-grammes that peek into the dysfunctional worlds of people with either obsessive habits, bizarre jobs or secret desires; a modern version of freak-pointing at the circus. Publicly we assert that we are impartial, but a good editor can cut a story to make our judgement forefront. Without a viewpoint the programme would be bland, and even though the viewers would cry out if it were proved we were biased, they are as complicit as us by not tuning to another channel. Secretly they know we only give them what they want, and the appetite of the masses for voyeurism never ceases to surprise me. It keeps David and me in immense comfort.

Neither David nor I are at the frontline of production or camera any more; from my desk I exec everything that passes through the office – no project gets the sign-off without my say-so – and David is the deal maker and confidence builder, his days stacked around forging connections with influential people. After months of tennis matches and boardroom breakfasts, we landed a major series, one we hope will sell internationally and get repeat commissions year on year – we hold out for these golden geese above anything that has BAFTA potential. David told me of the programming executive, 'I know all his secrets, all his friends who jumped the interview process, and I even know who he's fucking behind his wife's back. I could bring him down just like that.' He clicked his fingers and froze the gesture at the side of his head for several seconds too long after he'd finished speaking, the smile on his face in traction.

The result of all this work is that the money keeps piling in. We have all we need but we keep on making more, as hobbyists or collectors do, storing the excess and watching the numbers on the page grow bigger month by month, like sediment at the mouth of a river. But money's not the only currency that David deals in: power and charm are in abundance too, and he uses all these assets like a tool to be switched on and off dependent on the job in hand. Recent talk of expansion, of joining forces with another company overseas and making our brand international, was quashed without debate; he'd rather keep it local. David wouldn't trust another office without himself at the helm, infecting every deal with his purpose and insight. Plus another element would be missing, and that would be me: my ability to pick a winning pitch above any Arts Council frippery, but more importantly my knowledge of David and the ways in which we conduct our trade – all the above-board and the number of shady dealings to which I've recently been introduced. With David there's no definition of what he's chasing; he will never arrive as there will always be somewhere else to go. Men like him don't retire, they fall dead on a squash court, racket in hand, doing a deal, and we share and tolerate these and other unspoken secrets between us out of habit and shame, not only because we know each other so well, but because it's too late for either of us to change. There's too much history and too much to lose. These things make us unique and desirable. We are a team. I keep David's secrets and he keeps mine, although since the accident a dangerous imbalance has tipped in David's favour.

Yesterday's half-finished glass of water is on my desk. A membrane of dust lies between the air and water, reminding me of a chemistry experiment at school when the teacher pulled a thread of nylon from between two liquids and curled the strand round a pen. I swig from the glass of old water to wash down two pills, the period between painkillers getting less and less, then sit back in my chair and press my stomach. The pain has no one rhythm or position, but when I think of the homeless man and the caravan I saw this morning, the sensation peaks. Instinctively I know that until what I've done has been made good, this discomfort won't go away. Nothing and no one can alter the fact that a man has died, but where there are clues to how he lived, there could perhaps be some resolution.

The front door opens and shuts with a double clang. I jump in my seat. As I stand and peer from my office door, I see the cleaner pause by the silent alarm pad, scratching his head. He switches on the bank of lights and my eyes blink at the clock. 7.00 a.m. Opening the store cupboard, the man takes out the vacuum and untangles its lead from the trolley of dusters and cleaning fluids, all the while mumbling to himself, though I can't make out what he's saying. He turns on the machine as I walk silently to the glass banister and watch him push the nozzle over the wooden floor in slow sweeps. Intermittently he stops to stare out of the window and chat a bit more, as if the cleaning is interrupting an important conversation, then leaves the vacuum to one side and begins to dust the desks.

The phone rings. On impulse I pick up the nearest extension. The cleaner's head spins round. He sees me. His expression is vacant, and he stands with his paunch out and shoulders down. I'm on his time; normally I wouldn't care, but today I blush.

'Hello?' I say into the receiver.

The cleaner continues his dusting.

'What are you doing?' It's David.

'I thought I'd catch up on some things before the office got busy.'

'Have you seen my Hunters?'

I stare through the window. Grey light has bleached away the dawn.

'They're in the boot room,' I say. 'I put them there last night to dry out after you took the dogs for a walk.'

There's a pause, then down the phone line comes the squeak of David's leather slippers on the marble floor. An aside of skittering claws accompanies him, our two dogs probably curling in and out of his legs and jumping up. I visualize his route from the quality of sound down the receiver: across our tiled hallway and dining room, then through the kitchen to the back utility room we call the boot room. 'Naughty lady didn't take you out, did she?' His voice is muffled and I know he'll be holding one of the dog's heads, rubbing her soft ears and putting his mouth against her forehead as he speaks, imagining they share a telepathic connection.

David comes back on the line. 'If I'd known you were leaving so early I would've got up too. I won't have time to go to the gym now. I'll have to take the girls out instead.'

'David,' I say, 'let them out in the garden. The dog walker will be there at ten.'

'It's not fair on them. You should have thought this through before you left. Get Kelly to reschedule our lunch meeting so I can go to the gym later.' I hear him breathing down the line. 'I'll be in shortly to keep an eye on things there. You're becoming next to useless, Rachel.'

He puts the phone down and the hiss of quiet fills my head.

In front of me in my diary the day's tasks ladder down the page. I enjoy the tactile feel of paper and pencil, finding it easier to see what there is to do from pages smudged and scribbled over, like a dentist's appointment book. David always tuts at the sight of the computer sidelined to the back of my desk. 'What must it look like to clients when they come in,' he said once, 'you peddling away with your scratchy little pencil? That's the person I met, Rachel, with your two-ring cooker and baked beans on toast. It's not who you are now.'

I draw up a list of requirements for the day and prepare the paperwork and myself to sit next to David through all these meetings: shoulder to shoulder, interjecting only when I disagree with a client or filmmaker, the bad cop to his good. Anyone else would be honoured with the trust he bestows on me, but my talents have long been replaceable so I know it's more practical than that. The main reason we work together so well is that I understand him more than anyone else, I know what he wants before he's even thought of it, though sometimes I worry that I know too much. If ever I was free of David, my insider knowledge of the man, not just the business, would be of great concern to him. I've watched him win then fail then rise again, over and over, from student days with a sideline of a T-shirt stall, to promoting club nights and starting a record label, followed by a switch to production when he realized that young people only had a finite amount of money. He sat up night after night studying the workings of each new venture, taking higher-ed courses at obscure and far-flung colleges in camera operating and offline editing. I was the one who witnessed his humiliation at every setback, followed by his disbelief in the idiots who ran the business, those who were unable to recognize his potential. His incredulity was always followed by a volcano of ambition for the next pitch. What began as my support, bankrolling his humble and secret apprenticeship as I worked as a business administrator, turned into a pooling of our ideas and talents when I finally understood, as always, that David's plans had legs. I quit my job and became the financial and production partner to his technician.

In the early years the two of us pitched to commissioners and were mostly turned down, but the few jobs we managed to win enabled us to build our reel. Over time we gained more confidence and this was boosted by growing admiration in the industry. We expanded year on year until we achieved our current success in the Reality programming market. I have to applaud David's foresight – he stuck to this vision rather than pursuing more instantaneous but ultimately less lucrative avenues – but now we've reached the level we have, our TV formula a stylized roll-out to be adjusted to any unfortunate human dilemma, I sense that David's adrenalin is running low: more visits to the gym, impulsive sackings when a warning would have done, more frequent requests to top up his stash. I would be happy to sell the business, but for David our production company is family; if nothing else, he's loyal. So instead he'll branch out to other business ventures, whatever he can turn into success, whatever he can manage locally, and he'll hold on to what he's already created. Hence these new illicit openings outside of our known arena, such as David's involvement in Alex's development, which ticks more boxes than merely making money. When I questioned the lack of paperwork involved in our investment, unchecked by lawyers or traceable by the tax man, David told me to grow up. 'I'm trusting you to keep schtum on this, Rachel,' he said. 'I know you can hide this amount in your productions. This could be very profitable for us so I don't need any of your ethical hysterics.'

The first meeting today is at 10.00 with a children's charity who need a publicity video for fundraising, so there's plenty of time to organize myself for clients who are effectively asking of us a favour. We'll farm the project out to someone fresh and keen from film school, and the new recruit will give us their time for free in exchange for a foot in the door. For this appointment, David will wear his philanthropist's uniform of jeans and T-shirt, though in reality we'll be giving little away. In return we gain a stronger profile. Later in the day, David will change into the suit and open-necked shirt he keeps at the office for 'real' meetings. Today's was a late lunch with an ex-commissioner who's in between channels, though this will now be cancelled to make way for David's more import-ant visit to the gym. 'Small fry,' David has scribbled next to the woman's name in my diary.

A click and low rumble signals the heating coming on. I move to a radiator and press my hands against the metal as the warmth creeps up its surface. The stairs reverberate with the clang of the hoover plug announcing the clean-er's growing proximity, so I go into David's office where there's more space and an en suite, and lock the door.

David's large desk takes up a fair portion of the room. I sit in his chair and face the two banks of drawers which hang either side of the chair area. Some of these drawers used to contain stationery and other paperwork relating to current projects, though each one I pull now is locked. Usually David only secures the drawers containing financial information, and because I might need these statements, I was the sole person who knew where the keys were kept. I check behind our wedding photo on the windowsill, but the keys are no longer there. My hand runs over the rest of the sill and then across the shelves next to the wall, and finally I rummage through his spare gym bag until I hear the jangle of metal inside one of his training shoes.

As he clearly has so much to hide, it's time to redress the balance of secrets between us.

In one drawer there's a folder containing paperwork I've never seen before, detailing financial transactions between numerous companies, plus bank accounts I don't recognize. The first company that money has been sent to is in the UK and it's called Manorhall Construction, but the rest of the accounts are located in many different countries, and they amount to multiple transactions, the funds changing currency as they're paid on to each business, filtering through the various jurisdictions. I knew that David had stopped trusting me, but I had no idea the extent to which he had become involved in rinsing our money clean. Far greater amounts are detailed in the paperwork than was the original investment in the development, but this money hasn't been taken from any bank account I know of. There must be other sources, and I'm amazed and almost impressed at how fast David has taken to this new line of business.

Another drawer has a folder containing information on a man called Tyrone Aldridge. I recognize him as the leader of the camp of activists who was pictured in the newspaper at Mum's house. Here his mugshot is of a younger self with dreadlocks, and the paperwork details various arrests, mostly for dealing small amounts of cannabis, plus also his past memberships of various organizations: CND, Socialist Worker, Anti-Vivisection League; our debt collection agency has ways and means of sourcing more information than merely the financial assets of our clients. His first arrest was years ago at the poll tax riots, so he's older than I originally thought. In the bottom drawer is a notebook, exactly the same type as the one we keep at home for our household expenses. This one has only recently been started, and inside is a list of payments amounting to several thousand pounds. The first amount is dated the day of the accident. Next to the dates are the names of people I've never heard of, and pseudo-cryptic words that don't take a huge leap of imagination to work out: 'Fixer', 'Burn', 'Hush'.

There are voices outside the door, staff who've arrived early. The cleaner knocks and asks if he can come in. 'Give me a moment,' I call to him through the door. I scan as many of the bank statements as I have time for, my courage fading fast, then load the information on to a disk – another thing to hide from David, but I'll deal with that later. When I finish collating the paperwork, I put everything, including the background file on Tyrone plus the new ledger, back in the places where I found them, lock the drawers and hide the keys where they belong. I delete the scans and cancel the history on David's computer, then sit down on the sofa to settle my pulse before the day starts.

At 7.55 David pounds on the door. I've left the key in the lock and he can't get in from his side. Jumping up, I brush the creases from my clothes, flatten my hair with damp palms and instinctively sling my bag over my shoulder before opening the door. Kelly, our receptionist, is behind David. She holds a basketful of croissants, and peers round his back, her smile filled with questions. She has large front teeth and her top lip rarely seems to close over them.

'You look terrible,' David says. 'Great Willow will be here at eight fifteen.'

Another of the ever-popular breakfast meetings, our days stretched to fit in all the business that needs to be done, but the meeting isn't in my diary. I have a vague recollection of scheduling the appointment, though obviously didn't write it down. I forgot. It's not the first time recently. A month ago, before the accident, I never would have made this mistake, plus now I haven't got all the paperwork ready for the meeting. Great Willow Films are a rival production company who've fallen on hard times, mostly through their more traditional treatment of documentaries, and for some time we've been hoping to either put them out of business or absorb them. With their roster of work added to ours we'd be leaders in the Reality corner of the market.

David comes into his office and locks the door behind him. He sits at his desk and unlocks the middle drawer, taking out a small glass tube with a stopper. He examines it closely but it's empty so he goes back into the drawer and pulls out an oblong packet of folded-up paper, like basic origami, about three centimetres long. Next he takes out a mirror and a razor blade and unfolds the paper carefully, revealing compacted white powder. He scrapes a corner of the clump on to the shiny surface and, with manic little chops of the blade, turns the granules into a strip of dust. Inspecting the line with a couple of turns of the head, like a cat with a half-killed mouse, he puts the end of a small silver straw up one nostril, and with a quick loud sniff inhales the cocaine up his nose.

'This is a shit batch, Rachel,' he says, tossing his head back and pressing shut the other nostril with his thumb. He sniffs loud and shakes his head vigorously, more of a shiver. 'Bloody hell! It's cut with bleach or something.' He shunts his head forward and stares at me. 'If you score from the same dealer again, I'll break his kneecaps.' He pauses to let his words sink in. 'And I'm not joking.'

With his recent fast-tracking into the underworld – the man who disappeared my car, our dodgy investment in Alex's development, and now the reams of money that are leaving accounts I've never heard of – I don't doubt that if David has the inclination to find Will, it won't be a difficult task.

My phone is on silent but it vibrates with a text. I take it out of my bag and read the message. It's from Will: 'I miss you. Can we sort this out?' Perhaps there really is something to David's magical thinking, his thoughts crossing the ether to conjure people up. I hold up the phone, scanning the text and trying to read layers of meaning into Will's few words before I have to delete them, when I accidentally click on the camera option. In frame is a perfect shot of David sitting behind the clutter of his habit. He goes in for another line. I take several silent shots.

David cleans the mirror with his finger and licks the powder, rubbing what's left on his red gums, then he puts all the equipment back in the drawer before locking it again. He looks at me and pinches his nose clean, sniffing a couple of times. There must have been some coke left on his fingers as he's wiped a strip of white up his cheek, and has left a small rim of dust around one nostril.

'For God's sake,' he says, 'get yourself cleaned up.'

I go to reach for a tissue from the box on his desk, then stop myself and stand staring at him instead.

'Rachel,' he says. 'Get a move on. I need to prepare.' He shuffles through his papers. 'What's the matter with you? Take a shower or something.'

I wonder if he'll notice what's on his face before the meeting, and decide to leave it to fate.

In the bathroom, I wash my face and brush my hair. The strands fall in thick curls down my back. I've worn this same style – loose and long – ever since I was a girl and it never lets me down; every man I've ever met has fallen in love with my hair. The reality of the real woman underneath is a more complicated proposition. There's been little point to make-up recently, but no one is used to me looking undone, so if only to stop the cautious stares I put on mascara and lipstick, and dot some red circles on my cheeks. Before I spread the rouge up my cheekbone, in the mirror I see a little girl who's raided her mum's make-up bag.

Through the wall comes the noise of the clients filing into the meeting room, and Kelly chatting as she pours coffee from the big silver pot which sits at the centre of the table. No one drinks tea any more. I open the door from the bathroom into David's office and he stands facing me, holding out his folder, his eyebrows raised and the white powder gone from his cheek but still on his nose.

'What the fuck is this?' he says in a low voice so as not to be heard through the walls. He wafts the papers up and down. 'This is a mess, Rachel. You've left me totally unprepared for this meeting. Since you've failed at being a wife, the least you could do is live up to being my partner.' And he turns and walks out the door.

We enter the meeting room together and shake hands, making pleasantries about the weather, the pastries, David's squash match he played in which Ian James, the MD of Great Willow Films, was the victor.

'Hey, guys, Ian, it's so great to see you,' David says as he holds Mr James's hand for longer than the others' and guides him to his seat. 'Cassandra, Tanish. Thanks so much for coming in. We really appreciate you squeezing us into your busy schedule.'

Ian James sits down, smoothing both sides of his thick, greying hair with flat palms. Unusual, I think, for a man of his age to have so much hair. His colleagues sit on either side of him and across the table from us, their eyebrows raised. Then they look down. The younger man inadvertently pinches and rubs his nose, and repeats the action with a handkerchief. I watch David stroking down his shirt front and opening his folder, keeping his panic over my lack of preparation well hidden. He shuffles through the papers to find the relevant document, all the time relying on his presence to fill the room, but I can tell he's ruffled.

'So, guys.' David relaxes back in the chair and uses his arms to emphasize his words, sweeping his hand through his hair and smiling, everything but touch his face which would demonstrate weakness or fear. 'I think you know how excited we are to have you on board, and I'm more than confident that we can fulfil your existing commitments.' His smile is reassuring and warm. 'After the merger, we can start the process of combining your talent with our own company brand. You will of course retain autonomy over your productions, but we hope over time to unify our vision. In the meantime, you'll be under the safe umbrella of our name.'

The clients won't hold eye contact, their voices are low and rushed, and they gulp their coffee. In some circles of the film industry we would probably be chopping out the coke on the table between us, but we're not at the groovy end, we are suburbia. Ian James is known for being corporate and conservative, and for many years it's served him well, until recently when his fustiness has rubbed off on Great Willow's output. Even though his company desperately needs an update, David's 8.00 a.m. habit is clearly too radical. David fidgets in his chair, recalibrating his posture, aware of something chipping at the atmosphere. He widens the span of his arms, shows more of his teeth through his smile, and employs the best of his techniques to draw in the clients. I watch the theatre of his body, which I've seen so many times; David's talent for feigning greater ease and confidence in an accelerating crisis. This deal could mean a lot to us and the closer David gets, the more he wants to win, especially as he's under the impression that we're doing Great Willow a favour by taking on their ailing business. A light shine breaks out above David's top lip.

'All we need now is for you to sign off on the initial agreement and we can proceed with the first stage of the union.' He swivels the paper round to face the clients and places a pen on top, then sees he's put the wrong document forward. He shuffles through to find the correct one, puts it back in place for the clients, and reaches to pour himself a coffee.

A few stretched seconds pass where no one speaks. Great Willow look at one another. Mr James leans forward on his elbows and clasps his hands together in front of him, forming a V-shape with his arms on the table. His head is bowed at first, then he lifts it to David and looks at him properly for the first time.

'We have one other production company to speak to,' Mr James says. 'They're still preparing their proposal and should have it with us by next week. We'd like to wait until then. I hope you understand. We need to make sure our unique formula is competently handled.'

David leans forward and mimics the other man's shape on the table. Their eyes are centimetres apart.

'Right,' says David, 'I'd been under the impression this was a single bid. Of course, we're perfectly comfortable as we are with our existing output.' Another pause. He relaxes back into his chair for a final change of tactic. 'But with friends who share our vision, joining forces would make both our brands market leaders.'

David shuts his mouth and breathes a short snort. A speck of white falls from his face and on to his dark trouser leg. His eyes rest on the powder.

'As I said,' Ian leans back and begins to pack away his papers, 'we need to look at all of our options. We want to know we are in reliable hands.'

Great Willow get up, stretching across the table for more handshakes, then leave the room, closing the door softly behind them. We hear rapid breathy whispers through the door panel, followed by the speedy tap of shoes on metal as they descend the staircase. David remains in position, eyes staring straight ahead. He turns to me as I move the wheels of my chair away from him.

'That was a done deal,' David says. 'They were going to sign off today. You should have had the paperwork in order.' His voice is soft and slow but his nostrils are flared. He gets a tissue and wipes his nose gently.

I let out a small incredulous laugh. 'Their decision was nothing to do with the paperwork, David.'

He stares at me in silence for a few seconds, his body motionless and his eyes unwavering from mine. 'I have no idea what you're talking about.'

In a few years, the time we've been together will make

up more than half my life, and our familiarity is like that of conjoined twins fighting over shared organs. I know David so well that I understand it's easier for us both to blame me than for David to accept his own culpability. And the bigger problem isn't the loss of business or the damage to his integrity, it's that someone has seen beyond the sheen of business and peered into his personal world. They may as well have tiptoed round him while he was sleeping, sipped the water at his bedside and lifted the covers.

He slides a hand along my thigh to above my hemline and takes a chunk of my flesh in his grip. He squeezes. Hard. I take the pain with a sharp gasp. Twisted at an angle to him, I don't dare move further away but stare instead at the grey textured wall. David releases his hand.

'Again,' I whisper without looking at him.

'What did you say?'

I turn but my eyes won't lift past his feet. 'I want you to do that again.'

'You're losing your fucking mind, Rachel,' he says. He stands and strides from the room, closing the door behind him.

On the table is a pen holder with several ballpoints and pencils stacked inside. The writing tools have our company logo printed along their sides. I take one of the freshly sharpened pencils and lift my skirt to expose my upper thigh. With the pointed lead, I poke the end of the pencil into my flesh. A bubble of fresh blood leaps out and runs down on to the chair. I grab a tissue to mop up the spill then hold the paper against my skin until the flow stops.

In front of me the surface of the wall is like washed-out tarmac. I place my palm on the rough finish. It's the only thing holding me down.

11

HUNGRY DOGS

'I'm sure it's in here somewhere,' I tell the man behind the counter at the petrol station. He sighs. A queue is forming at my back as I go through my handbag one more time, the gritty bits of dead biscuits gathering under my nails. So many old receipts and tissues. My wallet is in my bag, but the slots where the credit cards used to be are empty. In the coin section is 23p. Finally I give up. 'I'm really sorry, I don't have any cash or cards on me. I'll have to leave you my address or something. What's the procedure?'

Behind me a man holding a large bottle of Coke says in a loud voice, 'Bloody hell.' A woman tuts and her toddler screeches as she pulls him away from the oasis of sweets displayed at child height.

The assistant takes a breath. He stares at me and breathes out slowly through his nose. 'You'll have to stand to one side while I clear the queue. I'll get the manager.' He rings a loud buzzer and speaks into an intercom.

'Manager assistance required at the till.' The tannoy beams across the shop and forecourt. I wait to one side as each customer reaches the till. Only the harassed mother tweaks me a smile.

This public shaming is the latest lesson from David. He doesn't know where or when the event will happen, and he won't be able to be a witness, but the thought of my humiliation will give him immense pleasure; a tit for his tat in front of Great Willow.

In the couple of days since that meeting at the office, a bright rage has flared between us.

'You'd be no one without me,' David says. 'You have no friends, no family. And I'd make sure you got nothing if you left.'

I know there are other jobs but David and our partnership is all I've ever known; without him I'd go back to being lost. I'd rather walk away with nothing than face the weeks of wrangling in front of his wall of lawyers, but then nothing is all I'd ever have.

At home we scuttle round each other, choosing alternate time zones, inhabiting separate beds and bathrooms, passing occasionally in the hall as one goes out and the other comes home, tag-teaming our baton of hate. Yesterday as I unbuttoned my jacket I caught David's eye in the mirror and watched the judgement slide over his features. He watched my reflection, not wanting to infect himself with direct eye contact, the world of opposites more tolerable, and my composure fractured momentarily. I imagined he could see through my skin to where my body is liquid, and to the rot which I know started long before the accident or before David came on the scene.

The pain in my stomach and back increases as I absorb David's venom, and with each attack I grow a step closer to the dead man, and the life I took away. Alex clearly wrote the man off as a simpleton, but the shopkeeper said he'd spent most of his life in institutions. Or was it that he'd been a musician? Living in a caravan is a long way to fall if he'd had such a stellar career, but then being incarcerated would explain why he endlessly walked the roads with no obvious destination, as if by the simple act of putting one foot in front of the other he was exercising his liberty. Most of all though I'm intrigued by what he was hiding, or hiding from. Instinctively I sense that by coming to know the real man – aside of all the Chinese whispers – and the place where he lived and died, an answer will be offered for both of us.

I fill out my contact details on a form at the petrol station, and they ask me to leave something of value. In my jacket pocket is the watch. I put it there this morning – not in my bag, thankfully, or David would have found it when he took my cards. Every day since the accident I've wound it and changed its hiding place at night, stashing it where David is least likely to look: the fridge, the ironing basket, the cleaner's box of chemicals. My habitual secrecy also ensured that I didn't waste any time the other day when I got home from work. David was working late as usual, so on the home computer I created a new email address and sent across all the information I'd downloaded at the office before destroying the disk and my browsing history. The photos of David taking coke went to the same place before I deleted them from my phone. A treasure trove of spite if ever I were daring. And if David one day decides to cash in the hoard he holds on me, at least I'll have some counter ammunition. I've always been careful, but in future I'll not be able to take chances unless I want to face the consequences.

I clasp the watch tight and leave it in my pocket, deciding instead to give the garage my wedding ring along with David's mobile number.

I'd left work early today with the intention of driving to Blackthorn Lane, but with the delay at the garage it's already 4.30 and starting to get dark. Back in my car, I drive fast and turn into a rudimentary car park, the closest point to where I'd spied the caravan which Alex said belonged to the homeless man. The homeless man who it turns out had a home. He was nearly there when he died and for a while lay on familiar ground. To die nameless and unloved is tragic, but to be apart from everything that mattered would be worse. After I read the article at Mum's house about the discovery of the body, I ordered a new remote for our TV at home, and I pick up local news when I can. I know that the police haven't yet identified the man or made the connection to the caravan, but it won't be long before they do. So before all this land is divided up to make way for new homes, I have a brief opportunity to stand in his shoes and experience what he knew, maybe discover something of his past and go some way to settle with him. Perhaps this way he can be rescued from rumour or anonymity.

The car park is empty aside from an unmanned digger in one corner. It waits for the go-ahead on Alex's development, the plans paused while Forensics conducted their search of the wider area. 'Terrible business,' Alex said when I saw him interviewed on the local news. 'We'll do everything in our power to assist the police in their inquiries. Of course the project is on hold. You can't put a value on a man's life.'

The trees prepare for their winter sleep, unaware of the threats that money and progress will bring, so in a roundabout way I've given this land and the activists a brief respite.

My car judders across the car park, over stones and into potholes, and an icy grit spatters the side windows. Soon it will be dark, but I don't intend to be long, and park on the opposite side from the lone street light in the clearing. There's no phone signal here so I'll have a break from the usual assault of texts – David's preferred mode of communication now that verbal exchanges between us have become so limited.

I know this place as David used to walk the dogs here, and in the past I came too, if we were having a good day. I'd grab these small holidays from his temper and judgement when they presented themselves, the respite a tantalizing view into what our marriage could have been.

David would take down his guard at the end of an extended period of difficulties, usually the point at which I was close to walking out, and he'd offer me the empathetic loving man I'd so long desired. He'd keep it up long enough for me to relax, and the possibility of a loving relationship was enough to make me stay. It's always easier to stay. I wonder if I could be fooled by his charm again.

Traditionally other factors have kept us going: sex, the house, money. Work. If we separated, David would fight me to the end for control of the business; the empire we've built together, which has David's name stamped on all the legal documentation. I've always bent to his reasoning, whatever it was at the time. He knew all about pre-nups before anyone else had even heard of them. Walking away from the house, with its chiselled luxury that sets order in my mind, wouldn't be easy. But if I lost it all and David relocated me to some festering little one-bed, his bile would continue and probably even grow, enduring out of spite from his failure to keep me in line. So I'd rather be present with a level of control than be the enemy.

The dusk is overcast but dry, the air freezing. A solo bird sings in a leafless tree. I get out of the car and lock the door then find the track into the undergrowth. The path stretches past dilapidated, ivy-clad farm buildings and into the acres of woods. Some of the trees are ancient but many have sprung up since this land was last used. The route branches and disappears, following the thrill of dogs chasing rabbits, and I walk for ten minutes to where

I think the caravan will be. There, at a grand horse chestnut with frayed nylon rope-swing, I peer north into the trees and see the home of the man I killed.

The passage towards the vehicle is like a memory of a path. In the five weeks since the accident, plants have reclaimed this space. Fallen branches, moss and leaves bed the ground. At first the bushes are easy to part, but the undergrowth gets thicker the further I go. Plants jag at my clothes. A thorn swipes my cheek, and fingers of branches tangle my hair. Looking down, my hands piece the way through the scrub until thirty metres forward the access opens on to a small clearing. Set at the centre, with the night closing in, is the dust-yellow caravan.

The oval structure appears flimsy, like a toy held together by Sellotape. Weeds crawl up and across windows towards the roof, and the caravan lists as if the vegetation is pulling it into the ground. On the other side of the vehicle is a barbed-wire fence, and behind that a ploughed field, ringed on three sides by the woods. The fourth edge of the field stretches across to a barn which sits at the foot of gentle hills. Above is a big open sky, dark grey and full. If it breaks, there will be sleet or snow.

A chill seeps through my jacket. I place my numb feet into footprints set in the mud, which guide me towards the door. The fossilized undersoles detail two sets of feet; one pair at least must have been male, but neither can belong to the owner of the caravan – the last time he was here, the weather had been dry. He never made it home to shelter from the rain that came.

A porch made from corrugated iron and old packing cases is attached to the side of the vehicle, and through this is the door to the caravan. Three wonky shelves stacked with bags line one side of the shelter: holdalls, handbags and supermarket carriers follow a size order – a system in the chaos – with big ones at the bottom and smaller ones up top. I pull one out and it falls. The rotten fabric bursts and books spill on the ground, pages rippled with damp. Air clogs with cold must. One hardback reveals a library renewal slip, last stamped in 1985. I bend down, put the books back in the bag then step towards the door, expecting the caravan to be locked or the door handle stiff, but it opens with ease on to a dark room. A wall of stench. With my eyes shut I hold my breath for as long as I can, letting the worst of the spores drift past before I refocus and enter with slow steps. The watch ticks inside my gloved palm, as if I've brought the man with me and am returning him home.

Directly ahead is a bed, heaped with blankets and an old hessian sack. There are two windows: one to my side and one over the bed. Below the window to my left is a small fixed table with seating for two. Opposite this is the kitchen. Pinned around the walls are pen-and-ink drawings of birds, rabbits and dogs. The pictures are naive but well accomplished, and many of the images are ringed by swirls and fractals of colour. Some of the pages have been pulled off and lie scrunched on the floor. I pick up a couple of the drawings. They are of trees, and have names written underneath: Olden Head and Greenscale. On all the flat surfaces is a brickwork of cans and bottles, some growing fur, and the space looks smaller than I thought, more claustrophobic for the clutter. There's a crushed can on the floor, and I pick it up and fit my gloved hand round the tin's creases where the man touched. Stepping over rubbish, I go to sit on the bed but a used condom is on the blankets – not his, surely, but kids. Interlopers. This bed. This stink. This filth. I doubt they thought it was worth it.

Outside, a bird screeches, then silence apart from the blood rushing to my ears.

Fitted cupboards hang open and rubbish spills out – someone has already been through the man's things. I reach into each cupboard, finding nothing but empty tins and newspapers, some porn magazines, and my gloves collect a tacky fluff. Only one door above the fridge is jammed shut. I yank at the handle until the hinge bursts open, and I stumble backwards, bumping into the table and dislodging a pyramid of cans to the floor. Brushing myself down, I find a crate, turn it over and stand on it for height. Inside the cupboard's dark mouth my fingers survey the edges, then hit on something cold and hard at the back, something that's been missed by the other tomb raiders. I slide it out. It's a box with a key – an old cash-tin – and it rattles as I shake it, though not with the clatter of coins. The lock shifts round in rusty jolts and the lid loosens, then opens with a squeak to reveal a sectioned tray designed to hold different denominations of money, only there's not a single penny here. Instead each compartment holds the complete skeleton of a small animal. One looks like a mouse, another a baby bird, all resting on tissue paper. The bones are bleached clean, as if they've been picked of flesh and left in the sun by someone who knew what they were doing, someone who regarded nature as a treasure. Two small pellets of bones, crushed up into ovals, sit in one compartment – parcels of regurgitated waste from a bird of prey. I clear a place at the table, remove my gloves and sit, carefully picking out the pieces of one of the creatures and placing the bones in the palm of my other hand. The skeleton weighs nothing. Each bone was once attached to muscle, the muscle covered by skin, and this collection of tiny parts would have made a living machine. I put the animal jigsaw back, then lift out the tray and put it to one side. Underneath is a stack of papers and a few empty envelopes with addresses from across the country. Some have hair cuttings and seeds inside. The recipient's name on the front is Seamus Williams.

I read the words several times. Seamus. Williams. My Seamus.

Sifting through the papers, I find several payslips addressed to Seamus dating back to the early 1970s. They are all from Manorhall Construction.

Even though the logo has changed, it has to be the same company whose letterhead I saw at the office; the business could have lain dormant all these years, until now when its bank accounts have again become useful. I flatten the papers on to the table to stop them shaking in my hands.

Beneath the payslips, yellowed newspaper articles talk about the aborted development here in the 1970s: WORKER THWARTS NEW DEVELOPMENT; UNIONS TAKE A STAND AGAINST UNSAFE WORKING CONDITIONS. The reports are hard to read in the low light, the print worn as if it's been handled repeatedly, but there's a small picture of a man, too pixelated to see his features, though the name credit underneath is for Seamus Williams. So the worker mentioned in the headline must be Seamus. I remember Alex saying that the man in the woods was part of the reason his family couldn't develop the land years ago, which suggests Manorhall is a Richard family enterprise.

At the bottom of the pile is an airmail envelope addressed to Seamus at a PO box in the village, and on the back is an address in Ireland. I unfold the thin sheet inside to reveal large handwriting with the dots above the i's drawn as hearts.

'Dear Pa, I have a cat now. She is called Mouse. She is black and white and I love her. When are you coming home?'

A photo falls to the floor with the picture facing up: a young girl standing in a garden next to a fence. There are daffodils in the flower beds and the girl smiles into the camera with letter-box lips, like someone has told her to be happy. On the back of the photograph is the name 'Claire' and it's dated 4 March 1976. She looks about ten. The same age I would have been that year, the same age

I was when my dad left. We could be long-lost twins, this the sister I always wanted. I wonder if my own father kept the letters I wrote.

Outside, the light is failing, but as I study the photo a late blanch of setting sun seeps through the dirt on the window and highlights letters etched into the grime on the glass: the letters spell 'Look'. I think of Seamus sitting here, pulling his finger across the dust to form the word, the writing left for me to see. The breath of a dead man brushes my neck. Behind the letters golden shafts of light fall through gaps in the clouds and travel at speed across the landscape, like giant legs keeping pace with the hurry of the wind.

From this position in the caravan, the whole field opens out to the horizon. Nothing gets in the way of the hills and sky. It's all mine to see. I imagine the man – my Seamus – sitting in this seat and watching for nature's details, the landscape altering at speed but at other times with such intricacy that the changes would be easy to miss unless you were paying attention. How easy it would be to replace every branch and insect here with uniformity. I wonder what happened to Seamus, and how radical he had to become to save this land from commerce. This must be what he fought for, and why he stayed. For the first time I understand why anyone would choose to live like this and why they would need nothing else.

It's hard to make out in this light, and at first I think I'm imagining it, but a small dot approaches from the direction of the trees and moves across the open field towards the caravan. The shape travels at a gentle speed, at times lolling to one side before righting itself. I can't make out if it's a person from this far away, and I panic as to whether it's better to hide here until they pass or make a run for it. I look round for something to crouch under, but everything is so filthy. As I watch outside, the shape comes closer until at last it morphs into a dog. No owner in sight. I put on my gloves, stuff all the papers in my bag, with the letter and photo zipped into the safe pocket, then I slide the container back into the cupboard.

The caravan rocks and squeaks as it releases my weight. I hold my breath and move slowly round to the barbed-wire fence as the dog comes closer, and we face each other in a stand-off across the rusty barrier. The animal's eyes are balls of dark jelly. Ribs push through its thin skin and jowls loop down from brown teeth in red gums. Long scabs run in parallel lines along the dog's flank, possibly made by crossing the wire if the animal had been forced to find a way through – if it had been desperate for food because its owner never returned. The dog is cautious but knowing and it lets out a low growl, but offers no other challenge as it paces the length of the fence. I take the scarf from round my neck and wrap it round my hand, then press down on the wire to climb into the field. The scarf is silk, my gloves soft, and a rusty spike goes through almost immediately, planting itself into my palm with a hot wet pain. I snatch my hand away from the fence. Blood blooms through the silk. I unravel the material, pull off my glove and instinctively suck the wound; the blood is warm and bitter, the flow strong, and the cut will need to be dressed properly. I strap my hand up tight, like a tourniquet, and walk away. Behind me the dog's bark is a rasp. I turn to see it paralleling the fence one last time with legs lean and flapping, before it turns and limps back across the field towards the woods, head bent to the ground.

Darkness overtakes me as I make my way back along the path of frozen puddles which crunch like broken glass. I take wrong turn after wrong turn, and panic I might end up here all night. How long would I survive in this cold?

After about an hour I hear voices and spy tents plus a series of walkways in the trees, set up like an adventure playground; the makeshift community of activists have bedded in against the development. A figure holding a lantern turns towards me, but he can't see me standing in the darkness. I pause to study the man, enjoying the luxury of observing without being seen. He's an older, shorter-haired version of the dreadlocked image of Tyrone I saw in David's office, and he's taller than in his newspaper portrait. Several people have gathered round a fire behind him, one with a guitar, another two are laughing. A grubby child bashes the ground with a stick before wandering over to its mother for a cuddle. It crosses my mind to ask them for directions. If I did, I could sit for a while to warm up; perhaps they'd offer me some tea, one of the women could dress my wound, then maybe I'd sleep out here in a tent, cocooned by the woods. The thought of David and Alex finding out I'd crossed over to the other side makes me smile, and I go to walk towards the group but a twig breaks under my foot. The man raises his lantern and shouts, 'Who's there?' I turn and flee.

From the camp I trace the direction back to the car park where the sallow glow of the street light filters through the trees. When I finally arrive I have no idea of the time; it could be deep in the night. Several other cars and a few people have gathered on the other side of the car park under the light; dog walkers probably, loading their animals after the last exercise of the day. A bit late, I think, but perhaps they know the area well. I get in my car and switch on the interior light to check my cut. It's still bleeding but has begun to clot. I sit with my eyes closed and my hands in my lap, focusing on the nub of pain in my palm. The sensation is satisfying, and I press the incision to amplify the sting.

A rap on my window. I jump and open my eyes, scrabbling for the keys in the ignition, but the car door opens and a man's head leans inside.

'It's all right, love,' he says, holding his palm up to face me, 'I'm not going to hurt you.'

He squats down on his haunches next to the open door. The stonewashed denim of his jeans stretches across his knees and thighs, and his face is large, hair short, clean and spiky. He places both hands on opposite sides of the door frame for support and shuffles in closer.

Cigarettes and beer on his breath, his body odour strong but not unpleasant. A distant trace of aftershave.

'I was wondering,' he says, 'if I could help you?' He looks at my face but hasn't noticed my cut, so I slide my hands between my legs as he shifts his position, spreading his own legs wider. 'We got a message that someone new was turning up tonight. So I came over, to see if you need a hand. You know, getting started.'

Words evolve in my throat and spit from my mouth, staccato and high-pitched.

'No. I'm fine,' I say. 'I was only stopping off before going home. I'm perfectly OK.'

'It's just that if you need an introduction, you know, I'd be happy to show you the way.' He sweeps one hand in an antique gesture towards the cluster of parked cars, and smiles, keeping his eyes on me, his etiquette belying the threat of his body which blocks my exit. On his forehead, a collection of busy lines hold moisture in their grooves. I try to smile. No other expression will come. Manners override my impulse to run. The man offers me his hand through the open car door – rough skin, scrubbed nails, palm facing upwards – as if he's asking for a waltz. 'It's often like this,' he says. 'You know, if it's your first time. Don't worry, we won't hurt you.'

He shifts his weight on to his other leg and I catch his eye. We size each other up, then I look across the car park. It's difficult to pick out details, but the vehicle at the centre of focus has its internal light on, and it contains forms, limbs, something awkward.

Saliva sticks in my throat. My breath is short and sharp.

'You have got to be joking!' I say. I reach for the handle of the car door and swing it towards me. It thuds on the man's back.

'All right, all right,' he says, standing, rubbing his back with one hand while still attempting to hold the door open with the other, 'no need to freak out.' He lets go of the door and brushes down his trousers, turns and walks back to the opposite side of the car park. 'Stuck-up bitch.' He doesn't shout but it's loud enough for me to hear.

I slam the door and start the car, looping the vehicle round to the narrow exit. My headlights blanch over the group of people and their faces light up like a clutch of neon balloons. The man walks towards them at speed with both his hands held out in front of him, gesturing a semaphore of 'no go'.

Out on the open road, I sling through the gears, only then remembering the cut on my hand. I press down on the steering wheel, stabbing at the pain like scissors.

12

STYROFOAM COFFEE CUPS

Bessie's been sick on the bed. Will's flat is equipped with an ancient washing machine into which he stuffs the duvet cover and sheet, but the quilt itself is too big.

'Have to take a trip to the launderette,' he says, bagging the grey material into a bin liner.

I gather my things and search for my car keys. My bag is empty compared to how full it's been this past week, stuffed with Seamus's letters and the newspaper articles I found at his caravan. It's been a challenge keeping everything hidden from David, and I've had to seek out new and obscure hiding places, the best one being the box in the garage where my dad's old clothes used to be, which now holds the spare tyre from my car. I've realized that David would never look in there; old things are dirty, they are infected with a past that existed before I met him and in which he has no interest.

On one occasion when I knew I wasn't going to be disturbed, I shut the garage door and used a torch to flick through Seamus's documents. Even though the newspaper articles were difficult to read, it was possible to glean that Seamus spent some time in hospital after an on-site accident on the old Richard development, and there was a battle for compensation, although it's not clear if he received any money. Perhaps Alex's family didn't pay Seamus off, and Seamus decided to get the unions involved, which in a roundabout way led to him staying on the land he'd grown to love. I put these articles back in the box and took out the drawings of the trees – Olden Head and Greenscale. Up close the penmanship revealed intricate details of bark and leaves.

Last night when Will was asleep I stashed all the papers at the bottom of a trunk of his gran's old keepsakes – he never looks in there, he says it makes him sad. If ever Will does find them they'll mean nothing to him.

I keep the little girl's – Claire's – photo in my back pocket, the watch zipped in my bag until I get home, and all that's left in my handbag apart from my keys, phone and medication is a small brown envelope. The packet has a rudimentary graph printed on the front. It's the type of envelope in which I used to receive my wages when I worked part-time as a teenager. This time though it's been put there by David. Inside are two five-pound notes and some change. He's called the money 'housekeeping' and he wants me to fill out the totals on the front, then transfer the expenses to our notebook at home. So far I've spent a little over £40 of this week's money, some on petrol but mostly in the pub last night – I'll need to find dummy receipts to cover the deficit.

'Give us a lift will you?' Will's eyes follow my hand movements. 'My van's up the creek.'

Last night was my third night away from David and only two weeks since my last stay, but I'd missed Will more than I thought possible. Plus he begged me to stay. Being wanted made the choice irresistible. I told Will it was a big risk for both of us, but more for him, and that I thought David was already looking for him. Will said, 'I'm a grown-up, Rachel, you don't need to worry about me.' When he was asleep I imagined whispering in his ear all the things I wanted to say.

The sun shines a square on the carpet through the window. Will clears his throat. 'We could go for a coffee or something while the wash is on.'

Nausea rises, telling me I need to get home – my working persona is fracturing, and there are no more excuses. I don't know what I was thinking by staying away again last night; or maybe I do. Something's got to give. I know no other way to make it happen.

I pull out the keys and put on my jacket. 'I have to get back.'

He moves closer, watching the floor, downtrodden. He looks like Bessie in the way some owners take on the manner of their animals.

'Look, if I really have to,' I say, my voice catching. 'I could drop you off, but you'll need to be quick getting your stuff together.'

'Come in with me for a bit. Please.'

I button up my jacket with shaky fingers. Will lifts my hands and kisses them.

'Spend some time,' he says. 'Let me look after you for once. I need to talk to you.'

David's anger will be as acute if I get home now or in an hour. It's more rational to spend the time with Will. Or maybe David will be out like last time and won't even know when I get home. Unusually I've had no texts from him overnight. Perhaps he's finally given up on me.

'OK,' I say, 'but I can't stay long.'

Will slips on his denim jacket and grabs the laundry bag, putting his arm across my shoulder as we walk out. I cough and move away. Bessie tries to follow but Will uses his foot to push her muzzle back through the gap in the door. 'You wait till later, girl,' he says to her. 'I'm not leaving you for another woman just yet.' He laughs and looks at me but I find myself turning the other way. He puts the bag of dirties in the boot next to the sack of dog biscuits I've brought from home.

Every time I've tried to return to the caravan to feed the stray dog, David has demanded a minute-by-minute itinerary of my movements – this listing of events the kind of conversation we can handle. I've hoped that perhaps the dog has smelt the camp fire by now and found its way to the group of activists. Last night, when the pressure of David's focus became too much, I caved in and came to Will's, though by the time I'd made my decision it was already too late to go via the woods. I knew I'd be able to pass by the caravan this morning on my way home and give the dog some food.

Will's road is in the suburban outreaches of town. The houses here are a mixture of styles and eras, ranging from pre-war bungalows like Will's, to 1960s purpose-built flats, plus a few modern terraces tacked on wherever land was available. Some of the more recent blocks are uniform bunkers with small windows, built for people with too little cash to complain, and the homes are connected by a helter-skelter of roads. Will is an incongruous presence among the families and elderly here, and if it weren't for him stepping into his gran's house – somehow winging it with the council to pass the place on to him after she died – then he would be based elsewhere; probably down in the valley among the pubs he inhabits most evenings, without the curse of the steep and drunken walk home.

Above the rooftops white clouds collage a blue sky. For once there is little wind. Hard winter light ricochets from the windows of the flats and, when touched by the sun, these drab buildings take on an air of calm and hope. I sit in my car next to Will and wait a beat before I start the ignition, allowing the moment to be the moment, and not the future or the past.

As I pull out, the sun sits low and cuts into our eyes through the windscreen. I squint and angle my head to see past the glare as we go round a corner. Will is watching me. I pretend not to notice even though I feel the prickle of his gaze on my neck. My expression is taut and I turn the wheel with a flourish, aware of his adoration but angry at myself for making it matter.

The launderette isn't far and we park directly in front of the window. Two large panes form an exterior wall on either side of a glass door, and the huge window displays money-off posters, some new, some old and bleached. Scraps of paper dangle from crusty Sellotape. Christmas lights edge the frame of the window, and at the centre of each one is a dot of lit colour, barely visible in the bright light. If it wasn't for this reminder I would have forgotten that the season of goodwill is beginning. There'll be bonuses to pay at the office, and David's displeasure will be signalled to those who go without.

Will hops on to the pavement from the small elevation of my 4×4, his movement practised but with a touch of cumbersome confidence, and he whistles, collecting the bag from the back seat. As he shuts the door, he spins on his heels to face the shop and we walk inside to a force field of thick steamed air; a chemical heat swelling to escape the building. Rows of tired machines edge the room, and a few customers stand beside them. Other people sit on a wooden bench that runs along the middle of the floor, and every one of them turns and stares. Will rests his arm on my shoulders and looks straight ahead, swaggering. We reach the back of the shop and sit on plastic garden chairs, where Will takes a phone call and swivels away from me to talk in whispers. His chair wobbles back and forth. The heat in the room weighs like a drift of tiredness, and my eyes lose focus as I stare at the industrial floor tiles. I'm reminded of the university laundry years ago where the floor tiles were exactly the same and where I first saw David.

My university was in the Midlands, and the campus launderette was where students brought card games and drinks to hang out and chat, like tourists in a club of domesticity; a world in which I was already a fully paid-up member. I was at uni to work hard, I had no choice, but most students were in it for the social life, and the launderette was just more recreation, test-running adulthood with tasks still too new to have become mundane. Posters of gigs and demos arranged by politics students plastered the walls and windows, and the room hovered in a permanent twilight – a happy arrangement for our nocturnal lifestyles. Everyone enjoyed washing their jeans, pretending to be that boxer-short boy from the advert.

A few weeks into the first term of my second year I was in the launderette doing my weekly wash when David came in with some friends. This was the closest I'd ever been to him, and I was intrigued by campus whispers about the cool new bloke who'd taken a gap year in America. He was dressed differently to the rest of us: he wore colourful T-shirts with big logos, baggy shorts and puffy trainers with the tongue sticking out. My shopping habits were built round limited funds, and I bought the bulk of my clothes from charity shops out of necessity, but for many others this impoverished style was merely an ironic nod towards the tasteless – anything new or sensible, especially bought by a student's parents, was distressed to hide the love invested. David and his posse – a group of five young men who tripped around him attempting to emulate his surfing-shirted, golden-haired style – were like a series of pastel-toned flares set off against the Oxfam-smelling greys and blacks of the rest of us. He was an apparition from an alternate universe, his clothing sending the subliminal message that there were places in the world about which we could only fantasize, where sunshine and positivity reigned free.

I caught fragments of his conversation across the buzz of the machines: the upward lilt he tacked on to the end of all his sentences, dropping in the occasional 'do the math'. I shook out my clothes with snaps of aggression, thinking David to be one of those backpacking trustafarians who received weekly food parcels from home and drove their gran's duffed-up Fiat. As David continued his chat, I could tell he was checking me out – the only girl on her own in the room – and I was struck by the continuity and persistence of his American dialect, and the sure and easy way he held himself: one foot up on the bench exposing a tanned calf, arms loose at his sides. If it had been anyone else I would have sneered at this impostor and his attempts to invigorate our sodden university with some transatlantic cool, but he was so unaware of his displacement, so convinced by his demeanour, that he actually carried it off.

A week later and his tray nudged mine in the canteen queue. 'Oh, gee, I'm so sorry,' he said, mopping up my spilt tea. Further down the line as we chatted, we discovered we were both on a Business Studies BA, him a year behind due to his sojourn in the States. There were white marks round his wrist and on a couple of fingers, as if he'd recently removed some jewellery; a cultural chameleon returning slowly to the style of his current pack. By the time we reached the till he'd asked me out for a drink, the invitation tacked on to a stretch as he reached across for a sachet of sugar, and his neck came close enough for me to smell his aftershave and see the tan line that framed his neck. The whole manoeuvre was casual enough to convince me that he asked girls out every day. The cash-desk woman – regulation paper hat pinned at an angle, red lipstick bleeding into the cigarette creases round her lips – was silent, waiting for my money, and for my answer to David. All I could think was that he was new around here, that maybe he hadn't heard about the steady line of boys who came into my bed, or of the wounded few who tried to see me again. I knew everyone talked about me, I saw the way they looked at me, so by now David surely had to know. Perhaps he simply didn't care. This was new; here was someone who operated along the same lines as I did, who pleased themselves and to hell with what other people thought. I was so shocked I said yes.

Now, a man walks across the launderette towards Will. Will stands. The two shake hands and the man claps the grip together with his other palm, Will's hand sand-wiched in the middle.

'All right, mate, how you doing?' Will asks.

'All good, mate, all good. Glad I bumped into you.' The man keeps hold of Will's hand, pumping the shake for a bit longer, then he stops and pulls Will towards him. His voice lowers but I'm close enough to hear. 'Been meaning to look you up to say thanks, you know, for what you did. It meant a lot.'

'No problem, mate.' Will coughs to the side and tugs his arm a little to loosen the grip, but the other man holds fast. 'I mean, enough's enough, right?'

'You got that right.'

Will slides his hand free and stands back to create a few inches between the two of them. The man nods his head towards me with eyebrows raised, and flicks a glance from me back to Will.

'Yeah, yeah, she's cool,' Will says.

The man wipes his nose on his index finger. 'Sounds like Darren won't be up to his old tricks after the state you left him in.' He moves a little too close again. 'Think he got the message, right? Last I heard he was heading for Timbuktu. Don't think you'll be welcome in that local no more though.' They laugh as Will looks to the floor, and the two men shuffle their feet. Will flicks me a shy smile and winks.

'Well,' the man says, 'a favour for a favour. Thought I should let you know someone's interested in your busi-ness, more than wanting a little slice. I'd think about switching venues if I were you.'

'OK, right. Cheers, mate.' Will scratches his head. 'I appreciate it.'

'It's only a rumour, that's all, but you can't be too careful.'

'I'll keep an eye out.' Will glances at me and I stare at the floor, pretending I'm not listening. 'Look, I'll catch up with you soon. You know . . .' I look up to see him tipping his head at me with a couple of nods. 'I better go.'

'Yeah, yeah, OK, but you should also stay away from that job rehousing those tree-huggers. Same crew's on their case that's been asking about you.'

Will straightens up. 'And which crew might that be then?'

'Can't say, mate, not my place, just keep away if anyone tries to get you involved. You'll end up on the wrong side of the fence, if you get my drift.'

'It was never my bag that one. Got nothing against a bit of peaceful protest.'

'Well, you know, can't imagine it'll be much bother, what with all their Gandhi bullshit.'

Will looks at me nervously and puts a hand to the man's back, turning the two of them towards the window. 'Look, thanks for looking out for me, I won't forget it. Keep in touch if you hear anything else, yeah?'

'Course, mate, course. No worries. I'll see you round.' He slaps Will between the shoulders and Will nudges forward a step. The man walks back to his machine, stuffs his clothes into a bin liner and leaves. He gives Will one last nod from the door.

Will looks at me and shrugs his shoulders.

'What was that about tree-huggers?' I ask.

'Nothing I'm involved in and nothing you need to worry about. Like I told you, I've got it covered.' He sits next to me and digs a finger into my ribs and wiggles it around. 'Think I've found a new name for you. Big Ears.'

I cover my mouth to suppress the snort, but a giggle bursts through before I can swallow it. He tickles me again and we both laugh. My cheek muscles creak. Faces turn to watch. I pull away from Will, straight-faced, and he lays his hands on his knees. We sit in silence for a few moments.

'As long as you're safe,' I say.

Will coughs and looks like he's about to say something, but he doesn't. He sits next to me for a few moments, his leg vibrating up and down, and I stare at him, waiting. Then he jumps up and says, 'Righto, better get the wash on then?'

He puts the duvet into one of the bigger washers and rattles about with the broken change machine, then decides to go to the shop next door for coins. A customer has parked her baby's buggy close to me in a dark corner. The little boy is sleeping, and his bare legs loll over the sides of the seat. His cheeks are fat and shiny like he's eaten butter and smeared it over his face, and he looks soft in his sleepy sweat, lulled by the drone of the machines and the warmth of the dryers whose drums puff a mist of cotton into the air. The child's romper suit creases and un-creases with each small breath he takes.

This is what it must be like to be a mother, to be watching always, aware of the nano-distance between life and death; a breath or no breath. I lean my head against the wall and close my eyes, daring to touch in and out of small waves of sleep, and I revisit a dream I had last night.

I dreamt of a bog – a big, deep, rotting bog.

In the dream I've bought a house on a new suburban estate. A circular drive connects all the homes. It's not the kind of place I would choose to live, but it's safe and happy – ordered – a place for goodness and new beginnings. Like I've come home. Outside a ground-floor window is a small decked area surrounded by a balustrade, and immediately on the other side of this deck is the bog. At its edge a crust curves round to form a lip which nudges the turf very gently. With the smallest rainfall the level will rise and the thick black silage will seep into the house and ruin the carpet and all our things. Even though I can't see below the lake's surface, I know objects are trapped and rotting underneath. The liquid ripples and a woman climbs out. She comes to me with open arms, but she's too filthy to hug. She whispers in my ear that the limbs of children have been thrown in the lake, and I need to get them out because they belong to me.

I'm startled from my half-sleep by Will coughing in front of me with two styrofoam cups of coffee. I take a moment to regroup, the edges of the dream still with me.

'The caff was really busy.' He looks flustered. 'I had to

queue and it took ages. I got us a takeout.' He sits next to me and hands me a cup. 'Sorry, I didn't mean to wake you.'

'Thanks.' I sit up in my seat and wipe a spit dribble from the corner of my mouth. 'I wasn't sleeping, just resting my eyes.'

The room has emptied and only a couple of customers are left: a man folds large grey underwear on the bench, plus the mother and her baby are still here. The woman stands by the window talking quietly on her phone. It's darker than before with the sun now behind a cloud, and the dim light is a blanket over the outside world. For the first time in for ever, I am with someone and in something I don't want to end.

Will and I take sips of the hot milky liquid, pressing the squeaky lids back on afterwards. He taps his knee. Leaning forward, he picks up a toy which has rolled off the buggy. First he places it on the hood of the pram, then changes his mind and puts it gently next to the little hand. The mother, still talking on her phone, watches with sideways eyes. Will nods at her and puts a finger to his mouth in a silent shush, then sits back in his seat with a wide smile. I lean over and press my shoulder to his. He is warm. I bend my head across to him and our hair touches. He puts a hand on mine. I turn my palm upwards. Where my wedding ring used to be, the skin is pinched and sunken. We interlock fingers. I smile.

'It's OK, you know,' he says.

'What is?'

He puts his cup on the floor and, with his other hand, leans across and brushes hair from my face. 'This.'

I shift up in my chair. 'And what do you call this?'

He looks around the room. Outside, it's started to drizzle.

'Happiness,' he replies.

Will's hand is warm and I squeeze a bit tighter. The space between our palms disappears.

'There are things about me you don't know,' I say. 'I don't deserve you to be so good to me. I'm not what you think.'

'Try me.'

'I wouldn't know where to start. It's complicated.'

'Rachel, you can trust me.'

'I want to but I don't know how.'

In my bag my mobile rings. I pull my hand from Will's to get the phone. David's name flashes up on the screen and hot-wires me back to reality.

'Oh, for fuck's sake.' Will tries to grab the phone but it falls from my hand and spins on the floor. Parts of the casing scatter but the phone carries on ringing. The noise bounces from the walls like a siren, and wakes the baby. I put my cup on the chair and the coffee spills into a puddle on the seat. On my hands and knees, I gather the bits of the phone, reject the call then stand to leave.

Will grabs my hand and looks up. 'Where are you going?'

'Home.'

'Why?'

'Because David will be angry.'

'You don't have to put up with his shit. Why don't you leave him? You could if you really wanted to. I can help.'

'What? Help me get away from David?'

'Yes.'

'You don't understand. You have no idea what kind of man he is.'

Will stands and paces a small line back and forth. 'Well, maybe I do, maybe I know more about him than you think. What d'you imagine that bloke was talking about just now? Someone's on my case, been putting out feelers as to where you go to on your nights off.' He stops to look at me then paces again. 'I'm one step ahead though.'

'Why didn't you tell me?' I hug my waist, the temperature sucking from the room. 'How close is David to finding us?'

'Not very. There are enough people covering me for now, but I've only got so many favours to call in.'

'When did you find out?'

'About a week ago. I know people who know people. But like I said, I'm on it. Why do you think we met at a different pub last night?' Will looks me straight in the eyes. 'We could go, we could leave, together. Soon it will be too late.'

'I don't know.' More breath than words come out of my mouth. 'David will find me, I know him, he won't give up.' I move away from Will and look towards the

door, then back to Will again. The customers in the launderette are watching and I drop my voice. 'I'm scared.'

'Then let me help you.'

'How?'

Will pulls me down on to his chair and kneels in front
of me. 'I've told you, down at the docks. It's easier than
you think to slip away, it happens all the time. Tell me
that you want to and I'll fix it.'

In the corner the mother jiggles the buggy and the
baby is quiet. The dryer pauses in its cycle and the man
searches through coins in his palm to feed the machine.
For one moment there is a brief and complete stillness.
I think of David at home waiting; the habit of us, even
though it's painful, is like cement, and I can't believe I'd
ever be free of him. Then there is the possibility of a life
with Will, the two of us grubbing away in the arse-end of
God knows where. And lastly there's the man whose life
I took. He has no choices any more. Perhaps I shouldn't
either. Bad people get what they deserve.

Tears rise in my throat but I won't let them through.
My voice is a whisper. 'I'm sorry. I should never have
come here, it was stupid of me.' I push the hair back off
my face with shaking fingers. 'I can't see you any more,
it's too risky for both of us. I have to go.'

I stand and walk towards the exit as the dryer starts
again.

Will stands, grabs my arm and holds me as I pull
away. His voice is low. 'This is it, Rachel. I'm tired of this
same argument – you're always so cold – but I'm offering

you a way out. Us together has become dangerous. If you feel the same way about me as I do about you, now is the time to leave. I've put myself on the line, but I won't do it again. This is your last chance. You need to decide.'

Without a second's pause, I pull my arm from his grip and walk towards the door.

Will calls after me: 'Yeah, bugger off then. Remember, next time you come knocking, I won't be here.'

The underwear man looks up at me with a blank expression, as if this kind of heckling is a regular pastime in these parts. The door is stiff and I tug it a few times but it only opens a couple of inches.

I hear Will behind me, opening the machine and clunking the door shut. 'Fucking hell,' he shouts. I turn to see him kick the machine. The metal shudders.

'You need to push,' underwear man says.

With my shoulder, I release the door into the biting air, and my back prickles with the three pairs of eyes I sense are watching. Behind me, the door swishes back and forth, and the noise from the machines pulses through the gap. I get into my car. Before I start the engine a text comes through from David.

'Baby, where are you? I need you. Something's happened to the dogs.'

13

DOG FOOD

As I open our front door, David rushes to me and throws his arms round my shoulders. His head is hot and his clothes are damp with sweat. For once his body odour is unchecked.

'Rachel,' he says, 'I've been going out of my mind. The dogs, there's been an accident.'

'What's happened?' From somewhere inside the house come manic barks but I can't see the animals.

'Portia ran into the road. I think she's OK. It's Petra I'm worried about, she went after her and took the full impact of the van.'

'Oh my God, why didn't you take them to the vet's?'

'It's only just happened. Stupid gate's not working and they got out of the garden. I'll sue the arse off whoever's to blame.' He grabs my hand and pulls me into the house. 'They've been going crazy. I need your help to get them into the car.' He leads me towards the kitchen. 'I'm so relieved you're home.'

'David, I'm really sorry.' Relief bubbles up. 'I was scared to come back, I thought you'd be angry.'

David stops and turns to me briefly. 'You don't need to be scared of me, baby.'

The heating is up full blast. In the kitchen I pull off my jacket and throw it over a chair, and leave my bag on the table.

'David, I want to explain, about last night.'

'Don't worry about that now,' he says, pulling me towards the boot room. 'There'll be time later to sort everything out.'

In the boot room, the two dogs are tied up. I expect to see blood but there's none.

Behind me, David backs away and locks the door. I swivel to see him on the other side, watching me through the glass panel at the top. His face is passive but he holds up the index and middle finger of one hand and points them towards his eyes, then he points the two fingers at me. He repeats this action several times before walking away.

I run at the door, shaking the handle, but it won't budge. As I stretch my neck, I see David leave the kitchen.

'Let me out, David!' I shout. 'Don't do this, please. I'm sorry.' I bash my shoulder on the door as behind me the dogs bark louder, gasping at their leads as they try to leap away from the wall. I rattle the handle and kick but the door remains solid. 'David. I can explain.' The noise of his car starting up is just audible above the barking, and I press my ear to the door and listen as the engine recedes at a gentle pace. Then it's gone.

Through the glass I see my jacket on the chair, but my handbag has been taken and with it my phone. The call history's been erased and the few photos I've taken have already been forwarded to my new private email before being trashed, so if anything David will be suspicious about my lack of activity if he checks my calls. Links to electronic phone bills are deleted as soon as I receive them. What can he do without evidence?

I turn back to face the room and sink to the floor until I'm eye level with the dogs. Their barking whips the air. I cover my ears, but it does little to help. With my eyes shut I try to concentrate on a plan, and then remember that Seamus's watch is also in my bag. David will have found it by now, he'll be touching it, maybe turning it over in his hand before throwing it from the car. I am bereft, as if I've betrayed Seamus; I've handed him over to the enemy.

The dogs snarl and I recognize their noise as hunger. I stand and edge round the room to the cupboards where the food is kept. Inside are three large tins and a bag of biscuits. Each dog-food tin has a label on it – 'day 1', 'day 2', 'day 3' – and the top of the biscuit bag has been rolled down to leave about enough for three days inside. No food has been left for me. I dish out the smallest portion for each of the dogs – the smell thick and sour, reminding me of an overcooked school dinner – and put the bowls in front of them, leaving the animals leashed. They chomp their food down in lumps.

Off to the right of the room is a small toilet and I try

the door but it's locked from the inside. I'd need a screw-driver to turn the latch from this side, but everything has been emptied from the drawers and cupboards. I use my nails, jamming them in the groove of the latch and twist-ing my fingers until they hurt. My thumbnail bends back and rips across the skin. Now the idea of the toilet is in my head, I need to go even more, and I cross my legs. There's a large tray on the floor by the back door filled with litter. We got it from the vet when the dogs were puppies as they had to be kept in the house after they were spayed. It hasn't been used for years. It's clean and freshly laid. I listen again for David's car. Only silence. He knows I'll have to use the tray, but he doesn't want to see his wife sink that low – that would put him off for good – and I have a small debt of gratitude for him sparing me this humiliation. Outside, it's quiet. I take off my tights and pants, put them to one side, squat over the tray and piss. The dogs watch me. I stare back. 'Fuck off,' I say.

The first day is long and I keep the dogs tied up for some of the time to have a break from their restless pacing. David has left the heating on, the thermostat probably up full as the room is baking, and I take off most of my clothes apart from my underwear and top, and make a bed out of the dogs' blanket on the hard floor. My patch is on one side of the room, the dogs' on the other. That night it's hard to sleep as, without my drugs, the pain in my body finds new places to settle. I listen out for David's car, even though I don't really believe he'll come home early; he's set on his plan. David must have cancelled the cleaner and the dog walker, and the post is left at the gate. Only a fire would bring him home, and if there were matches I'd hold the flame up to the smoke detector which links directly to the emergency services, but the room has been cleared so thoroughly it's as if we've moved out. I am sealed inside a box. I could starve and the dogs would eat me and no one would know, except that David has made me a deal of three days. Three days to prove to a woman that she is a dog.

David hasn't left the animals' chews, so the dogs gnaw on their beds, grinding them with their teeth and leaving long scars on the plastic. When they get hold of my blanket they shred the quilted fabric, and feathers scatter across the floor. Once Portia and Petra sleep though, the silence is pure, and my heartbeat slows to a steady rhythm. That night there's the occasional hoot of an owl. Two foxes fight like screaming babies. I've never taken the time before to notice that we have real wildlife in our garden, I'd assumed the grounds were as sanitized as the house.

The next day when I wake, a small calm settles; with life reduced to basics and nothing expected of me, I become docile. Even the pain becomes bearable. From experience I've learnt it can be easier to allow the bad things to happen, like holding my breath under a passing wave. I slip into routine, creating a slow pace by measuring out the amount of time I have left, and the dogs' feeding times help to punctuate the days. After their twice-daily frenetic leaps to get outside they seem resigned to the space, and sleep a lot. I follow their pattern. The litter tray is too small for them but they do their best, and at least David has left some plastic bags, though even these are rationed. There's drinking water from the tap, but by the afternoon I'm so hungry that the dogs' food begins to smell appetizing. I won't eat the wet food though, and munch instead on a few biscuits, swilling my mouth out afterwards to get rid of the taste. It's only meat and rice, I say to myself. I think of the starving dog at the caravan, its stomach aching for food, and how in my panic to get home I hadn't stopped at the woods. Portia and Petra watch me and whimper as I pick morsels from the bag. I share some with them and they eat the biscuits, keeping their eyes trained on me, but their focus has softened. For the first time it seems as if we could be friends.

Claire's photo is still in my pocket, and when I take it out and look at her, she too seems trapped; my distant twin in a shutter of time. I try to imagine what she's doing now. Sometimes I dream of Will touching me, and the sensation is so real I try to pinch myself in my sleep but my hands won't move until I wake. When I come out of the dream, I remember Will's anger, and how I've already cut my last tightrope to normality. Mostly, though, I dream of Seamus. He sits here in the boot room, one arm round each of our dogs, with his muddy laces skimming the ground. Water drips from his coat into a pool on the floor, as if he's walked through a storm to get to me. Outside, the dog from the caravan leaps up at the window and scratches the glass with its paws. 'It's locked,' I shout, but the animal keeps trying to get in. When I wake and open my eyes, the muddy prints remain on the window and Seamus is still in front of me, and it takes several blinks before his image disappears.

On the evening of the third day, I pace the floor. The food has run out and the dogs are hyper having had no walks, so I tie them up and put their bed near the hooks on the wall. I use the washing-up liquid next to the sink to wash my face and hands but don't bother with the rest of my body as there's not even a towel in the room. The litter tray stinks; there's so little that's unsoiled. Hunger mixes with fear and becomes nausea. I bury my head under my blanket to stuff up the noise and wonder if, when David returns, this will be the end of my punishment, and what will have changed in my world when I emerge.

In the evening when I finally fall asleep with my mother's cover over my head, I dream of nothing. A big blank space. As dawn breaks and the dogs start up their usual barking, it's like no time at all has passed since last evening. I pull the blanket tight round my ears, but after several minutes of their noise I wake fully. The animals seem unusually agitated, and I stand and peer through the door to the kitchen. Everything is the same apart from my handbag which sits on the table. I try the door. It's open. I run into the house, and from the kitchen window see David's Jaguar retreating at speed down the driveway. I check in my bag and my keys are still there. Even though I'm in my underwear, I grab the keys and race to my vehicle, firing up the engine and taking the car down to the metal gates which have wound shut behind David. A large stone sits in the middle of the driveway which David must have used to hold open the mechanism and enable his speedy escape. The gates shudder and whirr as they begin to reopen for me, but the action is in slow motion, and by the time I get through there's no sign of David.

The dogs' fevered barks reach down the driveway. I reverse back up to the house. In the boot room I unclip the animals' leads and let them out into the garden. Wind brushes through their coats like water, and I envy their seamless return to normality; they'll need no decompression – next time they see David they'll lick his hands and jump up as enthusiastically as if he'd never abandoned them. I check in my bag and find the envelope with exactly the same amount of cash in it as three days ago, plus my wedding ring from the garage; the band of gold now part of this transaction, the same bringing to heel as the constraints of poverty. My phone is inside, plus the remaining painkillers and a fresh tub of diazepam. In the zip pocket there's the watch. Its glass face is scratched as if it's been rubbed with wire wool, and the inscription on the back is erased by deep lines, the kind you'd make with a school compass. Claire's words to Seamus, a daughter's message to her father, gone. Did Seamus thank Claire for her gift? I think of her rushing to the letter box each morning to wait for his reply.

The action of the watch's winder is stiff as if it's been forced, and I hold the timepiece to my ear then bang it against my palm a few times. It's broken. At the kitchen sink, I dry-retch.

Before I shower I clean out the litter tray, emptying the contents into a bin liner and pushing the sack to the bottom of the wheelie bin, replacing the older bags on top. After I'm clean and dressed, I get in my car and head to the office; it's the only place David could be, he never misses a day of work. En route I rumble with what to say, rehearsing the accusations that will come out in front of the staff who'll bear witness. When I finally reach the forecourt my whole body is shaking with the story as if I've already delivered the news.

I walk inside. The room hushes. Heads turn one by one. Kelly rushes to me and hugs me.

'Rachel,' she says, 'I can't believe you've come in.'

I take a moment to process before replying. 'No, nor can I.'

'I mean, don't you think you should take some more time at home?'

'No, I want to be here.'

Kelly releases me and lowers her voice. Heads crane over workstations.

'I know what you're going through,' she says. 'You shouldn't be ashamed. It's more common than you think.'

'Really?'

'Yes. But we've got everything covered here, so you can take it easy and not worry.'

'Where's David?'

'Um, well, he's in his office running through things with the new exec.' She starts to gabble. 'David's so sweet, he's had him lined up for weeks now, ever since he knew you were a bit . . . well, you just took on too much, didn't you? That kind of pressure would make anyone a bit wobbly.'

'David's said I'm wobbly?' My voice is a shout.

Kelly looks towards the watching staff, grasping at them for help, but their eyes turn down. She angles her own head to the floor, starting a sentence, stopping, then coming forth with, 'You know, sometimes the person who has the breakdown is the last to know they're in trouble.'

'I haven't had a breakdown. David locked me in the fucking utility room.'

Some of the staff are standing up now. Panic tracks across Kelly's face. David told the one person in the office he knew would be unable to keep the secret.

'We're all here for you, Rachel,' she says, reaching for my hand, but I pull it away. 'You don't need to be paranoid, we're on your side.'

'For God's sake!' I shout.

David's brogues come clanging down the stairs and he leaps forward and holds on to me. 'Don't worry, Kelly, I'll take it from here.'

'You fucking bastard.'

'Rachel, baby, I told you not to come in, it's too soon. You've been through so much.'

'Too right I have.' I lunge at him but he wraps me tighter in his arms, stroking my head with rough hands.

'Shh, baby, it's all right.'

I break away and race up the stairs to see another man in my office sitting at my desk, all my things stacked in a cardboard box at the side. David chases after me but can't reach me before I get to my desk.

'You didn't waste your time, did you?' I say. 'How long have you been planning this?'

'Rachel, this is crazy, you're not thinking straight. You're my wife, I love you.'

The man at the desk looks startled, and he stands with his arms stuck to his sides. My diary is open on my desk in front of him.

'What are you doing with my stuff?' I ask him.

'I was inputting your appointments to the computer. You know, to make it easier for when you come back.'

I pick up the book and hurl it in the man's face. The diary hits his temple and he cries out as he holds his hands over his face, expecting more. David comes up behind me, clamps his arms round me and frogmarches me into his office. He locks the door behind him and takes out the key then walks behind his desk. I stand in front of him shivering.

David remains standing and breathes in and out slowly. He leans over his desk, balancing his weight on to his steepled hands, and looks at me.

'No one will believe you, Rachel.' Another breath. 'You have no friends. Even your sleepover buddy won't be answering his phone any more. Or dealing his shit coke.' He delivers his words with slow ease, and I hold my hands together tight in front of me to stop them from shaking, turning over in my mind the three days David's had to prepare for this moment, and what could have happened to Will in that time. David stands up straight. 'This is the end of it, the last of your behaviour I'll tolerate. If you don't stop you'll see that your little holiday with the dogs isn't the worst I can muster.'

I blink so the tears won't come. I open my mouth to speak but there is nothing I can say and no way I can win this. I turn from David and rattle the door. 'Please, I want to go home.'

David comes round to the door and stands in my way. 'Why don't you go to the bathroom and get yourself cleaned up. Have a little self-respect. Even for a nutter you look terrible.' He opens the door and walks out, shutting it behind him. Through the panel I hear him say, 'Graham, I'm so sorry. Guys, everyone,' he calls to the office. 'I'm sorry you had to witness that. Rachel's going to be OK, she just needs some rest, it will take time, that's all. We'd both appreciate your discretion in this matter while she gets her life back on track.'

I go into the bathroom to throw some water on my face. As I look in the mirror I realize David is right. I do look insane.

14

BONES

Every time I've tried to contact Will these last few days, his number rings out then goes to voicemail. I keep telling myself no one else would bother to keep his phone charged, but without hearing his voice I'm desperate to know for sure that he's safe. In the absence of any other course of action, I've forced myself to believe that David hasn't yet got to Will, and the meaning of Will's silence is simply that he does indeed hate me.

There's been a fire at the protestors' camp in the woods. No one was killed but two people have been hospitalized with burns. Accusations of arson and thuggery fill the headlines of the local news. The leader of the protest movement is in prison accused of supplying class A drugs. The police found a huge haul at the camp when they were investigating the fire, the drugs somehow having danced away from the flames. It will take some time to get the accused, Tyrone Aldridge, to trial, but it will be long enough for the trees to come down. Tyrone's previous record was for dealing cannabis, and will probably contribute to the weight of evidence against him, although its seems that class As are a whole new venture for a man who claims to need little of what money can buy.

All of David's phone calls are taken in private these days, but I catch snippets of his conversations with my ear to the door when the dogs don't give me away. Enough to tell me he was involved in these events. David's constant snuffling nasal drip tells me he's still sourcing coke, only now it must be from a new connection, and without having to ration his intake in accordance with my ability to supply, he's clearly upped his daily quota from functioning to dependent. He jumps when the dogs bark, and scratches as if there are insects beneath his skin.

Local news bulletins talk of children from the camp being taken into care, and their tearful mothers plead to the camera. It terrifies me to think of loving someone that much – it's far easier to turn in on myself, or squash things down. This long-held practice of denial cultivates flashpoints of pain in the day-to-day mechanics of eat and sleep, though there was a soft place I used to visit when I thought of Will. This has now gone, replaced by an ache which at times grows so vast even I cannot endure it, and the only thing to topple it is alcohol. So I drink all the time now, whatever I can afford, which is generally supermarket own-brand spirits. Being back at home in the aspic of order and David's rules, I bear the self-loathing in a creeping fog of booze. Compliance is easier than trying to outwit him, and there's a simple reassurance in the habit of our relationship, like returning to my natural state. In the sterile environment of our home, my subjugation is a martyr's weight, the cloak of David my own self-imposed muzzle. It's only at night when the hungry dog visits my sleep that I'm reminded it's still possible to put some things right.

It's a Tuesday afternoon and David's at work. He's on location today with a recently appointed head of TV for a satellite channel. She's turning up to check in on a production, and David's gone under the guise of the big overseer of the project, but really he's there to pitch new ideas. It's the first day David hasn't called me at home on the hour, every hour. I received only one call this morning and then one at lunchtime, so I take this rare opportunity to drive to Blackthorn Lane. The petrol gauge flashes red. I park in the same car park as before, where three padlocked Portaloos have joined the digger at the edge of the tarmac. The route into the woods is wider now, scarred by Caterpillar tracks and lined with tree stumps and piles of logs. This woodland has seen more action in the past couple of months than it has in the last few decades as Alex's grand scheme for an estate of detached houses, fenced and gated to keep out the rabble, has finally been given the go-ahead.

In the back of my car, I lift the boot cover and take out my dad's old winter coat from its hiding place. The jacket I've been wearing up until now is lightweight, and when

David cleared my clothes he didn't leave me anything warm. Or perhaps that was part of his plan to keep me at home. This coat is broader than my shoulders and the hem touches my calves, but beneath it's like I've disappeared. With the musty wool close round me, I make my way from the car park and into the woods in the direction of the caravan. The burnt-out camp is further up the road, but the faint char of wood still hangs in the air.

Rain has blackened the trees with a steady patter that echoes against the bare walls of nature. Deep swallows of mud-soup suck at my boots. There's barking in the distance but it's too energetic to be the dog I'm looking for, and moments later an excited Great Dane bounds from the trees. The dog's fur and paws are filthy, and it leaps up to my height and covers me in dirt. I push the animal away but it growls. A man strides from the woods in knee-high wellies, his angular body pressed inside a scuffed waxed jacket. It's Alex.

'Get down, get down,' he calls from a distance. 'Suza, come here.' Then he shouts, 'DOWN, GIRL!' The dog scampers back to him. He holds her lead in his hand like a whip and fastens it to her collar. 'I'm so sorry,' he says as he comes closer. 'Rachel? Is that you? I didn't recognize you.'

'Hello, Alex.'

'Are you OK? God, I'm sorry about the mess.'

I look down and wipe my front with my gloves, turning the paw prints into streaks. 'I'm fine. Nothing the cleaners can't handle.'

The dog jumps and barks again. 'Stop it,' he shouts, but she's still trying to get at me. 'Enough!' He smacks the dog's nose with the end of the leather lead. She yelps and falls into line. 'The bitch gets very excited when she's in heat.' Alex moves closer to me, his complexion cracked with red veins. 'Does David know you're here?' The animal's whine is high and she pulls at her lead, rasping for air as the collar pinches her windpipe. She sparks up again and barks, making me jump, and Alex re-swipes her nose.

'I don't know what's got into her,' he says. 'We don't come across many people on these walks any more, not since the diggers moved in. I like to come up here and check on progress as much as I can. My family's been after these woods for years now, so it gives me great satisfaction to see all of our hard work finally coming to fruition.' He studies my face and I look down. 'Are you sure you're OK?'

The dog circles his legs, tangling her lead round him so that he jolts and spins to retain his footing.

'I'm fine,' I say again. 'I needed some fresh air, that's all.'

'Yes, I see,' he says, leaning in. 'I heard you'd been having a few . . . um. Well, not been feeling yourself.'

The wind sweeps a fresh blast of drizzle into my face. I pull the coat round me and Alex watches my hands near my chest for a second too long. His mouth opens to a slit. Inside the hole of his lips it is black.

I take a couple of steps back. 'I'm sorry, I've got to go.' The dog sniffs my leg and moves up to my crotch. I push hard at her muzzle and walk away.

Alex nods in the direction I'm travelling. 'You'll not get far up there. An area's been cordoned off but the police have finished with it now.' He begins to walk towards the car park as the dog yanks him along. 'Nasty business. Still, no one that'll be missed. They'll be doing us all a favour when they shift that pile of junk anyway,' he calls. 'You should be careful out here after dark. It's not the safest place for a woman on her own.'

He disappears into the trees. Only the barking and his calls travel back on the wind. I worry what he'll say to David. I'll call Alex later, I decide, and ask him not to mention having seen me.

I have an extra bag, heavy with dog food, wire cutters and a torch. The strap slips from my shoulder. I hoist it up. In the distance, a horizontal white line shudders in the wind, and as I get closer the material comes into focus: white plastic striped blue with the words POLICE and DO NOT CROSS. It circles the trees around the caravan, and closer in, next to the vehicle, more tape is propped up on metal canes. Some of the strips of plastic are broken and they flip and snap in the wind. The police have linked Seamus's body to the caravan during my three lost days, but I already have everything of importance – Seamus's paperwork, plus the photo of Claire – so they'll still have problems identifying him. For now Seamus belongs to me.

At home I've been researching Manorhall Construction on the internet, the company from which Seamus received payslips, and the business through which David's money has been filtering. Information is scant; there were only a couple of archived news items from the seventies relating to this same land – a large area was to be cleared to make way for flats to house the overspill of employees at a new cement works. After a protracted court case over Seamus's on-site injury, the legalities unearthed other business malpractices, but from there the online trail goes dead, almost as if the information's been deleted at source. I imagine Alex would hate having this damning information in the public domain, and he has enough money to erase his mistakes.

The treasure Seamus discovered in these woods is again in danger, but there would have been little he could have done this time round to stop the encroaching development. Even so, he gave the woods an extra thirty years. I think again of Claire. If Seamus was my father, it would matter to me how he lived.

I look behind and around me, and when I'm confident I'm alone, I duck under the police tape and track the now well-worn path towards the caravan.

My torch shines through the windows to where the walls have been stripped and the surfaces have been cleared of cans and clutter. The mattress is uncovered revealing a topography of stains, but everything else is gone, the caravan an empty shell. Seamus has been erased. One of the tiny skeletons he collected is outside on the ground. Broken. Small fragments of bone are pressed into the mud by the imprint of a shoe. I reach down and collect the pieces, trying to put them back together, but they're too damaged. I slip the bones in my pocket. Around the caravan the ground has been scuffed, and in places dug to below the mud where there is tarmac. I work at the patch with my boot and see that the grit extends underneath and around the caravan; the vehicle is parked on hard standing. This could have been part of the original construction, and the track probably extends all the way down to Blackthorn Lane. How else would Seamus have driven a caravan here? Nature has worked fast over the years to make good and reclaim its territory.

As I walk to the other side of the vehicle, I look past the fence to the empty field and the distant hills where a wall of heavy cloud moves closer, dragging underneath it a streak of rain that smears the gap between land and sky. The landscape is more beautiful now than when the sun shines; the undisguised brute force of bad weather is the true face of nature, not the coffee-table books of butter-flies and flowers we admire from inside our centrally heated houses. A rush of wind from across the open ground catches my coat. I undo the buttons and the material shafts up and open. This is how Seamus lived. I sense him here. Putting my bag on the ground for a few moments, I hold my arms out on each side to let in the weather.

The elements bluster through me as an ecstasy of feeling. I am alive.

The barbed-wire fence is rusty and the cutters slice through the layers of metal with ease. I tug back the fence with my thick gloves and stamp down the spikes, clambering over the wedge of weeds that's grown between the fence posts. The soggy earth of the field is like deep glue. Tufts of hardy grass shiver. Then the rain hits, as if the clouds have dropped their skirts.

I look to the distant trees for the dog but nothing comes. It's hard to see in the darkening weather, and I trample further into the field towards a small elevation of mud. As I get closer, I see that the mound has hair and limbs. An animal is on its side, ribs forming miniature hills and valleys through the soaking fur. It's the dog. Its mouth is open. Tongue like old ham. Still. Dead.

I sit down next to the dog and hold Seamus's watch in my pocket. There are no more steady ticks to filter time, and the minutes pass slowly, as they would have done for Seamus and his friend before I took them both away. Wet earth soaks through my clothes to my skin, until I'm chilled fridge-blue.

Hills emerge from the clouds as the worst of the rain leaves the field as abruptly as it came. A bird swoops and hovers, helicoptering steadily in the air before diving down, but it's too far away to see if it caught its prey. How fast the mechanics of nature reveal themselves. If I lived here I would learn to judge what was coming, its beauty or its ferocity, but I don't live here. I inhabit David's world.

The clouds drift to another field and in their place comes a quiet dusk. Shadows fall like tired old bones.

Two dead now, and both my fault.

Deliver me from evil.

Let the worst have me. Let me feel.

15

1980

It's nearly the end of the summer term and I'm doing my homework on the dining-room table when Uncle Peter calls round. Mum's still at work. Peter asks if he can sit with me for a while and have some water – it's hot and he's thirsty. He takes tiny sips from the glass, watching what I'm doing, and says he can help me; geography was his favourite lesson at school, 'not as long ago as you think, Rachel. God knows how I ended up working in the police force.' His eyes follow my hand and my writing comes out messier than usual. Peter pulls his chair close until the wood of our two seats squeaks together and our bodies almost touch. His breath smells of burnt sugar and tobacco. With his right arm curled round my book on the table, he leans his left side towards me, and his other arm relaxes in the space between us. His hand is out of sight under the table in between our chairs and his fingers brush my skirt.

The homework is glaciers and oxbow lakes. Peter's

forgotten his glasses so he moves closer to get a better look at the words, then he flicks through the textbook one-handed. Some of the pages don't turn first time and he has to give them another prod with his fingers. All the time his other hand is a still lump next to my leg. He asks about school and friends and what other subjects I plan to choose for my O levels. Then the fingers of his secret hand spread out like a slow spider and climb up my skirt and on to my thigh, and at first I don't think it's really happening. The hand slides over the top of my leg and down into the middle. I shake. Then I stand up. The book I'm holding drops to the floor.

'Would you like a cup of tea?' I say.

He leans back in his chair and pulls his pipe from his pocket. His legs flop wide open. 'Yes, that would be lovely, thank you, Rachel.' He fills his pipe without looking at it, keeping his eyes on me, smiling.

I go into the kitchen and boil the kettle. It's quarter to five and Mum's due home soon, so I decide to peel the potatoes for supper. In the afternoon heat, the mud from the vegetables dries quickly on my hands and makes my skin all tight and cracky. The peelings go brown. Next I remember that the larder's a mess so I decide to take out all the tins and bottles and stack them on the table. Uncle Peter comes into the kitchen and leans in the doorway watching me, lighting his pipe with long whistling sucks. I crouch down, putting all my effort into getting the last things out of the cupboard, and then I hear the clunk of his pipe as he leans it in the ashtray next to the sink.

Peter's legs crack like sticks as he bends his knees and settles behind me, curling his body beetle-shell round my back. His thighs rest along the outside of my legs and his breath is on my neck. I put my ear to my shoulder to get rid of the tickle. One of his hands is on the floor next to me, his fingers spread out to steady himself, and he brings the other hand up to my chest.

The back door rattles. Mum's home. Peter stands up. I look sideways to see him grab his pipe and lean against the kitchen worktop. The hair that covers his bald patch hangs forward over his eyes, but he doesn't touch it, only smiles at Mum as she comes through the door. I turn my head to see her wide eyes flicking between the two of us.

'Peter, darling,' she says, 'whatever are you doing here so early?' She drops her bags on the table and fiddles with her hair, looking in the mirror by the back door. 'I really wish you wouldn't surprise me like this, I'm not remotely prepared.'

'I'm on earlies this week,' he says, 'and my shift's ended. Thought we could go for a drive or something.' He stands in exactly the same position, legs crossed out in front of him like a ski slope, back against the counter, and he sucks on his dry pipe. I don't know why Mum hasn't noticed it's not lit. 'Anyway,' he says, 'Rachel here's been taking care of me, haven't you, sweetie?' Finally he smoothes his hair back across his head with a steady hand.

All the food from the larder is out, stacked on the floor around me, and I sweep the dusty corners of the cupboard, glancing over my shoulder to see Mum check-ing her face in her compact and dabbing her lipstick with a hanky. She stops mid-action and looks at me.

'Whatever are you doing, Cinders? And change out of your school uniform before it gets dirty.'

In the larder I brush all the crumbs, cobwebs and hollow woodlice into the dustpan. It's even hotter in the cupboard than in the kitchen. I turn to Mum and say, 'I'm not hungry. Is it OK if I go to my room and do my homework?'

'Do what you like. As long as you clear that lot up first. I'm not putting everything back after my day at work. It was hellishly busy.'

'Oh, my poor darling,' Peter says as he slides over to Mum and puts his arms round her waist, pressing himself to her. 'Did all those ladies queuing for their groceries give you a hard time?'

Mum swipes him with her hanky and pretends to struggle away. 'You terror. Just because I'm not arresting bank robbers and duffing them up in the cells.'

Peter draws her close and tries to plant a kiss. Mum shakes her head from side to side a couple of times, but she's smiling, so Peter puts his hands on both her cheeks to hold her steady then kisses her on the lips.

It's silent for a bit, and so I re-stack the larder, clang-ing the tins on top of each other. Behind me I hear Mum and Peter moving into the sitting room and I turn to see their backs as they go through the door. Mum holds his hand and leads the way. She walks sort of slinky like a little girl. Then I hear the *clunk clunk* of her shoes as she kicks them off. I imagine her sitting in her favourite position in the lounge: legs stretched out on the footstool with the seam of her tights stretched over her toes, the material dark from the damp inside her shoes. She'll have an arm flung in a loose semicircle over the top of her head.

'Bring some ice through, will you, sweetie?' Peter calls.

'And make sure you take your books upstairs with you,' Mum adds. 'They're all over the dining-room floor, you messy little princess. The house is in such a state. It looks like there's been an intruder.'

I clear my schoolwork from the dining room and take it into the kitchen, where I finish stacking the cupboard. Mum and Peter are giggling. Then the noise stops. The back door's still open from earlier when Mum came home but inside the house the air doesn't move, like I'm stuck in hot jelly. I look into the garden at the grass and flowers still lush. It hasn't rained for ages and the garden won't stay looking so nice for much longer. Next to the sink, the potatoes and their skins have turned orange. I throw them all in the bin – if Mum doesn't see I've started then she'll probably forget all about food tonight.

'Ice,' Mum calls from the sitting room.

I get the ice tray from the freezer. It's metal and solid. My fingers stick to the aluminium container as I pull the lever to break the cubes apart. The handle is jammed with the cold and the squeaky noise makes my teeth go funny. Daddy used to hate this ice tray, so he taught me how to use it. Mum and her friends call me 'Big Chief mixer and chiller of drinks'. I run the hot tap, holding the tray under the stream. The water scorches my skin but the metal warms and unglues my fingers. Too hot and too cold at the same time. I wonder if it would be worse to die in a fire or from cold. I know you go into a kind of sleep when you're freezing, but fire's probably quicker, and if the smoke gets to you first, it would be painless. Ice cubes rattle into the sink.

As I walk into the lounge, Mum slides off Peter's lap and sits back in her place on the sofa. Her hair is messy and she prods at it with her hands, but it doesn't make any difference. After I leave the room, she shuts the door behind me.

Girls at school say Peter's good-looking, and they ask if I fancy him, but I don't know, I've never had a boyfriend. Most of the girls in my class are going out with someone. Melanie Blacksmith's boyfriend is seventeen. He left school last year. He waits for her outside the school gates in his white van. I saw the back doors open once as she climbed in, and there was a mattress and a dirty duvet on the floor. She smiled at me as she shut the doors, then he sped off and did a handbrake turn at the junction. I thought about her rolling around in the back of the van next to his tools, and how cross she'd be, but when I saw her again she boasted that they'd smoked pot and had sex. Sometimes her boyfriend's older brother waits with him at the gates. His name is Mike and he's nearly twenty. He has a motorbike, and keeps asking if I want a ride. I tell him I prefer to walk. Last time I refused he took someone else. She came to school the next day with love bites on her neck, but they looked all blotchy as the cover-up she'd used was the wrong shade.

Dad's old study is my bedroom now. I used to sleep next to Mum's room, but since I moved, if I hear her and Peter at night it's through several walls. Mostly though I stay under the covers and lean into the side of Nanna's old desk, the one that used to be in the hallway. It's like a piece of Dad has stayed in the house, which is just as well as he's getting married again and his fiancée is already pregnant. In his last letter Dad said that money will be tight from now on, and I should ask Mum if I need new clothes. There's about enough room in here for my bed and the old desk. 'Perfect,' Mum said when we got everything in, 'this room was made for you.'

In one of the desk drawers are Dad's old fountain pens. I like to leave them in their places on top of the leaky ink circles so it looks like he's recently put them there, even though they roll out of place when I shut the drawer. There's a writing pad too. The top sheet is heavily lined, and I slide it under the cartridge paper to keep my writing in straight lines. Apart from Dad, I write letters to my guardian angel. I ask for new school shoes with a wedge, hair that doesn't frizz in the rain, more time with Mum on her own and a change from eggs on toast for tea. Sometimes I ask my angel to come and visit me, even if it's only in my sleep. When I hold a page up to the light, the sun shines through the watermark.

Dad's left some of his clothes too, and Mum wanted to throw them away. I said I'd look after them in case he ever wants them back. I've put them in the airing cupboard that's in the corner of my room to keep them safe and dry. Mum never looks in there. There's a little chair in the cupboard that I use to reach the top shelf. Sometimes I like to sit on it and shut the door, and when everything is quiet I can pretend that the world has disappeared.

16

A STRAND OF PLATINUM HAIR

I wander the field, sit in the caravan and allow the damp to move into my bones. By the time I get back to the car park, night has set. A sickly mist haloes the bulb of the tall street light, and underneath is the same huddle of cars as before. I bang my hands together, blowing into the hollow between my palms, and glance at the warmth and safety of my car waiting to take me home, to another kind of hell. I pause and check my phone for a signal to see if David has called by holding it high in the air, but this is a dead spot. On the other side of the car park, bodies are close together, then faces turn to me and one separates.

A man walks towards my car. From his solid pace and the way his skull sits heavy and low on his neck, I can tell it's the same man from two weeks ago, the one who opened the door as I sat in my car. Closer, and what's left of the light illuminates a dusk of features: his eyes, nose and mouth are all too small inside the frame of his big head, as if he's been crafted from bad stock. He looks directly at me and I set my eyes with his. Neither of us smiles and there are no words of welcome or reassurance, no room for pleasantries in what will be this most intimate of exchanges.

We face each other for several long seconds in a duel of anticipation. The man is a good head taller than me and I arch my neck to meet his face, as I imagine I will do later when we are skin to skin, if it's him and not someone else. God, let it be someone else.

'Oh, for fuck's sake,' he says, and turns swiftly, 'make up your bloody mind.' He stomps back towards the group of cars, his breath in frantic clouds like a racehorse on its starters, until he disappears into the black void between the two ends of the car park.

'Wait,' I say, and go after him, meeting him in the darkness.

'Well, c'mon then,' he says. He stands tall and holds a straight headmasterly arm in the direction of the cars. I expect him to say, 'Don't worry, we're all nervous the first time,' but instead he says, 'Bloody hell, you look like you've been dragged through a hedge backwards.' I walk past. He follows a couple of beats behind, and I quicken my step to keep the same speed so we don't have to walk together.

About eight people stand around one vehicle – mostly men, but a couple of women too. A figure with his back to me walks into the trees. Perhaps he's had enough for one night. Several cars have their headlights on, and the

group of watchers is cast in a close cloud of light. Outside, the rest of the world disappears. Eyes swing up and
down my body. I am goods. They move aside to clear a
pathway to the car where a woman sits on the passenger
seat with the door open and her legs sticking out as she
adjusts her suspenders. The tops of her stockings are a
red nylon lace, scratchy and fussy – the white sugar of
erotica. Good idea, I think, less to take off. She stands up
and walks away, scrabbling in her bag for her mobile. A
man joins her and they get into another car and drive off.
I wonder if he's her husband and what they'll do when
they get home. They'll have put something in the oven
on a timer before they left. A ready meal they got at the
supermarket. Then later some sleeping pills.

The group of people stand in silence around the car.
In the middle of their huddle, I pull my damp coat close
to hide my shaking legs and stare at the ground. I wait.
Someone jingles keys in their pocket.

'Well . . . d'you want to get in the car then?' The man
who brought me over bends the front passenger seat forward so there's room for me to climb in. He smiles at me
with the stretched grimace of a boardroom photo. I'm
freezing but my face is red hot and I'm glad it's dark so
no one can read my thoughts. I begin to get in but the
man grabs my coat by the scruff of the neck and pulls me
back. The jolt is a shock. 'You won't need this,' he says,
'the heater's on.' I breathe deep to stop the tears and take
off my coat, handing it to him. He passes the coat to
another man – more elderly – who folds the garment and

lays it as a butler would over his arm, the action gentle and considered. His eyes smile, and I picture him with a Christmas hat on and a grandson on his knee.

I clamber into the back and sit on the blanket spread across the seats. The material is checked and fluffy, man-made, the cheap kind used to protect seats from animal hair and mud. The dull interior light blends all the colours in the car to various shades of yellow. The engine ticks over, its vibration steady, and the tremor travels through my thighs and up into my chest and head – the only thing moving through the stone of my body.

The man who brought me over gets in the car and closes the door. 'That'll keep it warmer. You can get undressed now,' he says.

'I'm soaking wet.'

'I don't care.'

'What should I take off?'

'Might as well do the lot.'

He folds the passenger seat down as far as it will go and perches on its back. Our feet touch and I snatch my legs into the opposite footwell. There's just enough room to slide off my boots and socks, and I roll down my jeans, which are wet from the field. The denim jams at my ankles so I have to shuffle the jeans up a little to get a grip on the tubes of fabric. My jumper and T-shirt peel away, and my hair dries a little and dances in static. I calm the strands down with my hands. Finally my underwear and then, when there's nothing left and nowhere to hide, I sit with my arms crossed at my chest and my feet on tiptoe.

I don't look up at the man, only at his legs. Miniature spears of fabric from the rug jab into my skin. Still sitting on the back of the seat, the man unzips his trousers, and with his penis in one hand he takes a condom from his pocket and tears the packet with his teeth, pinching the rubber tip to roll it down over himself. At least he's using protection. But then I don't really care. This functional pause makes what we're about to do belong to someone else. It helps. I inhale. Then I panic.

'I don't want to any more,' I say.

'Don't be ridiculous.'

The man moves towards me, pushing my shoulder with a steady force down on to the seat. I lever myself back by my elbows until my spine is flat. A damp animal smell rises from the itchy material. Three trees of air freshener dangle from the rear-view mirror and sway with the movement of the car. The man checks out of the windows, wipes off some mist and leans across to the front of the car, putting the screen heater on full-blast to clear the fog. Then he turns to watch my legs. Hot air blasts the glass and it's all I can hear above my pulse. Outside the car it's dark, but there's the occasional movement – shapes coming nearer. Faces.

Fucking morons, I think. I don't look again.

It's over more quickly than I could have hoped, and as the man pulls away from me I realize he hasn't looked at my face once since we got in the car. Now he's coughing into his hand and zipping himself up, but I can smell him on me; his sweat and breath have penetrated my skin. I am porous. I let all of him in.

In the seat well is a packet of baby wipes, and several have been used and discarded on the floor. I don't bother. My clothes are still wet and it takes longer than usual to put them on, but I use the time to absorb the climate of the car: the vegetable smell of damp, the smooth area on the back seat where someone smaller than me usually sits. Some of the figures outside have moved away, some still watch. A man's face looms closer to the glass for a second but I keep my eyes down.

My socks are too much hassle in this small space so I scrunch them into a ball and put them in my bag, at the same time wondering if the dead man knew this went on so close to his caravan. I slide my boots up bare legs inside my jeans and the leather is cold against my skin. Seamus's skin had once been brand new, a mother would have bathed and powdered him. Pieces of him still exist close by. He was being processed by the woods before the police took him away.

As I get out of the car, the man who has my coat holds it open and guides in my arms. I thank him and he smiles. 'No, no, thank you,' he says. He leans closer to my ear and whispers, 'Nice cunt.' I swivel round to him, teeth bared as I jam my fingers into fists. He's small so I'd have a good chance of punching him to the ground. When he was down, I could kick him and use my keys to stab him in the eyes. The impulse transfixes me, but instead of acting on it, I allow the acid of his comment to infuse, then turn and walk towards my car, passing a man in the shadows who sits with his head out of view. All I can see is the bottom of his scruffy coat and old, too-big trainers. He holds a can of beer in his hand. A briefcase is at his side.

The street light recedes, darkness folds around me and I disappear. Across the empty night travel the edges of a conversation. I recognize the voice of the man with whom I've just been.

'Nah, we don't get all the same channels as you. We're on cable. It's cheaper and we get our calls thrown in for the same price.'

As I get in my car my hands have lost their strength and I can't start the engine even though I'm desperate to leave. Snippets of events turn over in my mind. They come at me in jolts, like concussion, with no thread or timing: my unpainted toenails, the rhythm of the swinging air fresheners, the man's phlegmy cough into his hand. The strand of platinum hair stuck to the blanket: long and straight, not mine.

A car sweeps away from the group and pulls up at my side. The window opens and a face looms forward into the light. I see the flash of his smile. Then recognition.

Alex.

Dear God, it's Alex.

The man who, since joining our ranks, has initiated and fed the current of illegal dealings now filling David with such vitality. He saw me only a few hours ago in the woods – how stupid of me not to have thought he could still be here. My concern that he may tell David where he's seen me has now become a terror.

We sat together at my dinner table only weeks ago. He ate the food I cooked. His wife tried to be kind but I wouldn't let her.

Again he has witnessed the worst of me.

17

BALLS OF MERCURY

'What difference does it make?' David said when I told him the police had found Seamus's caravan. I was hoping to pre-empt David finding out from Alex that I'd been at the woods – the rest I planned to deny – but so far Alex has said nothing. 'Nobody knows who he really was,' David continued. 'And they've got nothing on you. If you're going to cover up something as big as this, you need to carry it through. God, you're so paranoid. Get a hold of yourself.'

David was on his way out of the house, our conversations these days shunted in between appointments or tacked on to exits, strategies that mean we need only scratch the surface. In front of the mirror, David's lips stretched wide around his lock-jawed teeth as he picked a piece of food from between his molars. He flashed his eyes back at me. 'What the hell were you doing up there anyway? Do I need to keep tighter reins on you?' He turned to go, collecting the pile of unopened Christmas cards on his way out. At the office he would have given the correspondence to Kelly. She'd have opened the cards, sent replies, and our house will continue to be free from the clutter of friendship.

Since my first time in the car park nearly two weeks ago, I've been online and discovered other locations – supermarket car parks, picnic areas in the woods – and I've been hot-wired back to my prolific student days, to before I met David. Away from my husband, I've not lost my ability to oscillate between my fractured selves. In the old days I'd believed that pleasure was the endgame of these encounters, but perhaps even then I was deluding myself, and this sport has always been a joyless addiction, a futile attempt to fill the void.

The circuit is very interested in single women; I'm an anomaly. So many texts come through that I keep my phone permanently on silent, and I haven't been able to fulfil even a fraction of the requests. I always try to get home before David suspects I've been out – he works late and has dinner with clients most nights, anything rather than come home to the wife he can't bear to be near any more. To keep me in check, my petrol money is kept to a minimum. I leave home when it's light and find the nearest pub to whichever secluded car park is hosting the evening's events, then park and go inside the pub for an orange juice. I top the glass up when the barmaid's not looking from the half bottle of vodka I carry in my bag. After I finish the drink, in case I'm being followed, I make my way from a back exit and find a bus, walking some of the journey along country lanes in my dad's big overcoat. The land rises up to greet each of my footsteps, and with the wind at my back, my pestering thoughts are calmed by the simplicity and rhythm of the pace. I could live like this always. If only I never had to arrive. If only I need never go back.

At home, things start slower for me these days now that the efficiency I used to apply to work – the compulsive order which kept me rooted and sane – is gone. There is no more Will to look forward to, and I do my best to forget the danger I may have put him in. Today is a Saturday, and I stay even longer in bed, sleeping off yesterday's hangover and topping up a new one with nips of vodka from my bag. There seems little point in doing anything until the evening's events. The soup of painkillers and alcohol dulls the pain, but today the concoction has created a complexity of remorse from which there's no escape. Hushed up in the airless hollow of the duvet in the guest-suite bedroom, I lie motionless, hoping to convince myself that all the days that have ever been, never were.

Brisk and energetic from his trip to the gym and walk with the dogs, inspired by the remote possibility of a warmer day, David comes wordless into the bedroom, opens the window then goes downstairs. I peep from the covers. Outside a tepid blue teases through a wrung-out sky, but there'll be more rain later. Enough is enough, the window says, so I get up and shower – my fifth since yesterday. Cold air amplifies my damp skin under the dressing gown, and I slide the window across, leaving a small gap in case David comes back in; I don't know why it matters to him what I do with my time, it's not as if we spend any of it together any more, but I no longer have the energy for a fight.

A text comes through from Alex: 'I'm losing patience. Do you want me to tell David?' This is the ninth text I've had from him since we saw each other that night in the car park. He wants to meet me on his own and keeps suggesting times and places, but I haven't replied, nor have I gone back to the same place where I last saw him. I swing between which would be worse: to go to Alex, or for David to find out how I spend my time. For now the car parks hold enough shame for my purposes, and I'm not sure I really believe Alex will tell.

Through the gap in the window comes the noise of a car pulling into our driveway. I must have been in the shower when the visitor buzzed at our perimeter gate. Peering outside, I see Alex's Aston Martin parking close to the house. He gets out of the vehicle and walks towards the front door holding his key behind him. The car locks with an electronic bleep. Hazard lights double flash. At the door he taps a friendly rhythm, and the dogs bark. I pull on the nearest skirt and top – flung over a chair last night, no time for tights or trousers – slip on shoes and run downstairs to fend off Alex, but David's footsteps are already clicking across the hallway. Circles of muddy paw prints trace his trajectory to the front door where he now stands with his hand milliseconds from the handle.

I freeze on the middle stair. On either side of the front
door is sandblasted glass, and through this barrier is the
motionless shadow of Alex.

David opens the door. 'Alex, how lovely! What a surprise.' The two men shake hands. 'I wasn't expecting to
see you until next week. Come in, come in.'

With the door open wide, David stands to one side to
let Alex through. The dogs are at our guest immediately,
barking and leaping. He walks through them as if they
are liquid and looks ahead at me. Behind him, David
shuts the door.

'I have some paperwork I wanted to drop off to you,'
Alex says, tilting his head to David but keeping his gaze
on me. 'Thought it would give you more time to consider
your options before we meet next week.' He turns to look
at David. 'Sorry to barge in on you like this. I tried calling
but my mobile had no juice.'

I hold the banister with one hand but can't move. Alex
brushes drizzle from his hair, and the moisture darkens
his grey, making him look younger.

'Very thoughtful of you,' David says. 'Do you have
time for a coffee?'

Alex has already begun to shrug the black mac from
his bony shoulders. He hands the coat to David. Rain
studs the waterproof fabric like balls of mercury. 'Won-
derful, thank you.' He looks at me again and smiles. 'I'd
love to.'

'Rachel, be a darling and make us a coffee, would
you?' says David.

'I have to go out,' I say.

'Don't be ridiculous.' He smiles at Alex then looks back at me. 'Your hair's still wet from the shower.' He walks towards the stairs and holds his arm out to me. I come down a couple of steps and touch his hand. 'Anyway, whatever it is you need to do, we always have time for friends, don't we, darling?' He pulls me to the bottom stair and pecks my cheek with gravel lips. Only his eyes betray the effort of this pantomime. 'It will do you good to have some company.'

The two men walk into one of our less formal lounges, David's palm flat on his friend's back, and I slide off to the kitchen. The dogs are in the boot room pacing for their food. After my time locked away with the animals, I let David do their feeds.

At this distance, the men's voices are a murmur: laughter, no silences – it can't be that bad. I relax a little and put the kettle on, heat milk and set a tray with two cups and a cafetière. The tray is melamine: bright red with large graphic flowers. The price of this tray would have fed Mum and me for a week. We didn't get new things. Like when our chesterfield sofa was ripped by scissors during one of Mum's dressmaking enterprises. Her designs were floaty numbers with scarves attached to the sleeves, like a toddler's dressing-up wardrobe, and the sofa was where she cut out the patterns. She planned to sell them at coffee mornings and town fetes, saying that once she'd made her fashion fortune we could buy as many sofas as we wanted. One day she strutted down the street to get a loaf of bread, dressed in a sheer creation with her feet bare. To me she looked so beautiful until she held two fingers up to Mrs Simpson across the road. 'Up yours, you old prune!' she shouted. Mrs Simpson stood with her hands on her hips and heckled back, 'You might enjoy giving it away to all and sundry, but the rest of us don't need to see what's underneath your clothes.' After that the scissors were put away, and the sofa was covered with the old throw.

A sudden burst of laughter from the other room. The kettle boils. I pour water into the cafetière and a dense bitter smell lifts from the coffee grouts, turning my stomach. There's a hiss from the milk pan as a wave of froth bulges over the sides and settles on the hob. The edges of the liquid char. I pour what's left of the milk into a jug and set everything on the tray, the china and glass chinking together as I carry it through to the lounge. David hears the rattle.

'Rachel,' he calls, 'we're dying of thirst in here. Hurry up, will you, darling.'

David and Alex are seated opposite each other on identical white leather sofas. In between them is a chrome and glass coffee table. Unread financial and interiors magazines fan out on the tabletop, and there's a pen pot identical to the one we have at the office with our company logo striped along the pencils inside. The men look as if they're in a casual office meeting, and it strikes me for the first time that everything in our house, even the artwork that was bought to match the decor, is corporate and flat. The effect of style without taste. I'd like to drive a bulldozer through the window, cover the floor with earth and watch how long it would take the weeds to grow.

The two colleagues sit with their arms stretched along the backs of the sofas and their chests full and strong. All that's missing are antlers. David's foot hangs on his opposite knee, and his leg lolls out to the side creating a confident triangle of space in the middle. Alex copies. A thin sun leaks through the clouds and sparkles on the glass table.

'At last,' David says with a smile as I walk towards him.

I put the tray on the coffee table and turn to leave. In the background the dogs' hungry barks have become more frantic. David twitches with each yap.

'You not joining us, Rachel?' Alex says. 'Do sit for a bit. Jane's been asking after you. I said I'd report back on how you're feeling.' He frown-smiles at David. 'Anyway, this might interest you too. I have the latest forecast for the completion of the development. We're finally getting through all the building regs and contractors' quotes, it's really steaming ahead.' He wafts a folder up and down, then slaps it on the table. 'Now all the opposition has subsided, there's nothing to stop us meeting our deadlines. The new broom sweeps clean, eh!' He leans forward and removes some of the plans and finance sheets, then angles his head to look at me. 'We've completely taken over the site now, no room for public access any more.'

'I'm in a bit of a hurry,' I say. 'I'll leave you two to talk shop.'

'Nonsense, Rachel.' David's voice travels up and down the syllables in perfect husband mode. 'It's a Saturday. Come and sit with us.' His eyes fix on me, telling me I'm not permitted to break the facade.

I go to sit next to David and trip on the rug, launching myself closer to him than I intended. Our legs touch. Immediately David springs up, the proximity too much to bear.

'I'm so sorry, Alex,' he says, 'I forgot to feed the dogs. If you don't mind I'll do it now before they drive us all mad. Please excuse me for a moment. Rachel, could you pour?'

He leaves the room and takes the shortcut to the kitchen. I stand also, but before I can turn Alex grabs my hand and pulls. It's a persistent drag not to be refused. I sit on his left. Still holding my hand, he leans forward and with his other hand pours himself a coffee – black with one sugar. He brings the cup to his mouth and winces – I made it strong – then he sets the coffee back on its saucer and heaps in another large spoonful of sugar. He stirs and the metal scrapes round and round on the china.

From where I'm sitting I can see into the garden, and the dogs bound across the grass and disappear into the trees. David must have thought it would be quicker to let them outside for now, and feed them later. There are growls and manic barks; not the usual noise of fun and play, more competition and pursuit. They've probably got another rabbit. David shouts at them, and I watch him striding across to the trees. The last time the dogs went on the hunt, we found bits of the animal across the lawn, torn apart and scattered but uneaten. The crows cleared what was left within minutes.

Alex continues to stir. 'Well, that's a turn-up,' he says, watching his cup. 'I didn't know how I was going to orchestrate getting you on your own.' He smiles and looks at me. 'I can't stop thinking about you, Rachel. You really are full of surprises.' He lets go of my hand and pushes my skirt up my leg towards my thigh. His palm is hot and damp and he holds his hand in place on my shaking leg, my skin a shade of blue next to the white sofa. Small blonde hairs sit upright. He takes the spoon from the cup and lays the scalding metal on my thigh. I jump but don't call out. Won't give him the satisfaction. He holds the spoon in place and looks at me. 'David doesn't have to know about any of this, but that's up to you.'

'You wouldn't dare,' I say.

'Man to man, he'd understand. I have my needs. I'd tell him I tried to protect you but you refused.' He moves his hand up my leg, closer to my crotch. 'Everyone knows you're losing your mind, Rachel. Who do you think David will believe? And how much more do you think he'll tolerate? He's not a man to be messed with, we all understand that. Some of the things we've had to . . . well, I never thought he had it in him, but then there's too much at stake these days.' His index finger skirts the hem of my knickers. 'I choose my battles carefully, Rachel.

I make very, very sure I'm covered, and this time, believe me, David will be on my side.'

His cheeks are flushed and freshly shaved. Inside each follicle is the poised black dot of a new hair. Above his mouth he's sweating. He glides his tongue over his top lip. We hear doors shutting as David comes in from the garden. Alex removes the spoon, puts it in his mouth and sucks. A red circle is left on my leg.

'I'll be in touch, Rachel,' Alex says. 'We'll have some fun. Bring you down a peg or two.' He takes his hand away from my leg and pulls my skirt down with a tug. 'Don't ignore my calls or I'll let David know. Bit of ECT should do the trick.'

As I stand, David comes back in. We pass each other across the rug, but David doesn't look at me. Instead he directs his focus to Alex with a frown and a smile, his arms wide in apology. 'I'm so sorry,' he says, 'the dogs have gone feral. These bitches need a good dose of discipline to bring them into line.' The men laugh and David sits back down. Alex pours himself another coffee. 'I hope Rachel's been looking after you,' David says as I leave the room, shutting the door behind me.

The hallway is dark in contrast with the glare of our south-facing lounge. I slip off my shoes and walk with bare feet on the cold tiled floor, the heating off. On the table by the phone is David's briefcase. It's open. David's need to appear the welcoming and relaxed host has caught him off guard. Poking out is a file and some other papers. I sift through them and find the ledger of cash payments from the office. Inside the book are many more entries, detailing a multitude of outgoings. Names, dates and brief descriptions as before: 'H' and 'Manpower'. 'Finder' is written several times next to the name 'Darren S'. David and Alex's voices trickle into the hallway, and I hear metal on china as another cup of coffee is poured. I tip the contents of the case on to the floor and drop the bag next to the pile, then run to the downstairs bathroom with the expenses book, which I stuff behind the toilet cistern. From there I speed into the kitchen and find the identical household edition in the drawer. My hands are shaking as I rip out the few pages that have already been written on. I shove them far down into the waste disposal, and tip the dregs of David's milky breakfast muesli on top. Later, when David's not around, I'll make a new book for home from one of the many blank spares in the study, and grind these old pages to a pulp. I hurry through to the boot room and open the back door, shaking the dog biscuits. The animals come running. I hold the household book out to them, tearing off blank pages which scatter in the wind. One of the dogs chases the paper and I hold the remainder of the book out to the other bitch. 'What's this, what's this?' I say in a playful voice. The dog snaps at the paper and sinks her teeth into the book. I pull back on it a few times to get her fever up, then let her have it. She runs off into the garden and disappears into the trees. The other dog joins her with excited barks. I leave the back door and boot room open, then scoot upstairs to the guest room where I've now permanently decamped. A few minutes later David and Alex come out of the lounge. With my ear to the door, I hear David's exasperated tones as he discovers his briefcase on the floor, though he maintains a genial timbre while Alex is in the house. The front door shuts. Alex's car drives away. Moments later, David is in the garden screaming at the dogs.

There are growls and yelps outside, but I don't expect the dogs have left David much of the book to salvage. From the hallway he shouts up the stairs: 'You stupid, stupid cow, you left the bloody door open. I suppose you did that on purpose. Have you seen what the dogs have done?' I go into the bathroom and lock the door. The en suite is the smallest room in the house, and I sit on top of the toilet seat with the light off and only the weak sun coming through the blind. The huge volume of the house presses against me, as if the space is filled with water.

From my handbag I take out the photo of Claire and study her face in the dim light: the way her mouth lifts a fraction at the edges from its letter-box smile, and her wide black eyes with no flicker of a shine, as if some-one's coloured them in with a biro. I think about where I would have been on this same spring day, who I was with and what I was doing. Maybe Claire and I were both writing letters to our dads at the same time, our pens in unison across the sea, scratching out messages of longing to men who were grander and more loved through their absence. Our mums played out their tra-gedies in front of us, but at least they didn't leave. The women's legacy for sticking it out is to get all the blame. But then maybe Seamus's reasons for leaving were more valid than my own father's, who jumped from woman to woman every time he felt the expectations of another family.

I wish I could take Claire by the hand and lead her through the quiet woods to her dad's caravan, and show her where his finger drew letters on the glass. 'Look'. I picture her focusing on the landscape beyond the window as I point out the trees and animals Seamus studied with such care. She'd understand something of how her father lived. He would have wanted her to see. If I went to the police, Claire would only ever have half the story.

When I am ready, I'll find a way to give up Seamus, but for now each shameful tryst in a car park and every hostile interaction with David decreases my debt, and I grow closer to the man I killed. No court or prison can give me the same.

PART THREE

18

BEER CAN

I've been stuck at home for most of the week having lost all appetite for the car parks, and without the routine of the office it surprised me to find that the thing I missed the most was noise; the background burble of life rolling forward. I envy others the even keel of their days, but somewhere inside me I know I wouldn't be able to settle for the worn-slippered evenings in front of the TV. The silence in our house soaks up my energy so I have to fill the space somehow, but music is too affecting, and I wouldn't trust myself not to play the sad songs over and over. The TV and radio are a good replacement for human contact though, and as our in-house sound system is wired into every room, I can beam through the chirruping discontent of international crises to wherever I may be. It helps. I pay special attention to the local bulletins. There's been no more about the fire at the camp, but *South East Today* reported a body found in a skip near to where Will lives. The man was in his forties and was known to be involved in the local drugs scene. My stomach lurched, and I gripped the back of the sofa to stop my legs from giving way. I stayed holding on until they flashed up his picture on the TV and I saw it wasn't Will. His name was Darren Spencer. He looked familiar, very possibly the man who Will had a fight with in the pub the night I was with him, though I can't be sure. I check again, and 'Darren S' is in David's secret ledger. I want to believe that David wouldn't go that far, but every toxic thing that happens now circles me back to my husband and the strong possibility that his flirtation with the underworld has become a marriage.

Since Alex's visit a little over a week ago, I've met with him twice in the daytime when David's been at work. These have been my only excursions from the house. David, clearly frustrated by the amount of time he believes I spend in pubs, has taken my car keys and left me very little money. Inadvertently the deprivation is a gift; there's freedom in this poverty. Without my car it's easier to disappear. I shrug on my dad's old coat, take the bus, then duck into a shopping centre, use the Ladies, find a different exit, take an elevator. After that I walk the rest of the way, and the weight and size of the coat steadies my footfalls and moors me to the ground. I doubt there has ever been any one day completely the same as another, and I witness each new combination of cloud and light, each swoop of a bird, as my own personal treasure, a safety hatch through which I can leap to forget about the real purpose of my journey.

Alex's rendezvous has been a hotel in Brighton; not the Grand, but a cheap and miserable B & B, a fitting addition to the sleaze. The first time we met, the sex was wordless and painful. On the second occasion, Alex laughed out loud as he fucked me. I blushed, and because there was nowhere to hide, the red spread down my neck. My embarrassment seemed to spur him on. Afterwards as he dressed he pulled his plaid socks to midway up his calves where the elastic pinched a circle of loose skin round his white furry legs. He put on his trousers and tossed me money: crumpled fivers and tenners, enough to keep my booze and transport fund going for a small while. 'I need more than that,' I said last time. He reached into his pocket for another note and some loose change sprinkled on to the bedside table. The coins bounced to the floor. He stooped to collect them but stopped himself, watching instead as I stretched from the bed to pick them up, then he said quietly, 'We'll keep these little meetings regular, shall we? Otherwise I'm not afraid to tell David about the car park, you know.' His face was close to mine and his breath smelt of last night's red wine, the taste of it still in my mouth from his tongue. 'You being there was nothing to do with me. And there'll be no coming back for you from that little revelation.' He straightened up into the room and shuffled his tie closer to his neck. 'I shall enjoy telling David about it almost as much as I enjoy doing what I do to you.'

After he'd gone, I took a big hit of vodka then threw up in the wastepaper basket next to the bed. Still naked,

I lay back and looked up at the swirls of Artex on the ceiling, yellowed to points like a baked meringue. The nylon sheets crackled with static and stuck to my legs. I drew out the time, sliding in and out of sleep, and had a dream where I sat with Seamus in his caravan sharing a beer. As I sipped from the can, my lips touched where his had been, and I drank down the lager with his saliva. The alcohol was warm and sweet, the fizz all gone, and it tasted like pineapples. Across the table between us marched the tiny skeletons of all the animals he'd collected. I couldn't work out how they were held together. One by one they dropped off the edge, and each time a collection of bones fell, Seamus caught the pieces as one whole in his hand and placed the creature back in its starting position. When the last one fell, I tried to catch it too, but my hand touched Seamus's with a spark of electricity and I jolted awake. When I was a child my mother used to say that if you fell and hit the ground in your sleep, then you'd die in real life too.

The ancient plumbing choked in the hotel bathroom, and the smell of the drain mixed with Shake n' Vac to create a third odour of fruity vomit. I went over to the window and pushed my cheek flat against the glass. From this position my own personal chink of sea came into view. Waves foaming and renewing. A windsurfer tracked through my frame of ocean, his board moving fast and strong.

As long as David was fighting to bring me back I would be safe, but my usefulness as a wife and business partner was all but gone. He would tire of trying to bring me in line, and I can only go on accumulating errors so long before he finds out. Either way, when his fixation with control and ownership switches off, he'll walk away from me as he would any other business deal that's stopped making a profit. Then there'll be no telling what he's capable of. It's been a long time coming.

I went home this one last occasion and packed a small bag with pants, a T-shirt, deodorant, the picture of Claire, Seamus's watch, plus the money from Alex. There were a few foil strips of pain medication left over, which I stuffed in my bag, but I didn't want the sedatives anymore, so put them back in the drawer of my bedside table. With so few belongings, I am weightless. The less I have, the less that David can take away, and I wished I could take nothing at all so that when he came home it would be as if I'd evaporated. I hid the bag overnight in the freezer along with David's book of expenses sealed inside a large brown envelope, and after David left for work in the morning, I took the bus into Brighton and did my usual shop-hopping until I was sure I wasn't being followed. Then I walked to the beach in Hove, where I now sit on a bench and wait. Hours have passed into the afternoon. My phone tings with a third message from Alex: 'I'm at the hotel. This is your very last chance. 5 mins before I tell David.'

This time I don't think he's faking.

My problem is I don't know how to get far enough away. It needs to be more than the distance of a drive, but plane tickets are expensive and can be traced. A boat could work, something small and local, the type that Will has spoken of in the past, if he wasn't making it up. Yesterday, I rang and rang until Will picked up, and I begged him to meet me one more time. At the sound of his voice something dead inside me drew breath, and I had to keep pausing while I spoke to swallow the tears. Now as I prepare what to say, I tuck back inside myself any belief that he could want to come too. After all I've put him through. But it's good to hope.

This stretch of beach in Hove is quieter than Brighton. It's off the tourist track with fewer cafes and amenities. Scrubby hedges line the north side of the walkway and the promenade parallels the sea to the south. In a big storm, waves throw stones over this path, and the following day tractors have to push the debris back to where it belongs. If anyone ever braved the waves when the weather was that bad, it would be the last thing they'd do. Today the sea is a rippled aquamarine, enticing me to believe it's warmer than the ice pool I know it to be. I fidget with my bag and coat, wondering if Will will turn up. I pace, then sit again on a bench and listen to the small waves hidden behind the breakwater. Pebbles clatter back and forth.

I check my watch – it's twenty minutes past the time we arranged – so I stand and dust my jeans, turning to walk back to the road, but Will is standing at the end of the path that reaches the promenade. He leans on a wall with his hair in its floppy mess. He tries to look angry, and I remember how badly we split last time and how I had to plead with him to come today, but his expression quickly changes to a smile. His teeth are set small and neat in his gums, like a child's. I want to kiss him.

'How long have you been there?' I say.

'Not long.' He shuffles his feet and kicks at the dust on the ground. 'Only a couple of minutes. Just got here really.' His head is bowed but he squints up at me through his long fringe, still smiling. 'You looked so thoughtful.'

A gust of wind sweeps up from the sea and flaps my coat. The light is failing and the cold makes me wish I'd packed my scarf. Will comes forward and puts his arms round my waist and kisses my neck. The action is a surprise, it's so long since I've been touched with care, and I flinch and pull away.

'What the fuck!' he says and stands back from me, throwing his arms open at his sides. 'What is wrong with you?'

'I'm sorry.' I tuck my hands in my armpits. In the distance behind Will, Worthing Pier is a finger of mist along the horizon. The jetty points at a ship, probably a tanker, but the vessel is the size of a dot. On board there are men far from home, and the boat tips over the edge of the world. 'I'm not myself.' I can't look at Will's face. 'This is really hard.'

Will paces the small piece of ground directly in front of me. He stops to speak, pauses, then carries on pacing. He stops again.

'Let me tell you something.' He points his finger at me

239

with little skewer jabs. 'I don't find this easy either. None of it. Nothing makes sense. First you hate me then you beg me to meet you. Make up your bloody mind. What is it you want from me?'

I hug myself tighter and look up at him. 'I'm in trouble.'

He crosses his arms. 'Well, of course you are, with a husband like yours. You should have listened to me when I said and left him.'

Words fall out like pepper. 'There's something else.' Eyes down. 'Something bad. Lots of things, actually.'

Will pauses. 'What?' His voice drops. 'What's happened?' My legs start to shake and Will comes closer. 'I need to know what's going on if you want me to help you.'

On the ground between us a crisp packet scratches across the path. 'I don't know where to start.'

'Try at the beginning.'

I breathe into my belly. 'I'm not what you think. I mean, I'm not the person . . . I've done bad things.'

'No shit.'

Gulls swirl and screech overhead. A last segment of the day's sun breaks through the clouds and lights the birds' bellies a postcard-orange.

'It's complicated,' I say. 'There's too much to explain now. You won't understand. I have to get away from here, that's all, but I don't know how. I need your help.'

'Great. Talk about shutting the stable door after the horse has bolted.' Will refolds his arms high across his body. 'It's OK for you, you're not the one that takes the brunt of your husband's psycho behaviour.' He snorts air through his nose.

A jogger and cyclist cut through our path and we separate on either side of the promenade. They chat as they pass. They look happy. Fit. Their voices fade and Will and I come back together, a little closer this time. I want Will to put his arms round me. I need him close, but I can't ask.

'It's not only David,' I say. My teeth chatter. 'There's more. It's worse than you think.'

Will grips my upper arms a little too tight and dips his neck to look at my face. He frowns. 'OK, I'm sorry. I'm listening now,' he says. 'What's going on?'

I look into the sky and inhale salty air, then drop my eyes to the ground. 'It all started . . . it was some time . . . oh God.'

Will's grip tightens. 'C'mon, Rachel. It's time. Please.'

I lift my eyes to meet Will's. 'I killed someone.'

'What?' He lets go and steps back as if he's been pushed. 'Who, for God's sake?'

It's out now, a relief, and the words spill from my mouth. 'It was an accident. I was scared. It was a homeless man. Nobody saw but I panicked and hid the body.'

'You? Don't be stupid. When? I don't believe you.'

'Some weeks back. It was raining. I'd just left your place and was still drunk. I didn't see him. He was on the road and I was going too fast. Things have got out of control with me since then, and I'm frightened. It's only a matter of time before David finds out.'

'Finds out what? About the accident?'

'No, he's known about that all along.'

'Then what are you worried about? Is he threatening you with the police?'

'I wouldn't care any more if he did.'

'Rachel, I don't understand. Are you scared he'll find out about you and me? Because I can tell you, that's all been dealt with, as long as you're not seen with me again.'

'No, it's not us, it's worse. There's much more. I've done bad things.'

'You're going round in circles. What the hell are you talking about?'

I move closer to Will. We stand together with the proximity of conspirators.

Will whispers. 'Tell me. If you want me to help you, I need to know what you've done.'

A breath. 'I went somewhere. I did something.'

'Enough of this. Out with it.'

'I'm sorry, Will. You don't deserve this but there's no one else I can turn to.' I bend my neck forward and curl my head into my chest. My breath dampens the fibres of my jumper.

Will strokes my head. 'Shh, it's OK.'

'Please try not to hate me.' I twist my neck to one side as a great sheet of starlings swoop low in the dusk and fly towards the dead pier. 'There've been others, other men. It was the worst thing, but it was nothing to do with you. I never meant for you or anyone to find out, but one of David's friends saw me, and he's going to tell David.'

'Saw you? Where?'

'In a car.'

'What's wrong with being in a car?'

'I was . . . you know. With a man. In a car park where people come to watch.'

Will's mouth opens a crack. 'You . . . ?'

'Yes.'

'You mean you've been . . . ?'

'Yes. This will be it for David. He'll put up with a lot if I keep my side of the bargain, but not this. I'm scared.'

Through the tiny gap in Will's lips comes a grumble of words. None form into shapes. Again, he holds me by the shoulders but this time he shakes me, hard. 'What are you telling me?' he says. 'What tiny piece of your brain thinks that it's OK to fuck with my head like this? After all I've done for you, all the risks I've taken. And you want me to help you after you've been doing this with God knows who?' His fingers dig deep into my arms. 'Why would I help someone like you?'

'I'm sorry. I'm so sorry.' My speech judders until Will stops the shaking. 'It was nothing to do with you. I hated it, it was the worst thing I could do to myself, that was the point . . . those men meant nothing to me.'

'You are fucked in the head, Rachel.'

'I know.'

'So enough of you and your shit.' He gestures at the sky as if calling on the heavens for sanity. 'I cannot believe I got taken in by you again.' And he turns fast to walk away.

243

'Please don't go.' I catch the edge of his jacket before he's out of reach. He pulls away but I grab more of the material and he stops with his back to me. 'Don't leave me.' My voice is a whisper through the tears. 'There's no one else who can help. I'm sorry for everything, for all those times I was such a bitch. I didn't mean to be like that, I just don't know how to be anything else.'

He spins to face me. 'It's a bit bloody late for that. You can't be bothered with me, then suddenly when everything hits the fan, and with this utter shit, you come to me and you need me? Is that all I'm good for? As a last resort? Is it?'

'No.'

'I've put myself on the line for you one too many times. And now other people are taking the flak for your stupidity.'

'What do you mean?'

Will's teeth scissor together. 'That guy in the pub, remember? The one I had a fight with that night.'

I look to the ground and my legs shake. 'I saw something on the news. I thought it was him but I wasn't sure.'

'That poor fucker, I never thought they'd . . . Jesus, I feel so bad. He was supposed to be out of town, for a long time. He'd had enough bloody warnings. If I'd known he was that stupid I'd never have fitted him up as your dealer. Even if they did catch up with him I thought a beating was the worst he'd get. That's all he deserved anyway, not this. What a fucking mess.'

'I'm sorry.' I rock back and forth under the radar of

Will's eyes. 'But at least it means you're safe.' I look up at him. 'Now that they've got him, I mean.'

'Jesus!' Will shouts. 'You don't care about anyone or anything apart from yourself, do you?' His mouth trembles and he clamps his teeth over his bottom lip. The incisors dent the flesh white. He comes towards me with eyes glistening and holds me up by the scruff of my coat so I have to tiptoe. Nose to nose, he bares his teeth. 'You, Rachel, are dangerous to know.' We stand like this for seconds, heat radiating from his body, then as fast as he grabbed me he shoves me away from him with a growl. 'You know what? You're not fucking worth it.' And he turns and strides up the path to the road.

I chase after him and stand in his way. He keeps walking and looks to one side of me, towards the line of parked cars.

'Will, please,' I say, 'I'm begging you, listen for a minute.' I put up both my hands to hold him steady as he strains against me, then settles. 'I'm sorry about that man. Really sorry. I knew David was dangerous, but he's never gone this far before. If I'd known how bad it was going to get I would have left when you said. Now everything's gone crazy.' I focus on the buttons of his shirt. The bulk of his ribs heaves up and down against my palms. 'I need to explain.' I take a breath. 'Always, even as a child, I've known I was totally alone. There was no one who could help. I thought you might know how that feels.' Will's breathing steadies. 'I don't know how to let anyone in, but I'm trying to change. Please believe me. I'm begging you, I know it's hard, but please forgive me. You're the only person I care about, the only one I don't want to leave behind.'

'Bullshit.' He stands back from me and my balance totters. 'God,' he yells, 'I could kill you right now.' He points at me. 'You. Have had. The last. Of me.' He knocks my hand away with the side of his arm. 'You deserve every bloody thing you get.'

'Please. I'm scared. I need your help.'

'The only person you need to be scared of, Rachel, is yourself.'

Will turns and strides to the road. He gets into his van, attempts the ignition three times before it starts, then swerves a U-turn back towards the city centre, not once turning to look at me. I stand at the deserted roadside and watch as he disappears into the effervescence of lights that line the coast.

Today it's almost the shortest day of the year, and even though it's only afternoon, the sun is fading fast. The beach is empty. Windows and balconies of the flats which overlook the promenade are decorated with twinkling lights; one set is a Father Christmas climbing a ladder. Curtains are drawn as people prepare for the evening's television. Oblivion. 'You're a long time dead,' my mother used to shout at the neighbours when they complained about the noise, and for once I agree.

It's coming at you, faster than you think. Almost here.

A seagull rides the air and I wonder if there's pleasure in the action, like play, or whether it's purely functional; to stay up from the ground away from predators, with a constant eye on the opportunity for food. Relentless survival.

I walk back to the beach. My hair blows across my face and I pull strings of it from my eyes. The sea has turned black as if it's sucked the slate from the sky. Waves push and drag, push and drag.

Faint footsteps. A man walks towards me holding a can of beer in one hand. He takes a swig. A skinny dog is beside him. The man's shoes are loose and they slap on the ground with each step. His coat sweeps up at the sides. He walks with a slow pace and a small limp, but it won't be long before he reaches me.

19

CHRYSANTHEMUMS

The B & B I've been staying in for a couple of nights in Brighton is cash only. It's a different hotel from the one where I met Alex, and this time I'm alone. In my single room with corner sink big enough for one hand at a time, I've been hovering between fast food and the rattle of daytime TV. I've rung and texted Will many times, but he's replied only once. His text said, 'Leave me alone.' So I have. David's made no attempt to call.

On the second morning when I wake, the television is dead, and I have to settle instead for stillness. Noises leak into the room from downstairs and next door: voices, a vacuum cleaner, doors banging. A group of young men call to each other on the street outside. They're lunchtime drunk, and they sing Christmas carols, replacing the traditional lines with swear words and jokes. Their voices lift up past my window and bounce from the bricks, travelling higher, dissipating and softening as they meet the vacuum of space. I swig from the bottle of gin I bought yesterday before I try standing up, but the movement is awkward, as if my body is solidifying. Turning to salt.

The voices of the men outside recede, after which there's another kind of quiet into which my thoughts drop, back into the hole of my past. I pick at the muck in there but it doesn't go away. With the layers peeled back, I'm surprised at the density of the anger, but there's no specific focus, nothing concrete to kick at, only a need to go back as far as I can to the beginning and extract the rotten tooth. Cauterize the infection. The persistent taps of memory, brushed off by years of distractions – men, work, marriage, booze – have latched on. The truth is crouched and ready.

After all this time the hardest part is remembering his surname – he was always just Uncle Peter – but with some concentration the name slides into my consciousness like a whiff of his pipe smoke. After this, tracking him down to a nursing home takes only a few phone calls. All these years he's been on my doorstep. He still lives in Brighton, close to my office and the house I shared with David, as well as to the town where I grew up, so he hasn't strayed far; not much of an adventurer, more of a man who finds his security and pleasure in familiarity.

I pop to the corner shop for some gifts to take with me, choosing an ugly plant and some lardy chocolates, then order a taxi. En route, the cab passes Teller Productions. The windows of the building flash back the sun, and in the forecourt there's the usual jam of expensive cars. One of them is David's. With the small separation of three weeks away from the office since my very public shaming, the place appears smaller, foolish in its over-blown formality on this crappy feeder road into Brighton. I used to believe we were so swish, but really, who does David think he is?

It feels as if the taxi is glowing with my presence, and after my first glance I sink down in my seat and look the other way. David's inside, most probably at his desk marshalling his troops in the money trenches, and the thought of him in there perpetually pursuing matter and quantity, widens the few metres between us as if an earthquake has wrenched open the ground. He's welcome to his cold soul which knocks about inside his chest. It's all he deserves.

Twenty minutes later and the cab pulls up outside the nursing home, Chantry Hall; a mock-Tudor mansion on an avenue of grand houses, the kind of place designed in Victorian times for a family with live-in servants. Most of the houses have now been converted into flats or day-care centres, and phone masts line the busy road. The old and infirm are the new gentry, the nurses their underpaid servants. Anyone with money today would choose to live elsewhere.

I step out of the car and on to the driveway. Unpruned shrubs – the relics of a mature garden – compete for status among tall weeds. A tree reaches above the roof and salutes me with a swoosh of pine needles that fall as the wind gusts. Next to the lion's-head knocker on the front door is a plastic doorbell that chimes a Big Ben melody inside the house. Footsteps, then the door is opened by a flustered woman in a grubby apron. Behind her in the hallway there's a trolley with a gigantic teapot on top, plus a selection of beakers with lids.

'Hello. Can I help you?' she asks, wiping her hands on her sides.

'I've come to see Mr Davis.'

'Peter? Peter Davis?' She looks at my pot plant and chocolates. I nod. 'Matron's not here to sign you in, but I'm sure it'll be all right. Come on in.' She turns, walks to her trolley and begins to push. I follow. 'Family are you?' she says.

'Yes, he's my uncle.'

She nods. 'He'll be very pleased to have a visitor. No one's been for quite some time.'

Ammonia mixes with a fog of TCP. The smell will stay on my clothes after I leave.

'I'm on my way upstairs,' the woman says. 'I'll show you to his room.'

We enter a lift, its concrete shaft protruding from the panelled walls like a bedsore. The trolley clunks over the entrance lip and a beaker falls to the floor. I pick it up and put it back next to the others. All the spouts have been chewed as if they've been drunk from by teething toddlers. We arrive at the first floor and walk along a corridor. Open doors reveal crumpled people, some in bed, some on chairs, and the noise of their TVs merges in the hallway into a manic opera. One lady catches my eye and waves. I wave back. She's wearing a too-tight nightie, and wisps of grey hair stick up in electric shocks from her pink scalp, like she's been plugged in.

At the end of the corridor we turn a corner and reach a door where the trolley lady pauses. 'Here he is,' she says, and steams her vehicle through the door. 'Peter, dear,' she shouts, 'you've got a visitor!' The man in bed opens his eyes for a second then shuts them again. She pours a cup of milky tea with two sugars into one of the beakers, puts a lid on it then rests the cup at his bedside. 'I haven't got an ordinary cup to give you a tea,' she says to me. 'Don't suppose you'd want to drink from one of these?' She holds up one of the translucent containers and smiles.

'No, but thanks anyway.'

'You can have a lovely catch-up when he wakes,' the woman says as she leaves the room. 'The tea should get him going.'

I follow her to the door and shut it as she leaves. Through the walls I hear her rattle into the next room. 'Hello, duck!' she bellows.

Next to Peter's bed is a red cord with a triangle of plastic on the end. I ravel it into a bundle and tie it high and out of reach. He'd been about ten years older than Mum, which means he's closing on eighty now, but the years of alcohol, tobacco and canteen breakfasts make him look even more ancient. Layers of blankets cover the old man, and his lungs heave against the weight of fabric on top of him. Underneath I imagine the raisin of his body. His breath sucks in and out of crumpled lips and a clock ticks an infinity through the mud of heating in the room, but it's taken me a lifetime to get here so I can wait.

Through the window is a view of the back garden where an empty bird table stands. No one has bothered to put out food so no birds will come. Peter must have thought he had the best suite in the house when he got here, tucked away nice and quiet with a lovely outlook, but he's on his own at this end of the corridor, and to see through the window he'd need to twist his neck.

He coughs. Lips part. Tobacco teeth with a few spaces. He splutters again and wakes, turning his head, starting when he sees me. Bushy brows push worms of skin up his forehead as he struggles to sit up.

'Hello?' he says, wiping his mouth on the back of his hand. 'Do I know you?'

'Yes, you do.' I press his shoulder back on to the pillow to settle him. His skin is loose under his pyjamas, and I snatch my hand away.

'I'm sorry.' He lies back and wheezes. 'My memory's not what it used to be. Have you come to do my assessment? Remind me of your name?'

'It's Rachel, Rachel Teller.'

He looks at me for seconds, squinting. 'I'm sorry, dear. You look familiar but I can't quite place you.' The skin at his jowls shivers. 'Do I need to fill out a form?'

'No, that's not why I'm here. I'm an old friend. Well, a friend of a friend. You would know me as Rachel Sharp.'

His cheeks freeze.

'Yes, Patty's daughter,' I say and sit up straight with my hands clasped round each other in a double fist on my lap. Outside a crow calls. 'Is it still OK to call you Uncle Peter?'

His eyes steady and his hands grasp the sheet into little balls. 'No, I'm sorry, dear, I don't recall you.' He pushes to sit more upright, joints mashing. 'Patty, you say?'

'Yes, Patty, your girlfriend.'

'I don't have a girlfriend. My wife died some years back.'

'And Patty's dead now too,' I say, leaning a little closer with a tight jaw. 'I think you remember. I think you remember everything.'

'Rachel, you say?' His eyes jump towards the door as the clatter of the woman's trolley disappears down the hallway. He looks to the side of his bed for the emergency cord and his vision scrolls up towards the ceiling where the thread hangs in a knot. With his elbows holding him up, he looks back to me. 'I've forgotten so much.'

Anger rumbles in my belly. 'You were Mum's boyfriend. Patty, my mum. You were with her for a couple of years. Back in the seventies.'

'The seventies? I was a policeman then. Worked for them my whole life, but they didn't bloody look after me when I retired. It's criminal, the pension I got. Criminal.'

'Peter,' I raise my voice. 'I'm here to talk to you about Patty. Patricia. My mum.'

'I don't know any Patricias. What is it I'm supposed to know?'

I lean closer, smelling his boiled-sweet breath, and say in a low voice: 'What happened? I want to know what you did to me.'

'Did to you?' he shouts. 'Whatever are you talking about?'

I sit up straight. 'When I was a girl.'

'I don't understand.'

I jump up and the chair falls back. Peter yelps. My arms are stiff and straight at my sides. 'You don't have to understand, I just want you to remember.'

'Remember what? I think you've got the wrong person, young lady.'

He sits more upright in the bed, trying to pull the bed sheets off, and the sticks of his legs edge towards the floor. I throw the covers back across him and hold him by his shoulders, pushing him down on to the mattress. Peter scrabbles at my arms with ribbed yellow nails, but I press harder, feeling the loose twigs of his bones inside the sack of skin. Tears spring up in his eyes.

'I'm sorry for whatever it is,' he says. 'Believe me, I'm truly sorry.'

I lean in close and spit my words in his face. 'You can't be sorry unless you remember.' He struggles as I press down, then with his teeth bared he stills under my weight. His breathing speeds up, lungs hungry for air, and tears roll down his cheeks. Me on top, him underneath, the reversal of how it had been all those years before, and the memories tumble out. All of the times. Each and every event rushes at me as a fresh incision.

'Please forgive me, for whatever it is you say I've done.' He wheezes and his face turns from grey to white. 'I'm just an old man.'

Under Peter's head is a stack of pillows. I could put one over his face and hold it there; he's weak and it wouldn't take long. Who would know? I have already disappeared.

'Oh God,' he says, 'please go. Please leave me alone.'

'That's what you should have done to me.'

Under my pressure his shoulders bend into the mattress, and his fragile bones remind me of Seamus's limp body as I dragged him through the woods. From the bed there's the popping sound of a ligament. Peter screams. My hands spring from his shoulders, and I grab one of my fists with the other and restrain the pair against my chest. The old man's cheeks are wet and he rests shaking hands over his face.

I slump back in the chair at his side, watching Peter until his hands slide off. He looks at me and his body shudders, then he sputters and retches, grabbing a tissue from his bedside table. He spits. Damp green leaks through the thin paper. As I lift up my hands to run them through my hair, Peter screeches with the sound of a little girl and fumbles to the other side of the bed, almost falling off. He grabs the sheets to haul himself back. Again he sobs and I chuck him the box of tissues. He blows his nose several times, focusing on the bedding in front of him, before he flits a look at me. I catch his eye. He turns his face back to the bed.

'What do I need to do to make you go away?' he says in a quiet voice.

'Tell the truth.'

He wipes his eyes and sighs. 'It was . . . you know. All those notes. What did you expect?'

'Notes? I don't know what you mean.'

'The letters in my jacket, the ones I used to find in the mornings after I'd stayed with your mother. You were persistent, I'll give you that. I thought you wanted me to . . . Well, Patty told me to sort it out.'

Another piece of the story breaks off and slides into place. My father's writing pad on the desk in my child-hood bedroom. The letters I wrote to my dad were pages long, telling him all about what I'd been doing, asking when I could see him again. I used his old fountain pens, thinking they made my writing more grown-up. When Dad wrote back I was so excited, but over time the replies became shorter, replaced by the occasional postcard, until Mum told me he'd moved abroad.

Absent fathers, letters unanswered. 'Pa, when are you coming home?' Was it the same for Seamus; easier to hide his mistakes and pretend he didn't have a family? Let the women do their growing up in front of the children.

It's a sin for the woman to leave, but damn the wife who tries to contain her man. Like my own dad who bounced between lovers and wives, siring children along the way, his offspring passed over like puppies for the pet shop. When the forwarding addresses for Mr Sharp changed to 'Return to Sender', he got the freedom he'd always desired.

So in the absence of my dad, the letters to my guardian angel became prolific. I'd sit in my room at my nanna's old desk, creasing the pages of the writing pad with my fingernails painted red and tearing the paper into tiny pieces to make it last. I'd fold these notes over and over then hide them around the house: behind picture frames, wedged into gaps in the skirting board, tucked into shoes and jacket pockets. If they'd disappeared by the next day, I knew the angel had found them.

In front of me on the desk where I wrote was my school photo. I'd been tall for my age, stretched, but not all the pieces of me had grown in sync: my teeth were too big for my head, my hands and feet huge on the end of skinny limbs. Small breasts and a child's narrow hips. Pieces of a woman tacked on to a girl. Where was the mother to guide me until I was ready?

The pot plant I've brought is on Peter's bedside table: chrysanthemums, cheap and colourful, the same kind he used to buy for Mum. I always hated them, and I know Mum did too, but she was afraid to tell him in case he stopped buying her flowers altogether. The yellow petals are as bright as if they've been injected with dye, and they suck the colour from everything around them, turning the universe of the room insipid and grey. In the heated room their perfume is a chemical vapour.

I pick a small flower, one recently opened from a bud, and roll the stem in my fingers. The petals bruise along opaque lines the second they are bent. I put the flower in my pocket next to the little bones I found outside Seamus's caravan, then stand and stare at Peter. He sours into the bed. When he goes to speak I press my hand hard on his wet mouth, remembering the adult currency he traded with a child's infatuation. I think of him one day soon reverting to his base elements, as my mother has already done: oxygen, carbon, hydrogen – the molecules separating and no longer able to do harm.

Let him fester, and rot, and disappear.

20

1981

A layer of soft hair covers my face and body. It's grown quite slowly over the last year but mostly it's on my forearms. Luckily it's quite fair, not like the hair on my head. I like to pinch some of the strands together and roll the hairs between my fingers so they pull a bit. My skin looks like it belongs to a newborn calf, but I don't feel very pure. More of a beast.

Around my chest, I strap myself up with lengths from a torn sheet, then a tight vest over which I wear a baggy top. I've tested the look in the mirror and I'm flat like a plank. Girls at school chant a rhyme when I pass them in the corridor, 'She's so boring, she's got no tits, she never puts out, and she never gets her kicks'. The boys tease me too, they call me spaghetti. None of them have asked me to go out with them; none of them would want to if they knew. Only Mike gives me lifts home on his bike. He French kisses me with a pointy tongue when he drops me off. Mrs Simpson over the road watches through her net curtains. I think Mike's my boyfriend, but Melanie Blacksmith's going out with his brother, and she says that Mike's not interested in girls who are frigid.

For supper Mum's cooked what's left in the fridge: a mishmash of cheese on toast, some cabbage and half a pie. We sit opposite each other and I eat slowly, worrying about how long I can leave the food in my stomach before it gets absorbed. Now that Uncle Peter's stopped coming round, there's nothing to break up the evening, and the meal seems to take ages.

'How was your day then, darling?' Mum says in a squeaky voice, pecking her food with a fork. The cutlery clangs on the china. She won't finish the meal, but she'll expect me to finish mine.

'Fine.'

'Did you get your homework in on time?' Her words are all shaky. 'I expect to see great things from you at the next parents' evening.' That'll be the first one she's ever made it to then.

Mum dabs her mouth on an ironed napkin and her lipstick prints satsuma shapes on the cloth. Earlier today before I went to school, she opened the front curtains, placed herself by the window and wrestled the rusty ironing board open. When I came home, everything from the laundry basket had been ironed, even the dress I wore for my twelfth birthday which no longer fits me. She's hung it in my wardrobe anyway.

We finish the meal in silence. I scrape my knife and fork together and put them to the left of my plate. Mum lights a cigarette and inhales a big lungful of smoke. She looks out of the window and flicks cylinders of ash into an ashtray. Normally she uses her plate.

'You know, you mustn't talk about this,' she says with a sniff.

I stare at my plate.

'There's just no need.' She pulls on her cigarette – it's nearly finished, in record time – and she stubs out the butt and looks at me. 'It'll only cause a load of problems. They'll ask lots of questions, of me as well as you. No good will come from airing your problems. Mistakes are best hidden.'

Her eyes scorch into me. She fiddles with the packet of cigarettes then lights another. I wish I could smoke and take big breaths like that.

'Well,' she says, her voice all high-pitched, 'we'll have to make sure we concentrate on your studies now, shan't we? Get you into that university you're always talking about.' Her words start to quiver. 'Get all this sex stuff out of your head.'

The gravy from the pie has made brown rainbows on my plate. I think about the food in my stomach, mixed up into a thick sauce like in a giant food processor. No one would eat if they had a TV of their insides, they'd take space pills instead.

Mum's crying now. 'You didn't have to do that.' She wipes her eyes with her dirty napkin and a bit of lipstick smears on her cheek. 'Is it too much to ask, for me to have something for myself? The one good thing that's happened to me in all these years, and you had to come along and ruin it. After all I've done for you, after all I've given up.' She stands and paces the floor. 'Did you think we could share him? Was that your idea?' Mum looks at me but carries on walking and puffing on her cigarette. She holds the butt in the V of her fingers and jabs it at me while she talks. 'If you were a grown-up I'd call you a little bitch. But you're only skin and bones, a stupid little girl. I don't know what you think you've got to offer that I haven't.'

Raindrops of mascara trickle down her cheeks. She wipes the black on to her hand. At the kitchen window she stops and looks out, turning her back on me. Big yellow roses burst round the window frame. Their leaves are dry and the outer petals are starting to crisp. They'd last out a few more weeks if someone bothered to water them.

I stand to leave the room but my legs won't move. I run my fingernail up and down the edge of the table, making a small dent in the wood where the Formica has come away and gritty bits of old food are stuck. I wish I had a time machine to take me back to one of those other meals, before all of this started.

'You could be in so much trouble, young lady.' Mum sniffs back her tears, takes another drag and stubs out the cigarette, but she doesn't turn from the window. She fills the sink with water and washing-up liquid, and clanks the plates and cutlery into the volcano of bubbles.

'I love him.' I say the words under my breath.

Mum swivels on the balls of her feet to face me, her face damp and red. Soap suds are on her hands and up her wrists.

'What did you say?'

'He said he loved me.'

'Love!' she shouts. 'What would you know about love? You're only fourteen.' Her head juts forward from her shoulders and she waves her hands in the air. White clumps of bubbles fly around the room; some land on my face. She screams and I'm glad the windows are shut, even though the room is hot and smells foodie. 'Look at yourself, Rachel. What do you see? I see a silly little girl flaunting herself in front of a grown man.'

'I didn't. I wouldn't have let him . . . I thought . . . I thought that's what I was meant to do.'

'Liar.' Her voice is getting louder. 'You're a liar!' I stare at the floor and mumble. Tears drop on to the lino.

'I only wanted—'

Mum flies at me and holds me by the shoulders, digging her fingernails into my skin. Her lips are shrivelled round her clenched teeth and her bottom jaw sticks out. She shakes me and my head bobbles back and forth on my neck until my brain goes fizzy. 'Wanted what?' she screams.

'A hug.'

'Liar. I bet you loved every minute of it. Don't tell me this wasn't your plan all along. You're jealous.'

My legs go weak and she pushes me away. 'Dear God!' She wipes her head with her forearm, leaving a line of suds on her hair. 'I don't know what we're going to do without your father's support. It's bad enough what you did, but why the hell did you have to tell him? You and your stupid letters. Did you think it would bring him back? Did you? Well, it won't. Your plan's backfired. He's disgusted with you. We're on our own now, Rachel, totally alone, thanks to you.'

I sink into my chair. I can't get enough air in my lungs.

'Now it's all down on paper; if anyone else finds out, you'll end up in prison. Peter is a policeman, he could lock you up and throw away the key. You'd be stuck in there with all those rapists and murderers, all those bad people like you.' I start to cry out loud. 'In fact,' she says, 'that's what you deserve. I rue the day I ever gave birth to you, you little demon. You're a thief and a liar.'

She grabs my hair. I scream and grapple at her hands as she pulls me out of the room, but she keeps on yanking and hauls me up the stairs, and I'm scared my hair's going to come out in a big lump. I stumble halfway up the staircase and she lets go and holds my arm instead, pulling me on to the landing and then into my bedroom, where she launches me towards my bed. I flop down and she slams the door behind her as she leaves the room.

Her footsteps clomp down the stairs, and when I hear the pans bashing in the sink in the kitchen, I get up and go over to the airing cupboard. Inside is the little chair that's too small for me now. I sit on it anyway, and my knees do a diagonal up towards my chin. On the back of the door is the padlock and hinge I bought from the hardware shop. I fitted it myself, sneaking Dad's screw-driver back into the shed before Mum saw. I lock up the cupboard and test the door – it's jammed shut. After a while I stop shaking and wipe my snot on my sleeve.

It's very dark in here, but the edges of the door make a square of daylight. On the floor is my biology textbook, my exercise book and also the torch I put in here earlier. I flick on the light to read about 'the bolus': 'A small rounded mass of a substance, esp. of chewed food at the moment of swallowing.' I have to put it into my own words, so I write: 'You chew and mix the food up in your mouth, then push the lump to the back with your tongue. Next, your oesophagus squeezes it down to the stomach where the acid breaks it down. It would even work if you stood on your head.'

My legs cramp. There isn't enough room to stretch out. When I was little I could squeeze behind the immersion tank, but once I got stuck and it took ages to get out. After that I put the chair in here and sometimes I fall asleep. I need a wee and I'm not sure how long I can hold it in, but mostly I worry about the supper I've eaten. I'll have to do more sit-ups tomorrow. From downstairs comes Mum's voice. She sounds like she's shouting through a pillow, but I can still make out what she's saying: 'You little bitch. I'll leave you and go on a long holiday, then you'll really be able to starve yourself to death. That's what you deserve.'

The outline of light round the door slowly disappears until there's nothing but black. The torch dims, then flickers, then goes out. It's so dark that I can't tell how far away the wall is, and I try to imagine I'm in a big room, but that makes me more scared so instead I put my hand flat on the wall in front of me and keep it there, holding myself up.

This must be like the prisons Peter talks about, where people who are liars, the ones who get other people into trouble, go to rot and die. No one ever knows what's happened to them. They disappear. Peter says the police can fix it so that whatever they say goes.

Everything is my fault anyway. If I concentrate hard enough I can make it like nothing ever happened.

21

A STRING OF STARS

Downstairs in the nursing home the trolley woman is talking to me, or at least her mouth is moving, but I can't decipher her words. On her third attempt she's tetchy and almost shouts, 'Do you want me to order a taxi?'

'No thanks,' I reply. 'I need to walk.'

Rush-hour traffic zooms past on the busy road as people return to homes and families and Christmas cheer. A damp dusk crowds the sky. I bend my head forward as if carving a route through the sea-steeped air. The smell reminds me of the last time I saw Will at the beach, and the same predictable ache twists in my gut. I've become strangely at home with this sole connection to Will, only now it's coupled with a hopelessness which gnaws even deeper, as if I'm being hollowed out from the inside.

Heading in the direction of the town and my B & B, I leave Peter behind, locked inside the walls of his decrepitude. My fingertips hold the slide of his loose skin, and I hug my dad's coat round me as I force my feet to move,

one in front of the other, to draw me into the meditation of walking, but my thoughts won't blank; a lid has
opened on the past. A tumble of images flicker through
my brain: Alex's calves pinched by the band of sock elastic, my colleagues' heads at the office bobbing above their
workstations, the brush of the old man's fingers in the car
park as he put the coat on my shoulders. The dead dog.
Seamus lying under wet leaves. Mum's sweaty face as she
stood over the washing-up. The taste of pipe tobacco in
my mouth.

My roll call of shame.

Echoes of memory bounce back and forth, but so
many at once it's impossible to lock on to any one. A car
beeps its horn and several others join in as a jam builds
up at a junction. The buzz of noise crowds the snapshots
in my head. The lid shuts.

A man in a ragged overcoat and oversized trainers
walks the crossing as the lights flash amber. The man's
pace is solid and relaxed, as if he has all the time in the
world. Even as the lights change to green for the traffic to
go, he ambles at his leisure before reaching the other side
and stepping on to the pavement. Waiting vehicles spin
their wheels to get away. One driver shouts from his
window, something I can't make out above the noise of
the traffic, but the man on the pavement takes no notice
and continues to walk at the same speed into the distance.
I run to catch him up, jamming my finger repeatedly into
the crossing button, but the signal phase takes too long
before I can cross, by which time he has disappeared.

It will take over an hour to walk back to the B & B, and I cut through the suburban outreaches of the city. Most houses have Christmas trees in their windows, and I picture a young Claire, like me, waiting for a Disney version of her father to walk through the door, full of apology and arms laden with presents. Claire's letter to her dad is hidden with the rest of Seamus's papers at Will's house, and if Will ever finds the correspondence he won't have a clue what any of it means. The police can't identify Seamus or trace his family without this information, and his daughter will for ever wonder what happened to her dad. I could turn myself in but then Will would be drawn into a mess he has nothing to do with, so it's better I remove the middle man and deal with this last piece of shame head-on.

There's a wall next to a big park. I sit. Detached houses circle the green, many with closed wrought-iron entrance gates leading on to a driveway where at least two cars are parked. The lights from all the entrance buzzers form a string of stars along the road. I take out my mobile and scroll through the numbers until I find 'Sister Williams' – I thought it would look as if I'd discovered the Lord if David found the number, and I hoped that in my current state of hysteria, David would believe I was capable of that.

A month ago, before I cut all ties with the office, I rang my contact at our debt-collection agency and asked Toby to put a trace on Claire. 'She was pretty easy to find,' he said when he phoned back. 'County Court judgement back in '92. Lives in Belfast, divorced and married a second time, three kids. Pay cheques go into her account from Tesco.' He sounded guarded, less friendly than the conversations I was used to – normally he'd have been breathless with the chase, so David must have got to him – but I'm glad he did me one last favour, and perhaps David is wrong; I do have some friends.

I dial 141 first so my number can't be traced, then put the call in to Claire. I get her answering machine. The message says: 'Hello, this is Claire, please leave your name and number after the beep.' It's the voice of a woman and it takes me a moment to connect her grown-up intonation with the image of the little girl in the photo. In the background of the recording is clattering and a baby crying. I don't leave a message but hang up and redial. On my third attempt she answers. I say nothing, but listen to her voice and the noises in the background: laughter, a TV up loud, children shouting. So different to my own life, so full. I want to sit with her on her sofa; we'd smoke cigarettes and laugh at the happy chaos around us. 'Who is this?' she says now. 'Tell me what you want or leave me alone.' My phone beeps with a low-battery warning – I'm so used to charging it in the car, I didn't think to pack my plug – and before the last bar of power disappears I hang up and copy the number on to the back of Claire's photo in my bag.

A few paces inside the park is a modern-style glass and metal phone box covered in graffiti. Its yellow glow is a beacon in the darkness. I walk towards it and open the door, avoiding the old spit on the handle. It's so long since I've used a public phone and the system has changed completely; I don't know where to start. From my purse I scoop a fistful of the coins that Alex scattered. Pounds and ten-pence pieces warm in my grip. I pick out and discard the coppers. A receiver hangs down vertically, not slung over the top like in the old days, and I lift it to my ear to hear the dialling tone; it's a relief the phone's still working and not been vandalized. Five pounds slide into the slot. I pause before dialling. This time I need to say something, but I've nothing prepared. Is it enough to listen to Claire again, the daughter of Seamus and living proof that he existed and he carries on? There's comfort in that alone.

I dial her mobile and this time I don't withhold the call-box number: now that I've heard her speak, I find I don't care any more if I'm discovered.

'Yes, hello?' Her voice is brusque and flustered.

'Hello,' I say, 'is this Claire Kenny?'

'Yes. Who is this?'

'Did you used to be Claire Williams?'

'Yes. Who wants to know?'

'I have some information about your father.'

'What?' The line crunches, as if she's changing hands, then her voice comes back clearer and more serious now. 'What information? Who are you?'

'I know where your father is.'

'My father?' Her voice crackles and becomes louder. 'How do you know my pa? That bastard's been gone for over thirty years. What makes you think I want to know where he is now?'

A pause.

'Hello?' she says. 'Are you still there? Who is this? Is this some kind of wind-up?'

'No, it's not.' I move the receiver to my other ear and take a breath. 'I'm sorry.'

'Look, who are you and what do you want?'

'I'm really sorry.' My voice breaks up. Words lurch and stutter. I hadn't expected this. 'It was an accident. I didn't mean for it to happen.' Not until we spoke did I realize what I was expecting. Resolution. Atonement. Forgiveness.

'An accident? What are you talking about, what's happened?'

'I don't know if I'll get another chance, but I wanted to tell you with my own words. I believe he was a good man.'

'If he thinks I'm coming to get him after all these years, then he's got another thing coming.' Her voice becomes cloudy, as if she's holding her hand over the receiver. 'Jesus, Paul,' I can make out, 'I've got some nutter on the phone, says she's got my dad. There's been some kind of accident.' I hear the man mumble, then she comes back on. 'Look, who are you? Where did you get my number?'

'I'm trying to tell you about your father. I know all about you, you wrote him letters, you had a cat called Mouse.'

'What the fuck is going on? How do you know that?'

'I know because I was with him at the end.'

'The end? What end?' she says. 'What are you telling me?' Then her voice is muffled again. 'Somebody help me here.' In the background something smashes and a child screams. 'Paul, get the police on the other line. No, do it fucking now!'

'No, please, don't waste your time,' I manage to say. 'They can't do anything, and I want to explain. I know what you've been through, I know what it's like to lose your father, but I believe he had his reasons. If you could see what I saw.'

Claire is shouting. 'You let me talk to him. You put my pa on the phone.' She's ranting, probably not listening, so I raise my voice.

'I'm really sorry. It was all my fault but I didn't mean to do it. He was just there on the road when I came round the corner.'

'What road, for Christ's sake?' Claire cries. 'Is he dead, is that what you're saying? Tell me what you've done to him!'

'Yes, he is. I'm sorry. He's dead.'

'Dear God.' Her voice becomes distant. Silence. Crackling, then sobs. A man asks her what's the matter. 'Leave me alone,' she says.

'Are you there?' I say. 'Can you hear me? I want to tell you I'm sorry, for everything. Please, forgive me.'

Back on the line now, and full volume. 'What did you say?' She's screaming and I have to hold the receiver away from my ear. 'You fucking bitch. Who are you to bring him back into my life after all these years, you have no idea. And with this! You ask for my forgiveness? How dare you! You deserve nothing.'

A man comes on the line. 'Leave my wife alone, do you hear? We've got your number and we've called the police.'

I bang down the phone. The receiver clangs on its support and the sound holds in the air like a tuning fork, then softens and blends into the silence of the night. I think of Claire and her husband left in their own noise and confusion, in another room across a sea. I pick up the receiver to call again, but I've said all I need to say so put the phone back on its cradle, softly this time.

As I leave the phone box, the door squeaks and thumps shut behind me. Cold oxygen fills my lungs. I inhale and exhale fast and loud, and do it over and again until I'm dizzy.

Behind me the phone in the box rings and I jump. It must be Claire. Or the police. I turn and stare at the receiver as if I can will it to stop, but it doesn't. The chrome and glass of the shelter chops the reflection of the trees into disjointed fingers, and a just-risen moon stretches round the contours of the metal. I walk into the big city park with a slow steady pace and listen to the phone drill behind me. It stops then starts again. The park is the kind of place where it's unsafe for a woman to be on her own at night. Trees lock round dark shadows. Leaves rustle. A swing in the children's playground squeaks with the ghost of the wind.

Time has been coming for me, always, trucking forward, and I've been fooling myself I could outrun it by hiding behind an upstanding life. And now the time has come to let go, it's a relief. There are no more decisions to make, and nothing else I can do to make anything right. I sense a large animal hidden in the undergrowth, pacing alongside me. Its eyes flash as if caught by the headlights of a car. Inside my pocket my fingers find a piece of Seamus's miniature skeleton.

In the distance the phone stops ringing. The clouds have cleared and the air chills. Two stars puncture the night. Later the sky will burst.

22

GRAVEL

There's only one thing I need from the B & B: David's ledger. It's already in a brown envelope, and I scribble Will's address on the front and post it from outside the hotel before I head towards the Downs. By car or bus it's a fair journey home, but I choose to walk the rest of the way. As I leave the city I look down from the hills on to the thousands of lights, each one a person in a room congealed into their daily routines. Rustles and squawks in the trees next to the road keep me company, and I decipher the night-time language: the quest for food and the defence of territories. Light footfalls crunch in the undergrowth as the creature from the park parallels me along the road.

About twenty minutes into my journey and the nightly bus I could have caught home if I'd waited passes me by. There's no pavement here, and the tube of tungsten swerves into the road to avoid me, blaring its horn. All around, the night erupts. There's not a single passenger on the bus, and from behind as I watch the vehicle recede into the night, it appears as if there's no driver either.

I'd made a pact with myself and thought I'd left David for good, but my only other option is the police, and prison seems pedestrian compared to what I have coming. Whatever David has in store for me will be worse than anything I can do to myself. Even so, as long as I keep moving the fantasy of escape still exists, and finally I understand Seamus's attempts to obliterate the insistent memory of family by putting one foot in front of the other. There's still some gin left in the bottle in my bag. I go to take a swig but can't face it, and throw the bottle into the hedgerow. My stomach grumbles but it doesn't matter; I'm cold but it doesn't matter. I pass through villages and back out into the countryside, mapping in my mind the islands of towns and the strings of access that tie them all together: Maudlyn Lane, Shooting Fields, Chanctonbury Ring, Spithandle Lane. I stop for a while next to a sand quarry of such enormous scale it looks as if the devil has dug his giant hand into the hillside and scooped out the earth.

From the barbed-wire perimeter the quarry stretches forward a mile or so and, even in this light, the earth is streaked with layers of sediment, like dirty gold set down by a prehistoric river. I squat there to piss. Steam lifts from my urine; my skin is ice but inside I'm still full of heat.

The moon is high, diminished in size now by the expanding miles of black sky. When a car passes I hide in the undergrowth, though for most of the way the roads are quiet. In the distance I hear a motorbike zipping through the gears, and a recollection from school days comes, of Mike giving me a ride home on the back of his bike – a noisy 50cc bullet. He'd followed me from the school gates until I agreed to get on. The faster he went, the harder I had to hug into him, and he approached a blind summit with such speed that we flew from its peak. At the moment of impact, when the wheels landed with a skid, I remember thinking, 'This is it, the end of my life,' and the finality was a relief because after that I wouldn't have to think about dying any more.

My legs are weak, my feet sore, and from here on the rest of my journey home is a slow surrender. It takes me several hours to reach our gates, by which time it must be at least midnight. On the road near our entrance, a crappy car is parked half-on, half-off the grass verge. David will be cross if it leaves tyre marks. He'll prob- ably line the verge with wooden posts to claw back these inches of territory.

Normally I'd use a fob to open the gates, but without my keys I have to use the keypad. The motor clunks into action and the gates pull open on to our gravel drive, lit silver. Trees are cut-outs against a backdrop of stars, and the ground is flecked with the black magic of frost. As I walk through, the gates buzz shut behind me. A light from the house filters through the bushes. It switches off. The bulbs on the gateposts extinguish. Darkness, lit only by the lamp of the moon. Skin the shade of death.

I approach the house where the twin beasts of mine and David's cars are parked with their eyes facing forward. I touch the bonnet of my car, remembering the thrill of the engine singing, changing down the gears for control round a corner, but always keeping the speed as high as possible as I explored roads and cut-throughs, getting lost, finding my way, creating an ever-wider map of the countryside in my head. My car was built to be driven this way, and I miss the times before the accident when I used to drive carefree as routine, racing forward, hoping somehow to speed into the future and leave myself behind.

A noise: the rub of the front door opening, but all I see is black. A few feet from the house, and a figure steps into the wash of the moon. The shape, the walk – it's David. But then who else did I think it would be?

His feet crush a beat in the gravel and his frame veers towards me. We face each other across the bonnet of my car. He opens the passenger door and gets in, into my private space. The vehicle rocks gently with his weight. He leans across and opens the driver's door.

'Get in,' he says. And I do.

We stare at each other. Moonlight catches the liquid in David's eyes. Moments ago I was on the open road, I was safe, I still had a choice. Or did I? Have I ever had options or was it always leading to this? Somewhere in my mind I knew the ending, as if time had made a contract with me, and I should have cut out the middle years and been done with it.

'I knew you'd come home,' David says.

He snatches my bag from me, opens and inverts it, and sprays the contents over his lap. Coins clatter to the floor. My wedding ring spins for a second on the dashboard then drops. Claire's picture slides through a gap in the seats. We both scrabble for the photo, but David gets it first and holds it away from me as I reach for him. He pushes me with his free hand back into my seat as he squints at the picture, flipping the paper over a couple of times. Then as I lunge at him, the gear stick jabbing in my hip, he rips her down the middle, then in half again. I'm on top of him trying to grab the picture and I swipe his face, but the photo is already in pieces. David throws the confetti to the ground and grabs my wrists so tight that my hands fizz, and he shoves me back in my seat. My shoulder slams against the door and my arms go limp. Blood sparkles back through to my fingers when he lets go.

He points at me. 'Don't. You. Move.' A fleck of his spit lands in my eye.

I freeze as he wipes his face with the back of his hand. The blood on his cheek smears black. From his pocket he takes a tissue and wets it with his mouth then dabs his cheek, flicking down the sun visor to check the cut in the mirror. A small light comes on and yellows his skin. His eyes flit between me and his reflection. When the scratch is cleaned, he pats the visor back up to the ceiling and rounds his gaze to me. Once again we are moonlit.

The contents of my bag lie at his feet. He catches my

glance and follows it to the watch. He leans forward and picks it up, then brings it slowly to the middle of the space between us.

I shoot towards him but he's prepared this time, and before I reach the watch, he holds his hand up flat and pushes me back in my seat. With his other hand he smashes the face of the watch on the dashboard. The glass shatters. 'Enough,' he says, 'I've had enough.' He throws the broken pieces at me and an edge of metal cuts my forehead. 'All this junk!' He holds his hands up and shakes his head. 'I don't know what any of it means, but I'll bet most of it's got something to do with that fucking tramp.' I grab the remains of broken cogs from the floor and hold them tight. 'I know you got a number from Toby,' he says, and he nods at the pieces of the photo scattered on the floor. 'Who was she anyway? Have you called her yet? Does she know where you are?'

I don't reply, but stare at him, trying not to cry.

David sits back and breathes deeply for several seconds, smoothing down his jacket, patting his hair, composing himself as he would for a client, making sure all outward signs of battle are concealed. If nothing else, it's good to see that I've rattled him. David touches the scratch on his cheek. The blood is nearly dry but a piece of the tissue has stuck to his face, as if he's had a shaving accident. He picks the paper off and flicks it to the floor.

'The police called round,' he says, taking a few breaths before he's fully calm. 'They've found paint chippings on the dead man's clothes. The paint is from a car, the same make and colour as yours. They're questioning everyone in the area who owns or has owned one.' He angles his body directly at me and the car see-saws. 'It'll take a while to whittle it down, and even though we reported yours stolen, they'll need more information about where you left the car. They'll be searching CCTV footage of the area now too, but the state you're in you'll confess at the first opportunity. And then what else will you tell them? What other little revelations do you have up your sleeve? About me and the business? I'm sure you know less than you think, but I'm not going to take any chances.'

I breathe in short, shallow bursts. 'Then you need me more than I need you.'

David laughs. Watching him, I sense that this is his biggest performance to date, and without the satisfaction of having me at home he's been psyching up and rehearsing for days, testing his bad-guy-with-a-heart in front of the mirror.

'I don't care what you've done, Rachel, but I do care about the business. I won't jeopardize everything for some tiny incident you've managed to turn into a bloody catastrophe. Nobody gives a shit about that man, he was a drunk and a loser, but you've chased it and chased it. I don't know what you were trying to dig up but now this problem won't go away. All you had to do was lie, Rachel. I'm not going to get caught up in your mess any more.'

I grip the door handle. If I'm quick, I could run across the lawn and into the trees, but I know he's faster than me.

He reaches over and holds my free hand, pressing my palm into the seat with his meaty fingers.

'What do you want me to do?' I say.

He clears his throat and presses harder. 'There's nothing you can do.' With his other hand he rubs my arm, his movements exaggerated as if they've been prepared, and I wonder for whose benefit this little scene is being played. His skin is rough and in the corner of his mouth a nerve twitches.

Inside the car it's as freezing as outside, the day's scant heat streaming into a cloudless sky. A snap of twigs comes from the bushes, an animal probably changing its perch. I look at David and he's still smiling, as if he's experiencing pity and kindness at the same time, the same expression he uses when he clinches a deal; the generous and caring benefactor, the man who saved me from my student squalor and tolerated my chaos as long as I toed the line: that I satisfied only him and presented well.

'Why not?'

'Because,' he lets go of my hand and sits up, 'you've finally lost your mind.' He shakes his head from side to side as he turns to look at me. 'Alex told me about your little adventures in car parks. Can you imagine how embarrassing that was for me, and for him? I'm in business with the man, I don't need your personal life wrecking that as well. Good God, Rachel! What were you thinking?' With one hand he smoothes a strand of his hair that's flopped forward, and he stares into the distance. 'I can't have you in the office any more, and I don't want you in the house, let alone my bed.'

Awkwardly he stretches his body across the space between us and presses his mouth hard on mine until it hurts, then he parts his lips and holds my bottom lip with his teeth. He bites. A rush of hot iron in my mouth. I cry out and push him away. My blood's on his lip also. He spits in disgust.

'We used to be such a great team.' He wipes his mouth with the dirty tissue. 'But no one is irreplaceable.'

With the same tissue, he dabs my face. The paper is tacky.

'When they come looking for you,' he says, 'I'll say you lost it, you upped and went. There's no reason not to believe me. I haven't left a trail. Unlike you.'

He reaches over with both hands and prises my fingers from the watch. I fight back, but he's stronger than me and he almost gets it but suddenly he stops, as if he can't be bothered any more.

'Keep it,' he says. 'You won't be needing it where you're going anyway.'

And with that he gets out of the car, bending down one last time to peer at me through the open door.

'I'm not jealous, Rachel,' he says as he picks up my wedding ring from the floor and tucks it in his pocket. 'Because it's not love, it never was. You and me, we were just business.'

He turns and walks to the house, leaving the car door open.

'David!' I shout to him.

He stops. 'What?'

'This isn't over.'

He calls over his shoulder, 'Nothing you do or say can touch me any more, Rachel.' And he walks away.

Two figures stride from the shadows, one round to the passenger door to block my escape and the other man to where I'm sitting. One of them opens my door and hauls me out by my elbow. Smell of his breath. Face close. I know him. It's Will. I open my mouth but already his fist sling-shots forward and cracks my cheekbone, slamming me to the ground.

'For Christ's sake!' I hear David's voice. 'You idiots. Not here. Do it somewhere else. And make sure you clean up afterwards.'

Gravel sticks to my face, and from where I lie my blurred eyes see underneath the car to the house. David opens the front door and turns on the hallway light. Three amber rectangles stretch across the driveway: one shape is the light through the open front door and the other two are from the glass panels at either side. The middle oblong narrows to black.

I am lifted up. One of the men holds me across my chest and the other grabs my feet, but I can't tell which is Will any more. I try to speak but there's a hand over my mouth. Blood washes my face and eyes. Head like soup. The boot opens and the men fumble with something inside, then they slide me in and shut the hatch. I lie on plastic; I am a thing to be tidied away, bleached clean like a germ. The plastic is cool and crinkles under my body. Pieces of gravel have stuck to my clothes and they jab into my skin. I try to brush them from under my legs but there's no room to move. Then the engine rumbles. I roll forward on to my face with a crunch of bone. Backwards, forwards, lolling onwards. A hot liquid spreads between my legs.

My thoughts flicker on and off, frames of time stutter and break, and then I wake again to carbon-black, my body rocking, and I think for a while I'm in a bunk on a train. There's a dog in here with me, its dirty paws are on my school skirt. I try to shout but it's a whisper. Then I'm at Mum's house in a cupboard and it's locked. I've been in here for a long time and I don't want to come out. There's a sharp pain in my thigh, and I remember when I came home earlier, Mike's motorbike was in our drive-way, parked where Peter used to leave his car before he stopped coming to visit. I walked round to the back of the house and found Mike in the kitchen, bending down by the open fridge. When he saw me he stood up, but he wasn't surprised or embarrassed even though he was in my house without being invited. His chest was bare and his jeans were undone showing the top of his Y-fronts, and he was holding a pint of milk. I opened my mouth to talk but no words came. Instead I half smiled, thinking that in a minute he'd let me in on the joke. He pressed the foil lid into the bottle and dug his middle finger into the cream, then put the creamy plug of his finger in his mouth and sucked. After that he swigged the whole pint from the bottle. Little streams of white ran down his chin and spotted the floor. When he finished he left the bottle on the side. A fly buzzed round the top. Mike walked from the kitchen and up the stairs. I followed. Mum's bedroom door was open. He went into her room and sat on her bed with his back to me. Mum was facing the door and lay naked on her stomach on top of the sheets. On her windowsill was a pot of yellow chrysanthemums, smelling hot and syrupy in the sunshine. She held the bald stem of one of the flowers in her hand, then chucked it to one side on top of all the petals she'd already pulled off, like a game of 'He loves me, he loves me not'. She said, 'What's the matter, Rachel?' lifting herself up on to her elbows to light a cigarette. 'Cat got your tongue?' The ends of her fingers were stained blue and her breasts stretched down so that her nipples brushed the covers. I ran to my room, hid in the cupboard and put the padlock on. Mum had thrown my schoolbooks inside and all of Dad's letters and pens, plus some toys I'd kept from when I was younger. There were splodges of ink all over my stuff and on the carpet where Mum must have squeezed out the cartridges. I tried not to think about what she was doing with Mike in the other room, and I knew if I told anyone they'd never believe me. There'd be more lies to tell, one heaped on top of the other until I couldn't remember what was at the bottom any more. I didn't know if Mike would still expect me to ride home with him after school, or if he'd try to kiss me still. I picked up one of Dad's fountain pens. The nib curved into a sleek point as if it had been sharpened with a Stanley knife. I pressed the metal tip on my thigh. It sunk like a slippery fish deep into my leg.

The car passes over bumps in the road and the pain jolts me awake. I open and shut my eyes several times but it's as dark both ways. From somewhere near there's a red glow from the tail lights, and I try to kick them out but I've no strength in my legs.

Again sleep comes, no choice, less like rest, more of a black hole, as if I'm sliding down a mountainside of scree.

Blank it out, turn off my thoughts, bury them.

23

A FRAGMENT OF TIME

Voices wake me – Will and the other man – bartering.

Will says, 'Let me do it. You can keep your share but I want to finish the job.'

The other man says, 'I don't care, do what you want. Easier for me this way. What you got against her anyway?'

'Nothing.'

'Just like it, eh?'

'Yeah.'

'Please yourself.'

'I will.'

The other man laughs and I hear a door shut and a car drive away.

The boot is cold and my wet trousers cling-film to my legs. Underneath me the plastic sheet puckers as I feel around the space for something to use as a weapon, something I can swing at Will when he opens the boot. At his head or balls? I try to remember which is more effective, but I'll make it worse if I miss. My freezing fingers find nothing hard or long or heavy. Only fluff and bags. A pair of walking shoes. Dry mud crumbles under my nails.

I wait for Will to come, for the boot to lift open and his hands to pounce. My teeth and nails are ready. Fear bends seconds into eternity. And then the car starts again and we are driving. Disappointment. That I have to wait longer, that it's not yet over. Waiting for the inevitable.

The journey stretches across continents of time, only the noise of the engine and exhaust fumes, cold, some shivers of sleep, then a dawn of sorts, edges of light fingering the gaps through which my body can't pass. Gulls screeching. The car stops. Footsteps pace round the car. Silence. Click of the boot. Open, and Will's head bursting through an electric sky. I beetle into the farthest crevice but it's not far enough, and there's nowhere else to go.

God, let it happen. Be done with it.

His hands stretch in. 'Shh,' he says, 'it's OK.' My body is rigid, flesh and muscles nearly dead. Will's fingers are strong and warm, but he can't grasp the rock of my body.

'I'm not going to hurt you again,' he says. 'I promise.'

He grips my clothes, pulls, and I slide across the plastic, my broken face bumping objects hidden underneath. Nerve endings sense pain but it's distant, then Will's arms grab round me and he heaves me out and sits me on the ground next to the car.

I am solid. Then I shake and shake like I'll shatter.

Will takes off his coat and wraps it over the top of my

dad's, the layers heavy. The material falls and he crouches at my side, picks it up and lays the coat once again over my back. His face is close to mine now. 'I'm sorry I hit you,' he says. 'It was the only way they'd believe me. And I had to stop you from saying my name.' He looks left and right, then back at me. 'David doesn't know about us, do you understand? Not everyone's come out of this alive. Let's not give them any more fuck-ups.'

I can hear his words, but I don't understand them. Will stands. I flinch and cover my head with my hands. He scans the countryside, then relaxes down beside me again. I shiver and he holds the tops of my arms to steady me.

'Rachel,' he says, turning my chin gently and forcing me to look into his face. A shard of pain shoots through my jaw and I wince. 'Oh God, I'm sorry.' He lets go and takes a breath. 'Please understand, I'm trying to help you.' My eyes dart in all directions, but in the end there's nowhere else for them to rest apart from on Will. 'You have to trust me,' he says. 'We haven't got much time. This is it for you as far as David's concerned. I'm only here because I move in the wrong circles.' He sits next to me, but not so close that we touch, and he stares into the middle distance. 'I was so angry with you, Rachel. But I'd never . . .' He puts his head in his hands, and I can hear his heavy breathing behind his arms. Then he stands with a sudden energy and kicks the car. The door dents. He strides up the beach, taking a moment before coming back and standing in front of me. 'Look, I never wanted you dead, all right? I wouldn't go that far. I'm sorry I didn't help you when you asked me. But you really fucked with my head.'

Everything on my body shakes like it's minus forty.

'We haven't got time for this. If I'm gone too long, they'll know something's up.' He paces in front of me. 'They're waiting for me to get back with your car so they can get rid of it.' He leans down and tries to pull me up by my arm. 'Come on, Rachel, for God's sake, you've got to help me. You need to pull yourself together.'

He locks his arms round me to pull me up. His coat falls off my back, and his breath is damp and warm on my cheek. As soon as I'm standing he releases me again and looks away. His voice is small. 'I've never hit a woman before.' He sniffs and wipes his nose on the back of his hand. 'Jesus, Rachel, when will you learn that it's not all about you? How many more people have to get hurt before you get it together?'

My legs buckle beneath me and Will lunges forward. As he grabs me, I fling my arms round him and hold on tight. Will lowers his arms and they swing loose at his sides. We stand like this for a minute and for the first time I look over his shoulder to see where we are. It's the coast, a small bay. A few boats wobble on the water in the milky dawn. In the distance two spits of land curve round the water holding in the sea, and through the gap in the middle the horizon folds up into the sky: degrees of grey, ocean and ether one entity.

Will sighs, puts his hands under my armpits and

stands me apart from him, balancing me like a broken toy before he lets go and I'm standing on my own. He nods towards one of the boats: a small fishing vessel about thirty foot long, grubby, no sails, a cabin on top. A man stands on the deck and stares at us. Water fizzes at the back of the boat where the engine churns the water.

'John will take you across the Channel to Ireland, Wexford, or a beach thereabouts, but as close as possible to a town without you being seen.' Will looks back to me and stammers. 'When you get to the coast you'll have to lie low for a bit before you can get off, and when it's safe John'll take you to shore in the tender.'

My eyebrows drag into a frown and Will understands my question without me asking.

'It's a dinghy. You can't take a boat this big up to the shore. And you won't need a passport, no one will be checking where you're going, not that it's much of an issue if it's in a small port either, but just to be sure.'

'I'm scared,' I say, my voice rusty after such a long pause. 'I don't want to go.'

'Well, you've got no choice. You can trust John, he's family.'

'How do I know he'll get me there? He could do anything to me out on the sea and no one would know.'

'Rachel,' Will says, staring at me directly, 'if I wanted to kill you I'd have done it by now.'

A peep of sun rises over the horizon, and the man on the boat revs the engine. I wonder if John is the family Will has been looking for.

'Come with me,' I say.

'I can't.'

'Please.'

Will's face reddens. 'Look,' he raises his voice, 'you're taking the piss. If I don't go back they'll know something's up, then they'll really come looking for you, and I don't know if I can protect you again. This is the best I can do. If you think what I did was bad, you wait to see what other psychos David's got waiting in the wings. He can afford to do what he wants.'

'We could disappear, like you always said.'

'It's too late, Rachel. You can't keep playing me like this.'

'I'm not playing you any more. And I'm sorry. For everything.'

'No you're not.'

'Yes I am.' I shake again, but this time it's with anger, not fear, and I'm shouting. Will looks around and shushes me. My voice doesn't sound like my own, but the words keep rolling out. 'I didn't want things to turn out like this, I had no choice in the matter. Everything was taken away from me, years ago. You have no idea. Since then, all my life I've been treading water.'

'All right, all right. Keep your hair on.' Will flaps his hands at me. 'This isn't the time or the place.' His eyes are wide and they sparkle. 'You have been such a bitch to me, Rachel, and still you think I owe you something. Like I said before, I am done. This is as good as it gets, my parting gift to you. You have to go now or you're putting us both in danger.'

'Well, this is my choice now,' I say, my voice quieter, 'the first I've ever had, and I want you to come with me.'

'No.'

'As long as you understand, that what I want is you.'

Will scuffs at the dusty pebbles but won't look at me. 'It's time,' he says, and walks to the boat, stopping halfway when I don't follow.

The sun lifts higher and bleaches through the mist. I look directly at the light and my eyes go water blind until they hurt and I shut them. Bright memory spots of sun morph like hot oil under my eyelids then disappear. Yesterday was the shortest day of the year. From now on each day will accrue a fraction more light. As I open my eyes my vision clears and I step forward, then stride past Will to the shoreline. The man has left the fishing boat and is rowing a small dinghy towards us.

'You'll need this,' Will says, catching me up and stuffing an envelope in my pocket. 'It won't last for ever, but it'll keep you going for a while. Get you set up.'

I look down at the wedge of notes inside the envelope, all used fifties and twenties. The package sits in my pocket on top of the few small bones I'd picked up outside Seamus's caravan, and to one side is the crumpled flower from Peter's room. All the petals have come off. The stalk is mushed to brown with only the old seed head left on top.

Gulls circle and screech overhead.

'You can't come back, Rachel,' Will says as he tucks my coat pocket shut. 'Do you understand? David thinks you're dead. If he knows you're still alive, he will find you and kill you. He'll come for me too.'

I look directly at him: the whites of his eyes are stained red, and the features of a gentle boy are almost lost underneath his worn complexion. How different it could have been for him if he'd had a better start, if he'd had the safety nets he needed along the way.

'I'm sorry it has to be this way,' he says.

'It's not your fault. And it's not mine either.'

I have a sense of falling as the scaffolding drops away. My constructs crumble. Without the poisonous repetition of lies and blame, all that's left is a small point, dense with sweet and painful memory. I step inside my bones. I fill them, and I rise.

Will opens his mouth to say something, but no words come. He closes his lips tight. I move to him and lean my body on to his chest with my eyes shut. Rain dusts my face, the drops fresh and light. I reach a circle round his back and pull in tight. He pauses for a moment, then folds me in his arms. The warmth of him seeps into my skin.

No conditions in this moment, nothing hinged that will break off and cause an avalanche. Only this fragment of time exists. Pure. Like no other I have had. Time will move forward, but these seconds will always have been.

A scraping noise. I lift my head to see John pulling the small boat on to the shingle. Waves lap the rubber sides of the dinghy and the man stands in the water with rolled-up trousers jammed at his fat calves.

Will and I pull apart. From his pocket he takes a small pair of scissors. I flinch. 'For your hair,' he says. 'I need something to give to David. I'm sorry, I don't know what else to take.'

I grab the scissors and cut tiny clumps of hair, some of it matted with blood, but the scissors are small and blunt so I give up after a while.

'How do I look?' I smile, knowing it must be bad.

He holds me in his gaze before answering. 'You look fine. You look like you.'

I hand the tufts to Will and he stuffs them in his pocket, then I give him Seamus's broken watch.

'David knows I'd never part with this.' I close Will's fingers over the pieces of metal and glass.

As soon as I climb into the dinghy, John pushes us out into the small waves. He leaps on board leaving Will on the shore with inches of water sloshing round his trousers and shoes. The beach recedes.

'I need your phone, throw it to me,' Will calls. 'He can trace you through your phone.'

I dip my hand into my pocket and throw the phone to Will, watching him bend into the shallow waves to retrieve it.

'Sorry,' I shout.

He laughs, dripping wet. 'It's OK, I forgive you.'

It takes less than a minute to get to the fishing boat, and John helps me on board before securing the smaller vessel to the back. He gives me a blanket and pours me coffee from a flask. Hot sweet liquid spreads through the sponge of my chest, and the pain that's travelled round my body for months begins a slow trickle away from my gut. A radio in the cockpit crackles a carol, then a mono-tone voice echoes a prayer.

'There's a bit of room down there,' John says, sig-nalling to a space through a hatch. It looks cosy, and I imagine lying down and rocking with the waves into a deep sleep with the hatch shut, like a cat who's found a safe place. 'There's a bowl and a couple of bottles of water if you want to get cleaned up.' He lifts the furred anchor and makes his way to the wheel, revving the boat with a judder. I stand. The boat moves out into the sea. I lurch and sit again, watching the shoreline drift and bob.

Will's figure is a silent pillar on the beach. He stands for a few minutes, then turns and walks to my car. The vehicle doesn't start immediately. I measure the land between my finger and thumb, and it's an inch high before the dot of my car twists in a circle and pulls away from the beach.

24

HOPE IS ENOUGH

No one asked many questions when I arrived in Ireland a little under six months ago, they knew better than to pry into the life of a windswept woman with cuts on her face. My appearance told all the stories they needed to know – a bad marriage, abuse, violence – and though dramatic, my situation was not unique; how many women are squirrelled away in desperate homes. No one needed to know how deep my own story went, but if anyone did ask, I simply moved on to another B & B or cheap hotel. By the time I found this house, my face had healed. There's a light scar on my lower lip, but over time it's fading.

The room I've taken is small; it's all I want and all I need. It was luck really that found this place: the village across an ocean hundreds of miles from where I know, a notice in a post-office window and an elderly woman who needed help. Sarah gives me a little extra on top of my room and board. There's no tax to pay, no National Insurance. No references needed.

Sarah lives in a two-bedroom cottage on the edge of farmland, built for farmhands, and she worked in the dairy all her life. After her husband died, the farmer let her stay on. She was two steps away from ending her days in a care home when she found me. Or rather, I found her. I beat her door down with kindness, knowing that this was the gift I'd been looking for. Sarah must have recognized the weary traveller in me and decided she would let me stay. I cook, clean, give her a weekly bath, and in return she asks no questions. Between us is the unspoken contract that our histories cannot be simplified into conversation. I've settled into this new-found freedom called anonymity. I am safe. And I've finally put my pin on the map.

It took me a couple of months before I had the courage to write to Claire. The letter I eventually sent was anonymous, and I explained I was in an exile of sorts, a fitting banishment for my crime. I told her how sorry I was, not only for the accident, but for the way in which I'd delivered the news on the phone that day. 'I was not in my right mind,' I wrote. I informed her of the town where they'd been holding Seamus's body, so she'd have been able to mark his grave by now, to release him from conjecture – my own as much as everyone else's – and return him to the ground. Let nature take its course. For a man who left his family for no good reason, that was the best I could do.

From the back window of Sarah's cottage we look out over a new estate of houses set round a crescent. Children cycle the pavements, their calls reaching high over the rooftops, and cars come and go in the mornings like busy insects. The farmer has sold off one corner of a field, but more land is set to go, and the beginning of another street is already laid; a runway through the grass that leads nowhere. Soon the low hedge round our back garden won't be enough to keep us private, and we'll have to put up a fence. Or perhaps I'll be forced to embrace community and discover that it's not so bad after all.

Each day when I've finished my chores and set Sarah up in front of the TV, I put on boots and my dad's old coat and walk into the hills. All those years I've spent locked inside watching the filthy weather, and it's never as bad when you finally get out. Sometimes I bus part of the way, but if I plan the route properly I can walk a decent stretch of the journey and make it back in time for supper. I've gained a good knowledge of the local landscape, so the challenge is always to go deeper, to find lost tracks and quiet hills. There I can witness the eloquence of the hidden world: snake lines of birds flipping and curving in the sky, cloud-shadows skating down a hillside, fat blades of grass luminescent with the sun on their backs. One day I came across the perfectly preserved skull of a rabbit. It was bleached clean and lay under a hedge, almost as if it had been placed there as a gift, but I didn't take it home. I have no use for dead things.

About once a week I take the bus to the next big town to do the food shopping, and while I'm there I book out the computer in the library to spy on David. I know all the passwords he used to use, and I'm relieved that he must truly believe I'm dead because the passwords are all the same: Portia; Petra; Rellet, which is Teller spelt backwards. He still uses the date of our wedding as one of the access codes, but I'm sure this is more out of habit than sentimentality; he never did have much of an imagination. Like air traffic control, I've locked on to the coordinates of his many online accounts and I am guiding him down to land. 'I see you, David.' He thinks he's flying to the Caribbean but when he descends through the layer of clouds he'll find he's not even left the airport. I stalk the numbers on the screen as they change weekly, the money filtering through the accounts, in and out of different countries, and I print off as much as I can. If I am able, I forward statements to my private email where I still hold the photos of David taking drugs. The embarrassment David will suffer from this outing of his petty habit will be worse than his shame over the conviction for fraud that's coming his way. And then, of course, there's the greater damnation of the ledger I posted to Will. Names, dates and amounts it won't be hard for the police to decipher, and which will put David away for longer than a bit of money laundering. I trust Will to guard these accounts until the time is right, but I can't act or ask anything of him until I know he is safe. Of all things, I wish Will safe.

I regularly check the feed of local news from where I used to live. Thankfully, Tyrone's conviction for dealing didn't stick, so already the police must have an inclination that something is amiss. And a pair of rare breeding birds have been discovered in the woods, forcing Alex's development to be put on hold, again. I like to think the animals are tucked into the branches of one of Seamus's trees, and the group of activists have ringed the nest with their camp. Alex will be furious at another obstacle to his family's onslaught on that land, and my plan is to get the incriminating evidence to the police before the chicks have left the roost. I wonder how long it will take for roots to break through the concrete that's already been laid, and for weeds to colonize the low walls of Alex and David's dream. Two men felled with one stone. Return the woods to Seamus. I owe him that at least.

Sarah is dozing in the other room in front of the white noise of the TV. Soon it will be time for her evening meal. As always, it's hard to draw the curtains against the outside. Through the window a light rain fluffs the air. I want the drops to fall on my face as they did at the bay with Will. Every time I remember those few seconds we shared, the moment comes back as an ecstasy of feeling. I would give everything to be at the source again.

Since I've been away, every few weeks I've sent Will an anonymous postcard, and on each one I've written a small part of my address buried in the text. First I sent the house name; next was half the street. Soon I'll send the town cut up across a couple of cards, then the postcode divided into digits. Not too much information at once – just in case he's being watched – but enough so he can piece the address together one day and come and find me.

If he wants to. Please let him want to.

On each postcard I place the stamp at a right angle next to his surname. The Victorians used this as code for words that were forbidden. The position and angle of my stamp means 'I am longing for you'. I've rehearsed the stolen phrase as a whisper. If I meet Will again, when I do, I will say it in my own words. After that I'll tell him the rest: how, when I arrived on this island and stopped searching for a place I couldn't name, what followed was a rushing backdraught to my former self, a refuge, where I am learning to be tender towards imperfection. For who are we if not the sum of our experience? We can choose what face to show the world, but there is only one face we can show ourselves. Seamus walked in incessant circles, and each evening he wound up as the same lonely old man.

A fighter jet thunders overhead. The plane's roar mutes all other sound for seconds after it's passed, then piece by piece life trickles back in: the canned laughter from the TV in the other room, a car driving into the distance, the fairy-tap of raindrops on the glass.

At any point I can choose to leave this place and enter the day, and all the days that follow. Time lays itself open in front of me. The future is a bold new country.

ACKNOWLEDGEMENTS

Huge thanks to my agent, Sue Armstrong, for her passion and guidance, and to my editor, Sophie Orme, for her kindness, and whose great insight has honed my words. Thank you to Maria Rejt for being a believer, and to all at Mantle and Pan Macmillan for their continued support and enthusiasm.

Eternal thanks to Kathy Andrew, Jacqui Burns, Laura Darling, Rosalind De-Ath, Glenys Jacques, Dionne McCulloch and Kate Wesson; my comrades in words. This book would never have made it past the first draft without your motivation, persistence and fine tuning.

Susannah Waters and Catherine Smith, most excellent tutors on the Creative Writing Programme, thank you for your continued guidance and encouragement.

Thanks to Phil Brigly, Mark Brown, Elizabeth Davidson, Dr Sam Fraser, Shawn Katz, Detective Constable Brad Lozynski, Julian Male, Rob Stapleton, Graham Tyler and Nick Watts, who answered my questions with patience and wisdom. All errors are my own.

To my mum and mad – Jean and Terry – who were as surprised as I that there was a book in me. Thank you for never telling me what to think, and for keeping the faith with an endless supply of chicken soup and childcare. To Ben and Luke, dear brothers, thank you for being at my side and teaching me the power of the gentle man. And to great-grandfather Charlie H – the bloodline continues!

ACKNOWLEDGEMENTS

To Bea and Billy. You are brilliant; you rock my world. Thank you for being so happy for me, and for your enthusiasm always to eat pizza.

And to Rob – *amore mio* – for love, support, friendship and jokes. Thank you for creating the space and time for me to write, and for refusing to let me give up.